THE UNTIDY GARDENER

By the same author

BUTTERCUPS AND DAISY
COWSLIPS AND CLOVER
YORKSHIRE RELISH
SWEET NOTHINGS

THE UNTIDY GARDENER

by

ELIZABETH CRAGOE

HAMISH HAMILTON
LONDON

First published in Great Britain 1982
by Hamish Hamilton Ltd
Garden House 57–59 Long Acre London WC2E 9JZ

British Library Cataloguing in Publication Data

Cragoe, Elizabeth
The untidy gardener.
1. Gardening
I. Title
635'.092'4 SB455

ISBN 0–241–10759–8

Printed in Great Britain by
St Edmundsbury Press, Bury St Edmunds, Suffolk

CONTENTS

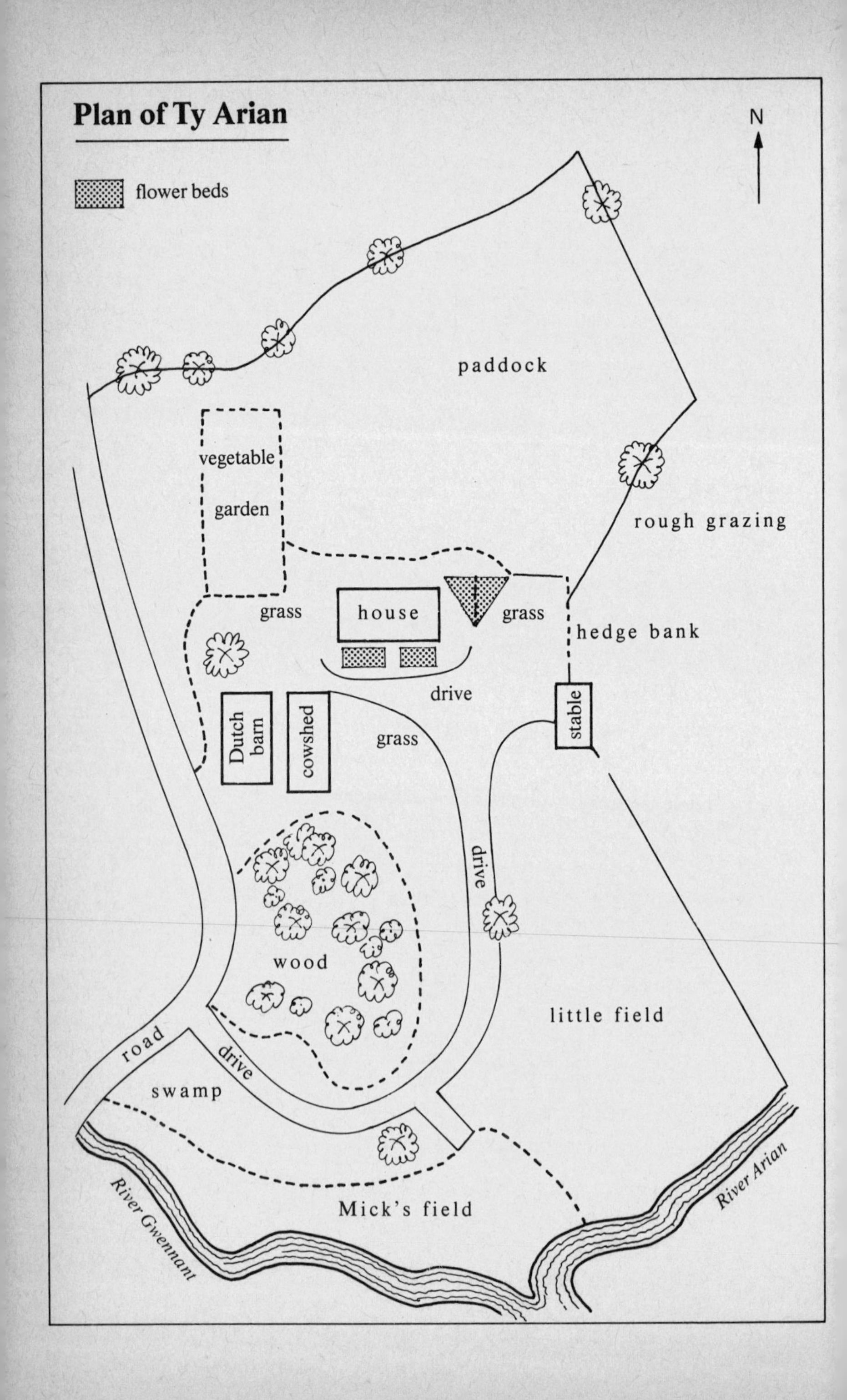
Plan of Ty Arian
N
flower beds
paddock
vegetable
garden
rough grazing
grass
house
grass
hedge bank
drive
stable
Dutch barn
cowshed
grass
drive
wood
little field
road
drive
swamp
Mick's field
River Gwennant
River Arian

I

The Untidy Gardener

It was all very peaceful. A wood-pigeon was cooing in the tall oak, his woodwind tones insisting over the sharp counter-point of a chiff-chaff. The sun shone; and the scent from the freshly-mowed lawn was like a blessing on the air. It was three o'clock in the afternoon. It was June.

Only my friend Sybil seemed out of tune with the month, the day and the hour. She was unappeased as she stood, tall and angular, on my terrace, and surveyed my little domain with a critical eye.

'It's so *untidy*, Elizabeth. It wants a total clear-out. And I know you; you'll *never* get around to it.'

'But I don't want it tidy, Sybil. Not really. Don't you remember that splendid house-agent's advertisement for that totally overgrown Georgian property, which said "The gardens are simply designed, and rely for their effect on a background of great natural beauty ..." That's the sort of thing I'm after. *You* see it as untidy and messy. But I'm like the house-agent hoped his customers would be. *I* see it as wild. And lavish.'

Sybil snorted. 'Lavish!' she said with scorn. 'Lavish! What a word! All *I* can see round here that's lavish are the weeds! What else do you call lavish? That?'

And she pointed at a little, fragile yellow rose that straggled, bent and sickly, across a corner of the border, next to the path.

I could see that she was getting cross, so I led her indoors and soothed her ruffled feelings with Earl Gray tea. But after I had seen her into her neat little car, and pointed her in the direction of her immaculate and sterile little town house, I went back to the little rose, and stooped to smell it, with something between a smile and a sigh.

It had not been there long. It was growing in some long, rough grass when Matthew, my son, discovered it, as he was extending the mowed area, that May, into previously unconquered territory. He saw the unexpected glint of yellow in the grass, stopped the machine, and called me over.

'Have a look at that! It's a rose – but isn't it a funny place to find one?'

I knelt and examined the tiny, slug-nibbled yellow flower. It had four peaky leaves, and a long stem, which lay almost prostrate on the ground.

'Poor little thing – it's almost at its last gasp. I wonder what on earth it's doing here? Perhaps we could dig it up, and put it in one of the terrace beds, and give it a chance. Where's its root? Can you see?'

Matthew was pulling away the long tufts of dead grass that were binding the struggling rose to the earth.

'Look,' he said. 'It goes under here. That bit of the old wall's tumbled down on top of it, and this big stone's flattened it. Let's see if I can get it off. There!'

The rose, revealed, was in a sorry state. Other tasks for the moment laid aside, we busied ourselves about its rescue. I fetched a fork, and lifted it carefully, its puny root still encased in a lump of earth; Matthew prepared it a planting hole in one of the terrace beds, with a sprinkling of bonemeal, and half a bucket of leafmould from the wood. Gently we lowered it into its new home, and firmed it in. Matthew rose to his feet and dusted the earth from his hands.

'I'll just go and put the mower away,' he said, 'and while I'm down there, I'll pile those fallen stones back on to that bit of the old wall. I *wonder* why anybody should have planted a rose in a funny place like that.'

Five minutes later, he called me over again.

'I know now,' he said. 'Look what I found when I moved the stones.'

It was a small square of slate, lying flush with the ground at the foot of the wall. On it was a simple inscription, in straggling letters, rather crudely carved. It said:

We looked at it in silence for a few moments. Then I said:

'Well, we've moved it now. We can't put it back. But I'll tell you what we'll do. We'll nurse it up as best we can, and get it healthy again. And then we'll take cuttings. Or layers. Or even bud it. And we'll give Tilly her rose back when we've got a good young bush of it again, in a year or two. Only this time, we'll look after it.'

Yes, Sybil, I thought, as I sniffed the sweet perfume that rose from the one bedraggled blossom; that's what we'll do. And it'll probably never be anything much of a bush at the end of it. It'll probably straggle. It may get black spot and mildew. I expect it'll be untidy. You can point the finger of scorn at it if you like; I know you wouldn't have it in your garden for a moment. But I like it; it's Tilly's rose. It can be as untidy as it likes – I shan't care.

But then, Sybil, like it or lump it, I'm an untidy gardener.

As the twig is bent, so will the bough be inclined. My father is a keen and knowledgeable gardener, and kept the one and a half acres that surrounded the house we grew up in full of flowers, trees, lawns and fruit; we three children, playing our days away in the dappled, shadowy green of it all, absorbed the love of gardens and the wish to cultivate them, as inevitably as the air and the food that made us grow. We potched around with our own small gardens, sowing packets of Virginia stock and marigolds, and never achieved anything the least bit memorable; but the seed that was really being sown in us was the love of gardening, a lucky sowing, I think; for gardening has been my most reliable joy ever since. If I were a fairy godmother, the love of gardening is the gift I should bring to any baby's christening, happy in the knowledge that it would last a lifetime, and would adapt to almost any combination of circumstances that fate might have in store for its recipient.

In spite of the Virginia stocks, I do not remember taking any very active part in gardening in my early years. I liked to *be* in the garden, to enjoy the flowers – fitting the tip of my little finger into the yellow velvet pouches of the calceolarias, or balancing tiny paper fairies among the sturdy pink cups of apple blossom; but there was no urge to alter anything. It was my father's garden. He decided what was to be grown in it, and where – that this bed should be turfed over, and another one dug here; that the bottom lawn should be made into a tennis court, and a row of cordon apples planted along the top of the bank – and we unthinkingly enjoyed the results of his efforts and ideas, in a spirit of appreciative acceptance.

It was when I was sixteen that I suddenly began to want to garden for myself. It was a conversion as abrupt as St Paul's albeit less dramatic. I was walking along a street in Leeds one spring day, when I saw, on the pavement outside a garden shop, a box of double daisies in full bloom. They were individually potted, nice sturdy plants, and their flowers were tightly quilled in pink, white and crimson. They looked fine and flourishing, sparkling as if they had dew on them; they looked as fresh as the spring itself. I fell in love on the spot, and laid out ninepence for two of them, a pink-and-white, and a crimson, which I took home and planted in a corner at the front of the big herbaceous border. Being pot-grown, they made no objection to the move, and, indeed, flourished mightily, and were still covered with flowers and promising buds when I had to leave them to go back to school. When I returned for the summer holidays at the end of July, I was charmed to find that they had seeded, and that there was now a vast progeny of little daisy plants growing all around them. With painstaking care, I lifted them and re-planted them in a long row to adorn the front of the border; but of course it was wasted labour, as anyone who is familiar with these flowers will know. All the offspring reverted to the wild type, and what we got was a row of carefully-planted out lawn daisies, which my father weeded out before I even got back from school the next Easter holidays.

In spite of this minor disappointment, I was now thoroughly inocculated with the gardening bug, and began to take an interest in the subject to the extent of reading articles in the paper. V. Sackville-West's contributions to the *Observer* were for many years my favourite bit of that paper . I also began for the first time to look at the beauty of our garden with seeing, rather than with merely looking-at, eyes.

It was a propitious time. The war was over, and the nurserymen of this country, getting back into their stride, were offering the nation's gardeners a vast variety of wonderful flowering plants. Starved as we had all been of colour and frivolity during the war years, when vegetables had perforce to take precedence in the garden, and flowers had had to manage as best they could, this new lavishness seemed almost a miracle, particularly in the rather grim climate and surroundings of the industrial north. My father bought Russell lupins, Bishop delphiniums, Symons-Jeune phloxes, Ballard michaelmas daisies, and shrubs and trees from Hilliers, and our garden flourished in an unprecedented blaze of colour. He also sowed and planted things we had never heard of – *leptosiphon, rhodohypoxis*, balsam – we looked, admired, and learned, and our horizons were enlarged.

In the curious state of hyper-sensibility that accompanies adolescence, I looked with fresh eyes at various familiar plants, and saw them in a new way. I remember coming into the drawing room one day when my mother had just put a jug of tall flowers down in front of the empty grate, and being absolutely struck all of a heap by a bright crimson snapdragon that was part of the arrangement. The brilliant, glowing colour of it, combined with its elegant rococco shape, its warm, summery scent, and the way the florets were set up the stem, diminishing into little green, unopened buds, seemed to me to make it one of the most beautiful things I had ever seen, and I enjoyed it every time I came into the room for as long as the arrangement lasted. Another time, I began to think about double red hawthorn in early March, and could hardly wait for it to come out in May so that I could feast my eyes on it, and check the accuracy of my mental picture of it with the reality. I suppose the variety we had in the garden, two trees of it, was Paul's double scarlet; there is a silveriness about the outside of the petals in this variety which is the subtlest thing, and a neat bunchiness about its florets that recalls rambler roses, very much miniaturised. On another occasion, I got lilies on the brain, and had to keep going out into the garden to re-appreciate their cool, deep beauty, and the cunning hinging of the anthers, so generously coated with golden or tawny pollen. It was lucky for me that my father was such a good gardener; I was able to indulge myself in these long stares at plants I liked, and I have always felt that in the end you come to a kind of intimacy with a plant, by doing this, that you never lose. The enrichment lasts for life.

There are many beauties in plants that you notice in this perhaps rather self-conscious cultivation of their acquaintance that might otherwise pass you by; and once you have got your eye in for that sort of thing, you do it without any effort. I remember discovering the particular beauty of buds, for instance. One of the trees my father had planted was an almond, and there was something about the flower buds that reminded me of jewels. This was nothing to do with their colour, for the best of the jewel effect was before the buds had unfolded far enough to show any petal. It was to do with the way they were set, in an exquisite bunch of round studs, not like faceted jewels but like carbuncles or pearls, rich because so many; they also had something of the pulsing life-promise of a stag's antlers when they are in the early stages of growing in velvet. These living gems studded the branches of the tree like garnets in the imagined crown of some Saxon king; I used to think the tree was just as beautiful in this stage as when it did eventually open into pink blossom. Another flower whose buds pleased me just as much as its fully opened flowers was the delphinium, whose blue, light or dark, slowly winning through the early sage of the green bud, went through a marvellous series of iridescent modulation – beetle-green, peacock, kingfisher, shotsilk sky, and finally the breath-stopping azure of the fully expanded floret.

It would be tedious to describe the way I cut my garden teeth once marriage and a place of my own gave me and my husband, Desmond, the opportunity of actually gardening, instead of only reading about it. He tended to be practical and commonsensical, I rather high-falutin and a bit of a garden snob; over the years each modified the other, to our mutual improvement, though I do remember him saying one day, in exasperation, that he thought I never really liked a plant unless it was very small, greenish-brown in colour, without an English name, and exceedingly difficult to grow! Two gardens on London clay and one on Hertfordshire gravel followed one another in quick succession, and then, after four years on the last, we decided to sell everything up and move to Wales to farm.

It was on the sixty-acre holding on Penllwynplan, where we lived for fifteen years, that I began to see where I wanted to go as a gardener. My first book, *Buttercups and Daisy*, is about the farming side of this adventure; little did I think, as I collected thousands of eggs, and wrestled to milk recalcitrant cows, that it was the gardening, then relegated to the status of a hobby for one's few snatched moments of leisure, that would in the end outlive the farming, and come to be, for me at least, the most important occupation of my time.

It began, as important things so often seem to, so very arbitrarily, during a conversation with a friend. We were talking about wild flowers, and I made use of the expression 'common wild flowers.' He took me up on the phrase. 'What do you call common wild flowers nowadays?' he asked. 'For example – when did you last see a cowslip?' The question gave me quite a pang. For, indeed, I realised, it had been years since I had seen that brave little flag of yellow fluttering in its wild and natural state among the spring grasses. It came home to me then just how threatened even the commonest of our wild flowers were. It was becoming rare, noteworthy, remarkable, to see a cowslip. How unthinkable that would have seemed to our forbears. Was it possible that perhaps in fifty years the dandelion, the buttercup, the field daisy – flowers that we took absolutely for granted, and accounted weeds – might in their turn become rarities? It seemed improbable; but then, the decimation of the cowslip, that everyday flower picked in clothes-basketsfull for wine, or heedlessly fashioned into tossy-balls, would have seemed just as improbable to our sun-bonnetted, pin-tuck petticoated ancestors of 1860. The continuing decline of wild flowers in a world over-full of hungry people seemed not so much a probability as a certainty; and in that moment, I decided to do whatever small bit I could to stop it, a decision that has kept me agreeably occupied ever since.

The first thing to do was to try to assess the situation. What was it that was killing off the wild flowers? I was unfitted both by personality and by circumstances to do a proper scientific study, but this was not too much of a drawback, because at the level at which I could hope to work, the answer to my enquiry was so obvious. You did not have to be Sherlock Holmes to see that what was killing off our wild flowers was primarily modern agriculture. A few seasons' experiment soon confirmed that the obvious was, for once in a way, true; wild flowers, in general, could not flourish under a regimen of high nitrogen, heavy stocking, and constant ploughing and re-seeding. The immense increase in productivity that we now demand from our land makes it, in my experience, absolutely impossible to grow wild flowers to any extent on the actual farmed bit. Farming and conservation are mutually exclusive, and any favouring of one must be at the expense of the other.

This established, what was one to do? If wild flowers were not able to flourish in arable or intensively cultivated grassland, had we perforce to bid them goodbye? Or was there a policy of conservation that could be followed that would enable them to survive round the edges of efficient agriculture, in woods and copses, on commons, in odd field corners, on road verges, farm drives, railway cuttings, and places like these? It seemed to me that there was such a possibility, and that if people who cared about them did what they could to save them, our everyday wild flowers might yet be preserved for our delight, and the inheritance of future generations.

But the cobbler must stick to his last. Knowing my own faults (at least, some of them...) I was well aware that it would be utterly pointless for me to try to organise anything, or even to take an active part in anything co-operative. Anything that I was to do, I had to do on my own. So I began, in the smallest of ways, to improve my acquaintance with the common wild flowers I wanted to see protected and thus to lay the foundations, I hoped, of the experience that would enable me to help them to get established in new and safe localities when their original habitats were overtaken by 'progress.'

I lay no claim to expertise in the matter; there must be thousands of people in the country who know a lot more about identifying, growing and re-naturalising wild flowers than I do. But in the six years since I decided to throw in my lot with the beleaguered wildlings, I have inevitably discovered a few things, and one of them is that there is an immense tide of interest in the subject throughout the whole country, and that people are anxious to know even such small things as a non-expert like me can tell them.

My aim in this wildflower business is simple. It is to develop this property, to which I came two years ago when my husband and I separated and gave up farming, as a wildflower reserve; to build up stocks of such wildflowers as I like, and as are suited to the ground; to learn how best to propagate them, and to make the resultant offspring available to anybody who shares my fondness for them; and, ultimately, to establish colonies of suitable species in places outside my boundaries where I think they will have a chance of flourishing. And, naturally, to publicise what I am doing as widely as possible, for enthusiasts can help each other a lot in this kind of business. Already, as a result of earlier books and articles that I have written, I have been able to exchange seeds and plants with other people, a traffic that I hope will increase as my stocks build up in both kind and number.

Another thing I have learned is not to be ashamed of the simplicity and smallness of my project. So – it is only three and a half acres, and I have as yet only experience of cultivating about fifty common weeds. But, so what? It is a beginning. In another six years, perhaps I will have re-distributed cowslips and wild daffodils all round the county, and will have experience of cultivating a hundred and fifty common weeds! Who knows? And by then, some of them may not still be so common. Shame at the inadequacy of one's efforts is false and damaging if it prevents one from doing one's own small best; and I am tempted to recast the words of the well-known aphorist – whose name just at present escapes me – and say that he who has made even one cowslip grow where only two blades of grass grew before has rendered a service to the state, not to mention to his own children and grandchildren.

2

A Place for Wild Flowers

Although as an agricultural unit, Ty Arian, with its three and a half acres, is derisory, as a garden it is a very fair size. Coats must be cut according to cloth; with most of my physical strength left behind in the first fifty years of my life, it is vital that I arrange matters here in such a way that I can hope to manage them not only now but in the years to come, when all that can be expected to increase is weakness. Luckily, the rather wild kind of gardening that I like can be set up in such a way that it can be kept going by occasional inputs of unskilled labour reinforced by appropriate machines; if I use the next ten or fifteen years properly, it should be possible to arrange matters so that an occasional burst by a jobbing gardener will keep it all reasonably nice to look at during the years of my decline.

It is a delightfully varied little property. There are two small fields; one, about one and a half acres in size, is partly flat enough to mow, and partly a steep, rough, flowery slope, running down to the roadside hedge; the other, all steep, follows the curve of the drive and runs down to the bank of the Arian river. The general slope of these little pastures is south and west, and as the lie of the land protects them from both the north and the east, they lie sunny and sheltered.

The drive, steep, stony and bosky, sweeps round from the road in a noble curve, sunk for half its length between high banks and overhung with trees –sycamores, ashes, hazels, hawthorns, willows and alders. It emerges into the sun just as it reaches the level of the low whitewashed cowshed, and divides into a flattened Y shape, the arms of which embrace the raised terrace on which the house stands. An old and partly ruinous stable building fronts the cowshed on the opposite side of the yard.

As all the property is on a slope, the only level bits are the artificially flattened platform on which the house stands, and a further shelf cut into the side of the hill at a lower level which accommodates the cowshed and the Dutch barn. Below the barn, the slope that fills in the curve of the drive is taken up by a charming little wood – or at least, that is what I call it, though various friends, looking over the place, have wrinkled their brows in puzzlement and enquired, 'But where *is* this wood you keep talking about?' Perhaps I do go on about it rather a lot. I have never had a wood before. But though it may not be very big, being a triangle whose sides are about fifty yards long, it is full of trees, and marked with little tree symbols on the Ordnance Survey map – and – yes, I *do* call it a wood. What else should I call it?

A sloping piece of land in a high rainfall area naturally drains off a good deal of water, and just inside the gate from the road there is a small triangle of land below the drive where this water collects. It is partly overgrown with willows, and honesty compels me to admit that it is not very nice. It is really neither one thing nor the other. The willows keep out the light too much for rushes to grow there and the water lies on it for about ten months of the year, which is more than grass can stand, so it is mostly an area of unlovely grey mud, surrounded by a rank growth of the poisonous water dropwort, and diversified by the gaunt skeletons of fallen willow branches which stick hopelessly up out of the morass draped with faded moss and tufts of sodden dead leaves. It is a swamp rather than a marsh; one can imagine evil miasmas rising from it more easily than kingcups. It will be altered.

A fair proportion of the property is in a decided mess. The mowable area of the larger field, usually called The Paddock, is clean, but there are several big drifts of bracken on the steep part, and thickets of brambles and little thorn bushes are beginning to encroach down the hedge that separates it from the wood. A large rectangle of this field which is wired off as a vegetable garden, is clear of the grosser weeds but totally overgrown with couch grass, except for the ten per cent or so that we have laboriously cleared by hand. Brambles and nettles together infest the wood and disfigure, in head-high drifts, the little field that runs down to the river. The people who lived here before me have also left me, in this field, the most awkward eyesore of all to deal with in the form of a sizeable scrap metal dump, tucked in behind what should have been the rather charming, tumbled, mossy ruins of a couple of nineteenth-century pig cots. 'Scrap metal' is a phrase, at first speaking, to bring a glint to the experienced eye, promising as it does visits from seedy merchants in flat caps willing to load it all on to their pickups and pay one for the privilege of taking it away. But the scrap metal left me by the Smiths is of the sort that you might describe as scrap de la scrap, being composed of rusty sheets of galvanised zinc, holed fuel tanks, derelict wheel-barrows, tangles of oxidised wire, bottomless dustbins, and sections of car bodies more than a little the worse for wear. Another smaller dump in the wood is more selective; it was here, it appears, that the Smiths disposed of their discarded car engines and milk churns. Their plastic rubbish they scattered generously about in a sort of sparse universal top-dressing, but this was relatively easy to gather up and burn. The metal could be removed by the Council, but only at vast expense; alternatively, I could hire a JCB and get it buried. But there again, it would cost money – money which must surely be better spent planting some of the hundreds of trees and shrubs that the place cries out for, so that they can be getting on with their growing. Rubbish, after all, will wait.

Another damaging thing that the Smiths did when they lived here was to keep goats, and, I believe, donkeys. I have nothing against either goats or donkeys per se, but as precursors in a garden, they leave a lot to be desired. The dozen or so full-sized trees on the place are unscathed, but almost three quarters of the saplings have been forced to grow awry by having large areas of their bark gnawed off; many of them will have to be cut down, and replaced with clean-grown young trees. This is less of a pity than it might be, because most of the damaged saplings are either ash or sycamore, and I quite welcome the chance of replacing them with a wider range of species.

But it is not entirely a bad thing to follow a family like the Smiths. There are compensations. As well as rubbish, they have left an immense number of delightful and useful things around the property, trodden into the soft ground, or overgrown with several years' weeds. So life assumes something of the character of a low-key treasure hunt as one trashes and slashes and digs about the place. So far I have unearthed a small builder's level, a mattock, an adjustable wrench, five shovel heads, a sickle, a pair of pliers, a trowel, two forks, a timber wedge, a short crowbar, and two goat-chains of considerable length not to mention various arcane pieces of equipment whose function I can only guess at, but which local opinion attributes tentatively to the craft of roofing. Buckets also keep turning up, from hitherto unconquered clumps of nettles; good buckets, too. I often wonder how they came to be scattered so widely about the many odd corners of the property. Perhaps they were used as water buckets for various tethered goats.

This account of the encroaching dereliction of Ty Arian makes it sound rather squalid. But it is not so. The metal tip is disgusting, certainly, but that is out of sight unless you actually go looking for it; and the weeds, the docks, nettles, brambles, and overgrown clumps of ragged cocksfoot, although not what I eventually wish to see, are not loathesome in themselves. Indeed, a good hearty bramble has rather a splendid shape, with its vigorous overarching sprays and dark, shiny light-reflecting leaves. If docks and brambles were rare, we should no doubt praise and conserve them; but as they are everywhere to be found, and are in no danger, I intend to get rid of mine, so that I can use the space for species that, in my fallible human way, I consider more beautiful.

Before any really serious attempts can be made at establishing colonies of chosen wild plants, then, there is a lot of clearing up to be done. This, on the face of it, is easy. There are tractor-drawn trashing machines; there are weed-killers; there is fire. But when you come actually to *do* the clearing, it is not so easy after all. There are snags to all the relatively uneffortful techniques; you tend to come back to the hard graft of hand work in the end.

Tractor-powered implements are out, for a start. The slopes where the bramble thickets lie are too steep, and the land is too rough, for tractors to move over it safely. A crawler, on tracks, could do so, but again, it would cost money that I haven't got, and the area is so small that no contractor would consider it worth his time.

Fire is the most primitive way of clearing away undergrowth and, even in this wet climate, is feasible during a drought. But I can't bring myself to use it. How can I forget that in every one of those thickets there are hundreds of mice, voles, hedgehogs and birds – not to mention insects? The destruction of wild life caused by accidental fire is bad enough. To be the deliberate instigator of that much pain and distress is more than my conscience will stand. I just can't do it.

Weed-killers remain, and I must admit that, to the consternation of some of my more conscientiously conservation-minded friends, I have tried some of them. In my first summer, I set out with a brand-new spray and a gallon of Trioxine, to bump off several hundred square yards of mixed nettles and thistles, and spent quite a busy day drenching the furry, grey-green shoots. I was disconcerted to discover, though, that my efforts were causing extreme alarm and despondency to a great population of beautiful green beetles on the nettles. They were long and narrow; some of them were jade, and some were turquoise, and all of them looked as if they had been lightly dusted over with gold while still damp from the hand of the creator. But they rushed away from the Trioxine spray as if it was scalding them, tried to hide under the leaves, fell to the ground, and made it pretty clear that what I was doing lay right across their path to a prosperous future. A little research in the library showed that they were the Green Nettle Weevil, entirely dependent on that plant for food, and doing no harm to anything else, and precious little harm to the nettle if the ranks on Ty Arian were anything to go by. Here, in a microcosm, was the whole dilemma of conservation. If I killed the nettles, I necessarily killed the weevils, for as every conservationist knows, destruction of habitat is the main cause of decline in wild life. But if I didn't kill the nettles, I couldn't get on with my other plans, and build up stocks of the lots of other lovely things I wanted – many of which were themselves, no doubt, host plants to similarly beautiful creatures. Perhaps it would be more open-minded to say simply 'to other creatures', and leave out the word 'beautiful', for a proper conservationist tries to avoid this kind of subjective judgement, and to keep the door open for the whole range of life.

It is all rather difficult. One is pushed into the position, for which one is obviously unfitted, of being God, and of dealing out life with one hand and death with the other, without the advantage of knowing the rules of the game, the object of the game, or even, when it comes to it, whether or not there is a game at all. However, the problem is more theoretical than real. When conscience is no guide, most human beings will follow the dictates of fancy, and that is what I did. I felt sorry for the nettle weevils and, indeed, for the various Vanessid butterflies that use the nettle for a food plant, but nevertheless I continued my work of destruction. After all, there were plenty of nettles on the other side of the fence, and I resolved also that I would leave undestroyed one or two drifts on my own land, in unobtrusive places. So far, however, I must admit that the nettles have had the last laugh. The ones I sprayed became pleasingly droopy later on in the day, and a week later had died right back to the ground. But a couple of months later they sneakily put up new shoots and, my efforts at the time being turned on to some other project, they quickly re-established themselves as hearty as ever. Obviously, I should have given them another dose as soon as they showed themselves. Next time, I shall.

Other poisons that I have used in my efforts to control the wrong kinds of vegetation on my overgrown acres have been Gramoxone, Tumbleweed, and even sodium chlorate. All of them have been about half effective. I have followed the directions on the packets about dilutions and areas to be treated perfectly conscientiously, yet what I always seem to get is a stun rather than a kill. The weeds, grass, or whatever, die back to the ground patchily, and then begin, almost immediately, to regenerate. Even sodium chlorate, which is supposed to render the ground poisonous for six months, seems to become harmless here after about two. Perhaps it is a result of our high rainfall. Anyway, there is one obvious conclusion to draw, and that is that one must do the job a little bit at a time, and not embark on an area so big that the prospect of doing it all over again, perhaps twice, is too daunting to contemplate.

In clearing brambles, I am sure that the only effective method in the end is hard graft. Brambles, so vigorous and spiteful above ground, turn out to have surprisingly little roots. Furthermore, when the main root is torn out, they do not seem to give much trouble by re-shooting from the bits that are inevitably left behind. The equipment you need for a good session of de-brambling is a garden fork, a pair of secateurs, and a stout leather left-hand glove. You cut off most of the top hamper with the secateurs, then loosen the root with the fork, and, once you can get your gloved hand round it, you just wriggle and drag and tug until, usually surprisingly easily, it comes up. You may have to cut one or two roots that are holding it into the ground, but there again, the bramble is a big softy when its bluff is called, and its roots cut easily. Disposing of the cut-off tops is one of the nastiest bits of this chore; they are endlessly anxious to catch you and, being of a sparse, open growth, are not very easy to burn, unless you can get a really good solid-hearted bonfire going. The rounded, knobby roots are worth saving and drying for burning on an open fire in the house.

Once you have cleared your patch of brambles in this way it will largely stay clean, but of course a yearly going-over for seedlings is a good idea. The only trouble about getting rid of brambles by the simple method of yanking them out is that it is so slow. They seem to like to grow at a density of about a dozen roots to the square yard, so one's progress tends to be unimpressive. There is a weed-killer called SBK which will kill brambles, and I often think that in the end I shall be driven to use this on the larger thickets, but it is extremely expensive, particularly if everything has to be sprayed two or three times over to get a complete kill. Perhaps a burning-over of the dead and stark remnants of poisoned thickets would not be too wicked a thing to do; the natural thinning of the cover that would happen as the plants died would ensure that most of the wild creatures had moved to other quarters before the holocaust took place.

Once the gross and disagreeable weeds are removed, or at least brought under control, it will be possible to press on with the constructive side of the plan I have for Ty Arian. The idea will be to garden it outwards from the house, so to speak, in rough circles of decreasing formality, the area immediately round the house being planted with conventional garden flowers, the outlying parts with wildings, and a sort of no-man's-land in the middle being diversified with those hearty plants that often naturalise themselves as garden escapes.

First of all, I have to consider the house itself. As it is long, low, white and facing due south, it presents a terrible temptation. There are so many things I would like to have that would enjoy a southern aspect; the trouble is that many of them wouldn't 'go' together. I have had to call upon my slender reserves of restraint and discipline; and I intend to keep the display to two colours only, lavender and pale yellow. I may bend this decision as far as *tone* is concerned but I propose to stay within its bounds in the matter of *tint* and exclude quite rigorously any true pinks, reds, or oranges.

The kingpin of the whole scheme will be a wisteria, which is already planted. This is shortly to be joined by a 'Gloire de Dijon' rose, a *Solanum crispum*, and a clematis or two, with the dark purple Jackmanii a strong contender. I am toying with the idea of a winter-flowering jasmine, which doesn't need the southern aspect but by the same token won't mind it, and which will extend the decoration of what is after all the most important side of the house through a difficult time of the year. There will also be room for another rose, but the choice is baffling. Ideally, it should be a pale clear yellow – with neatly-made double flowers – free-flowering – scented – perpetual – self-dead-heading – healthy – and with handsome, shiny foliage. No climbing rose variety that I can find in the catalogues seems to combine all these virtues; 'Emily Gray' comes nearest but is said, by her breeding, to be unsuited to growing against a wall. But I have no need to hurry. Sooner or later, I am sure, I shall hear of the perfect pale yellow house rose; and until then, I can enjoy my 'Gloire de Dijon'.

The house is surrounded at the moment with a neat and strongly-made concrete path, and it seems a shame to do violence to it for the sake of making flower beds. But no gardener could resist forty feet of prime south-facing wall, so the sledge hammer and the cold chisel will be called in again and, gradually, the dank, squashed, lifeless earth under the concrete will be revealed and coaxed back to life and fruitfulness again. Another reason for wanting beds right under the house wall is that the downstairs windows are broad and low, and seem to call for sweetly-scented flowers like pinks, wallflowers, mignonette or dwarf sweet peas to be grown directly beneath them. I love a summer room with the windows open and the scent of flowers drifting in through them.

The terrace in front of the house is already mostly flower bed. It was lawn when I arrived but, wanting somewhere to grow flowers, I dug two large rectangular beds and found myself beset, in so doing, by a most unusual difficulty. For the earth was full of broken glass. It appeared that there had once been a small conservatory on the front of the house, and that it had been allowed to decay *in situ*, or, indeed, had been destroyed; so tiny and so scattered were the pieces of glass that I sometimes wondered if the Smith children had been accustomed to entertain themselves by doing target-practice with stones on the remains of the unfortunate conservatory. Painfully, shard by shard, I extracted two plastic fertiliser-sacksfull of broken glass from that bit of soil. Even now, whenever I turn over a forkful of earth to plant something, or pull out a weed, I am bound to find some more. But who knows? Perhaps it improves the drainage...

In these two terrace beds I grow the ordinary things that nearly everybody wants to have in their gardens – delphiniums, lupins, dahlias, michaelmas daisies, bulbs, annuals, small shrubs, and so on – rather jumbled up. I have never been a planning, squared-paper sort of gardener, and I rather like the chancc-come associations that you get through sticking in your plants wherever there seems to be a bit of spare space. You have to take some slight precautions; I allocate certain areas to certain broad colour groupings, yellows and oranges at one end, and pinky reds and mauves at the other; this rather casual segregation usually prevents any really awful colour clashes. But in any case, I find that if you are unlucky enough to get something so misplaced that it makes an intolerable eyesore, you can usually move it, however actively it is growing, provided that you lift it with a really enormous lump of soil. Of course there are some things like brooms that won't put up with this treatment, but this spring, for instance, I moved a peony that was just making its flower buds, and instead of drooping and sulking, it went ahead and flowered splendidly in its new position. But when I say an enormous lump of soil, I mean really enormous; my peony was accompanied by at least twenty-five pounds of its immediate surroundings, and was dropped straight into a prepared hole.

I really don't think it knew that anything had happened to it.

I am anything but a purist in gardening – is there such a thing as an impurist, I wonder? – and my terrace beds contain plants that range from alpines to wildlings. Consequently there is something to look at every day of the year. One of the chief pleasures of gardening, I think, is going out in the morning after breakfast for a minute inspection of whatever the garden has to offer, so I always want something to be coming on, however unobtrusive it may be. Since my exquisite and heavily-stocked winter garden exists, as yet, only in my mind, I am often reduced in January and February to gazing at about two species crocuses and a constipated *Erica carnea*; but time is on my side in the matter, and with every year that passes, my dead-of-winter flowers will increase. Whenever the weather is warm enough, I actually eat my breakfast out of doors. Early this year, we constructed a very simple bench against the house wall of a railway sleeper laid on two eighteen-inch building blocks, and it is surprising how often the weather is fine enough for me to take my bowl of porridge out and eat it sitting there. With the dewy flowers at my feet, the birds singing in every tree in the valley, and the slanting rays of the sun illuminating every leaf with glowing light, nobody could wish for a lovelier place in which to start the day.

To the right of the house, if you are looking southwards, is a sloping square of mowed grass with a noble full-grown sycamore on it, in which the peacocks roost at night. About half this grass is dedicated to small bulbs, which have been carefully planted so that the line between the mowed and unmowed grass makes a pleasing curve during the months when the bulbs are ripening their foliage. We started with a small planting of crocuses, which reminded one, in their smallness and gallantry, of the Pilgrim Fathers setting out to colonise the whole of America... But, in just the same way, immigration is going on all the time, and this year they have been reinforced not only by some more of their own kind, but by Tenby daffodils, *chionodoxae*, grape hyacinths, snowdrops, and squills; while closer to the tree, a few *Cyclamen neapolitanum* and a solitary *hepatica* are tentatively testing the conditions.

The terrace beds, facing due south and unsheltered, are

sunny throughout the day, and it is surprising to find how many plants one wants to grow that really need a bit of light shade to do themselves justice. My front garden at Penllwyn-plan was about half shady, so the plants I brought from there included several that found the terrace too torrid. For these, and others that are still in their infancy, as cuttings or seed-lings, I am making an informally shaped bed at the top edge of the sycamore plot; working out the succession for it has been a great joy. I can never understand why so many gardeners seem to deplore shady spots. Beginning in January, my shady border is going to have as many hellebores as I can raise from seed – *niger, orientalis, corsicus,* and *foetidus*, with snow-drops, celandines and aconites as a groundwork. Four azaleas, bought as small potted seedlings at a nursery-man's closing-down sale in 1976, which all turned out to be shades of orange and salmon, will enjoy the light shade and the loose, leaf-mould-filled soil; round their feet I shall be able to repro-duce an effect I once saw in the garden of a friend, in which light blue forget-me-nots combined exquisitely with china-white-bluebells. I have a stock of the kind of white bluebells one buys, but they are not quite what I want. Their bells are short and wide and open rather widely, which gives a stocky look to the plant. The ones I am after have longer bells, with a long, narrow waist to them, and with petals that curl round and back. I have collected a number of albinos of the common bluebell, *Endymion non-scripta* from Mick's woods, with his permission, and I shall be interested to see how they flourish. I think they have the shape that I want. London pride and Solomon's seal are two more shade-lovers that I already have; they too might be worked in to this May picture. Later, I hope that white foxgloves and white martagon lilies will set off the grace of that most lovely of blue poppies, *meconopsis betoni-cifolia*. I have a mere six plants of this preparing to face the winter in pots, but once fresh seed is available, the whole business becomes a lot easier. July and August see the peak flowering of hydrangeas, hardy fuchsias, and some of the shrubby spireas; species cyclamen and pink and white Japanese anemones carry the scene along after that until the kindling of the autumn bonfire in the azalea leaves in late October and November. And from the time of leaf-fall, it is only a week or two until the opening of the first Christmas roses starts the whole cycle off again.

Another plant that is already flourishing in the beginnings of the shady bed is the almost black *Geranium phaeum*. This flowers towards the end of June. I found it, unexpectedly, growing in a massive stand at the edge of a remote lane; and when I tried to pull one stem, to take it back for certain identification, I found that I had got a bit of root as well. It really, truly was an accident! But, having acquired my piece in this chance-come way, I recalled the words of the martyr Latimer, and said to myself 'I will take it as sent from God.' It grew on in the most obliging way, and I hope will increase itself by seed soon, as well as by simply spreading. It is one of the few flowers I know that catches your eye by its darkness rather than its brightness.

Below the sycamore plot and the shady border is the bit of flat land that contains the cowshed and the Dutch barn; lower again is the wood. There is a certain aesthetic problem about the planting up of the space under the trees in the wood and down the edges of the drive. Is it to be garden, or is it to be wild? There is something so beautiful about a truly natural bit of woodland, growing only native species, that one feels oneself to be committing an act almost of vulgarity in contemplating the introduction of brilliant reds or oranges. There is the fear that such hot, vivid tints might kill the deep, fresh, chaste colours of the woodland. The rich glossy green of the ivy, the reddish tan of the fallen leaf, and the deep soft brown of the juicy dark soil – these are the colours that are germane to the scene, and when you introduce colours of a higher key, you spoil something, even in creating something else.

Richard Jefferies was aware of the problem when he wrote:

'Our English landscape wants no gardening. It cannot be gardened. The least interference kills it... The earth is right and the tree is right; trim either, and all is wrong.'

And the early eighteenth-century Lord Shaftesbury was saying something of the same sort when he wrote, in 1709 with a plethora of emphasis:

'Your *genius*, the *genius* of the place, and the GREAT GENIUS have at last prevail'd. I shall no longer resist the passion growing in me for things of a natural *kind*; where neither *Art*, nor the *conceit* or *caprice* of man has spoil'd their genuine order by breaking in upon that *primitive state*. Even the rude *rocks*, the mossy *caverns*, the irregular unwrought *grotto's*, and broken *falls* of water, with all the horrid graces of the *wilderness* it-self, as representing NATURE more, will be the more engaging, and appear with a magnificence beyond the formal mockery of princely gardens.'

In a way, I would have liked to be strong minded, and to have kept my wood and drive very pure, very native. But in actual fact, the decision was taken for me. We had planted in the garden at Penllwynplan several rhododendrons; and, ignorantly, we had planted them in the wrong place. Rhododendrons are categorised as A, B, C, or D, according to their hardiness and the degree of exposure they can stand. They are, after all, mostly derived from woodland species. A is the hardiest category, containing the ironclads, which can take anything you can throw at them, from blazing sun to cruel north winds. B is the next, and a 'B' hybrid, though it may maintain life in an exposed situation, really requires some shade and shelter to flourish.

Our rhododendrons were 'B's. They were all old varieties – 'Brittannia', 'Pink Pearl', and 'Madame Masson', and we made the simple-minded mistake of equating 'old' with 'hardy'. We planted them round the lawn at the back of the house, in full sun. They didn't like it. 'Madame Masson,' which is a white variety, with a fine freckling of dark gold spots in the throat, made a better fist of it than the other two did, but was unlucky enough to get trampled by the cattle when they all got out of the Atcost building one night, when I hadn't shut the gate properly. 'Britannia' flowered gamely enough but sulked in her foliage, growing hardly at all and always looking yellow and tatty in spite of a soil that should have been acid, and even, in desperation, a dose of sequestrene. 'Pink Pearl' nearly died. I have wondered retrospectively if part of the trouble was the soil Ph. The garden they were planted in had once been a kitchen garden, and may have been heavily limed over the years. Anyway, whatever the reason, they were a sorry lot.

As I bought my new place months before we sold the farm, I was able to take things from the garden without breaking any contract. Having a wood deep in leaf mould, facing west, sheltered and shaded, it really seemed too unkind to leave these three poor creatures languishing in an environment so unsuited to them, so I dug them up and brought them along. They were delighted. Despite a drought of nearly a month just after their move, they all 'took', and have showed, by the amount of fine, glossy-leaved new growth they have put on, how much they have appreciated the favour.

'In for a penny, in for a pound' is a good motto; and having introduced pink and Turkey red into my wood, it seemed sensible to abandon the idea of a purely natural picture, and use that kindly environment for a few other plants that would be beautiful in themselves, albeit exotic. I had a plant of the lovely semi-double camellia 'Adolphe Adusson,' which flowers in February and March, covering itself with three-inch-wide flowers of geranium lake, exquisitely gold-stamened; so I took that along, and bought for good measure, a small specimen of *Magnolia denudata,* which, if I am lucky, should in some years flower at the same time.

It is a strange thing how rarely you see this magnolia. *Soulangeana*, with its purple-stained buds and its yellowish young leaves, grows in every other garden, but *denudata,* the Yulan, is rare. I can't think why. Both kinds are early flowerers and at the mercy of frosts—both are quite easy, and begin to flower when they are quite young. To my eyes there is no comparison in their beauty. *Soulangeana,* as usually seen, tends to grow as a large bush, or if as a tree, then a sprawling one. *Denudata* is more upright, and when it is mature, takes on a gnarled, rugged, oriental shape that is a pleasure in itself. Then when it flowers, those crabbed, horizontal, pewter-grey branches are crowned all along their length with great upright snow-white chalices, which sit as lightly on the boughs as swans on still water, and with something of the same ruffling purity of effect. When I lived in London, my evening bus journey home took me up Denmark Hill, and I used to look out for a beautiful little specimen of *denudata* in Champion Park. Lit by the level rays of the westering sun, it would often be posed in the most dramatic and spectacular way against a bank of dark clouds in the east. It made a most perfect picture, and I hope that my slender three-foot-tall young hopeful may one day do the same.

Once one has admitted that one's wood is a garden, there is no end to the possibilities. My wood runs down beside my drive, which on that side is sunk about four feet. There was a hedge marking this boundary once, set about fifteen feet back from the edge. This has now become merely a row of gnarled hawthorn trees, twenty feet tall, with wide and irregular gaps between them, forming as it were the front rank of the wood, and keeping the worst of the sun's heat from the shade-lovers behind. I plan to use these trees as hosts for climbers, particularly for some of the more rampant kinds of clematis. They can keep their roots cool on the north side of the trunks, and wriggle their twigs through to the sunny south; it should be ideal for them. Then the actual precipice which goes down to the level of the drive can be clothed with things like periwinkles, and the fifteen feet of intervening sward carpeted with bulbs. It is quite an opportunity.

Bloody-mindedly, however, I still mourn, slightly, my natural and unaltered piece of Welsh woodland. I suppose the only answer (is there no end to one's greed?) is to have two little stretches of woodland, quite apart from and out of sight of each other, and follow the two plans separately.

Thus in the garden wood, as well as rhododendrons and azaleas, one could have plants in rich, glowing colours – shade-loving primulas, drifts of sky-blue *Meconopsis betonicifolia*, sheets of lilies, species hydrangeas, camellias, kalmias, and so on – while in the other one would stick to the quieter things that suit with what a better writer than myself has described as 'the Daemon of an English wood.'

There would be snowdrops to begin with. They grow round here in their millions, in any case. The climate exactly suits them, and there are many woods where they are to be found by the acre – funny, prim little things, more effective really at close quarters, where you can appreciate their fine detail and smell their faint scent, then in the mass – but welcome because of their bravery in flowering at that grim time of the year. '*Lili wen fach*' is the Welsh name for the snowdrop, 'little white lily'; I wonder if there has ever been anyone who failed to respond to this little flower, so cool, so sweet and so demure?

Then there are primroses and wood anemones. The beauty of this kind of gardening is that once you have got your stock well and truly established, there is hardly anything more for you to do. Primroses and wood anemones are so tough, so at home, so well adapted to life in a quiet deciduous wood that they will spread, given the chance, right up to its boundaries; all you need to do is to make sure that no gross invaders like brambles or nettles crowd them out. Their other enemies, whatever they may be, they have learned to live with.

Daffodils come next – and foxgloves – and campions – and wood goldilocks – and Solomon's seal – and lilies-of-the-valley. Honeysuckle and dog roses scramble through the bushes at the wood's edge and gorse and broom keep a note of sharp yellow going wherever there is sun. Of course this is only the merest sketch of the possibilities of such a wood, and I have mentioned only the most obvious things. But even if one were to grow nothing more recherché than this in one's wood – no heleborines, for instance, and no tutsan – it could still be a lovely place.

Even in winter there would be colour. Polished leaves of holly and ivy catch and reflect the sky's blue, oaks hold their tawny leaves, and the silver bark of ash and hazel is touched with the tender green of moss and lichen.

Perhaps more suited to the other, more cultivated wood, would be a little scheme that I have been thinking about for some years, which would be at its best from about mid-October to Christmas. This would depend upon a considerable concentration of plants whose chief glories lay either in the colour of their autumn leaves, or in their berries. There is immense scope. Female hollies of the wild kind would form the backbone of the planting, and, if they were tall enough to stand it, I would be tempted to run various vines and creepers up them. I remember a noble old holly in Hertfordshire that had been ascended, right to the top, by a Virginia creeper of some kind, whose leaves, either against the holly's dark polished green, or glowing with the light shining through them really almost looked in November, as if they were on fire. An inter-planting of the stag's-horn sumach, *Rhus typhinus*, would pick up the colour, and should be easy enough to come by, being such a willing suckerer. *Parrotia persica* is a wonderful autumn colour tree on some soils, though I must admit that the one I had for years at Penllwyn-plan never once turned a single leaf. Many of the cherries colour exquisitely; they, along with the yellow azalea *lutea*, which is another glowing bush in autumn, could be included not only for their autumn effect, but also to give another effect with their blossom in spring. Lower growing scarlet could be introduced in the form of some of the vacciniums, and some of the berberises, notably *thunbergii*.

Spindles provide both coloured leaves and beautiful fruit, and the climber *Celastrus orbiculatis* has the same splitting habit, with yellow fruits parting to show orange seeds, and a loose, scrambling way of growing. I would be happy to welcome pyracanthas to my berry plantation, both the orange- and the yellow-berried forms, but of course they would be grown as small trees, and would thus fruit much more freely than their close-pruned wall-grown relations do. To choose from the ranks of the berrying *berberis* family would not be easy; *rubrostilla, wilsonii* and Pirate King are all good kinds that I know from experience to be easy-going. Cotoneasters, too, offer an *embarras de richesse; simonsii* makes itself so much at home in this neighbourhood that it often occurs as a self-sown plant in field hedges, presumably by means of birds' droppings. The blue-bloomed berries of the vacciniums are pretty, but would probably be too early to play their part in the main conflagration, but in a good year the exquisite fruit of our common sloe would carry on the blue theme with fruits that persist for a long time; and I for one would not despise that cheerful commoner, the snow-berry. Three native scrambling plants, white bryony, honeysuckle, and woody nightshade are all reliable producers of splendidly glossy berries, and tutsan, that large wild St John's wort, joins in the chorus with its head of fruit that turns from green to red and, eventually, from red to black. Wild Arum, or Lords and Ladies, sticks up its jolly spike of orange berries at ground level, and the Gladwyn iris is another native with bright-coloured seeds that would appear to advantage in this kind of gathering.

I acquired my stock of this plant one snowy winter's day when, tempted by brilliant sun and an almost Alpine blue sky, I had taken my dog, Tip, out for a really long walk. We passed through some woods on the way home, and there, among the tufts of vivid wood-rush, I saw this hardy, tough-looking strap-leaved perennial that I didn't recognise at all. Using a piece of broken slate as a trowel, I managed to detach a bit of the rootstock from the edge of the clump (this was before the present legislation about the collecting of wild flowers was passed!) and, rolling it up as best I could in my handkerchief, carried it home. I planted it straight out into the garden, and in spite of the sub-zero temperature, it flourished and grew on. Two years later it produced the dingy purple little flowers that enabled me to be sure that it was, as I had suspected, the Gladwyn iris. The cut root is supposed to smell of roast beef, but I can't say I noticed it on the piece I had in my handkerchief. But then, of course, sub-freezing temperatures are not very propitous for smells.

The Gladwyn iris by no means exhausts the list of possible plants for my little autumn-colour-cum-fruit area. There are many, many other fruiting and berrying plants that could be used in a scheme of this sort. The Wayfaring tree is splendid both in leaf colour and in its transparent, red-currant-like fruit; many crab-apples retain their brightly-coloured fruit throughout the early winter months; and I have made no mention of the various roses and thorns whose hips and haws are among the most reliable of late autumn decorations. I think I shall have to try to get a berry plantation going in my little wood. It would be a splendid thing to enjoy in the last few months before one can begin to look for the earliest evidence of the turn of the year, and the approach of spring.

One bit of the wild garden which is already planted has given me great pleasure, though of course it will certainly improve as time goes by, and sparse plantings thicken up. This is a bit of hedgebank, about thirty feet long, running north and south, and sloping back to a height of perhaps four feet. The hedge that grows along the top of it is straggly and ragged, and is mostly composed of blackthorn, but contains also hawthorn, hazel, and dog rose. A sweetbriar, growing round the gatepost corner in the next field, is being encouraged to extend its long arms into the complex; brambles however, all too eager to join the party, are being snubbed, and gradually rooted out, as occasion arises.

All around the hedge roots, there is a splendid colony of primroses. There were about ten plants when I arrived, but by transplanting in seedlings and splitting up extra large plants, the colony has now been extended, and must now number forty or fifty individuals. There is plenty of genetic variety, too; differences in the size and shape of the flowers, as well as in floriferousness and in habit, can easily be seen among the many plants. Fifty primroses is a nice start, and makes quite a display flowering together, but I hope to have about fifty thousand in a few years; it is such a little darling of a flower that I should like to see it tucked into every cranny round the bole of every shady tree. I collect the seeds and raise plants with this aim in mind, but I am always surprised to find what a long time it takes them to ripen. It is July hereabouts before the capsules reach the 'burst and scatter' stage; which is a long time, when you consider that the flowers begin to appear in February and March.

To flower at the same time as the primroses, I have introduced some white wood anemones. These grow very freely round here, in sunny as well as shady situations, the flowers becoming larger and silkier as the season advances. Their leaves are pretty too, and I hope that before long they will have seeded themselves as thickly as the primroses among the roots of the hedge. A third participant in the March display is the charming celandine, a flower that I look out for eagerly every year. Its formal, varnished discs seem to me to be the true harbingers of spring, because it never seems to throw odd out-of-season blossoms as the primroses and violets do, but waits for the lengthening days, and the return of true hope. The blackthorn opens its snowy, almond-scented blossom above the flowers as April closes in, and the pace quickens as flower after flower opens to the first really warm sun of the year. Purple ground ivy, tiny but brilliant, adds a new colour to the tapestry; cowslips, dandelions, and wild daffodils augment the yellow of the hazel catkins. Dog violets, taken from the astonishing violet turf of the rough grazing, blue the green in their patch of grass; and ladysmock, taller than all the rest, threads its graceful lilac heads into the lowest branches of the hedge. There is one small patch of double ladysmock, much cherished, a gift from a very old friend; doubling spontaneously is a delightful habit with the ladysmock, and makes it look like a lovely little version of the garden stock. In mid-month, the first vivid magenta spikes of the early purple orchis appear; I have been lucky to acquire individuals both much lighter and much darker than the average, and up on the flank of the slope they display themselves to the best possible advantage. Stitchwort, so white –

how shall one describe it? Salt-white? Gull-white? Cloud-white? – rambles everywhere, its pristine flowers and neat green leaves the perfect foil for the other flowers.

Nor does the onset of May see any diminution in the beauty of the little stretch of bank. Seeding daffodils are succeeded by bluebells, and the strong pink of campion overtops the brilliant silken embroidery of sky-blue bugle, germander speedwell, and a carefully selected burnt-orange form of bird's-foot trefoil. Unless felled by the slugs, the tall spikes of the spotted orchids rise above the lower flowers, and as May lengthens into June, the brilliant yellow of the horseshoe vetch takes over from the earlier species that are now rapidly fading. The lovely sweet vernal grass, growing thickly among the flowers, scents the air with its haunting and pervasive fragrance. In the hedge itself, the first buds of the dog rose overlap the last fading petals of the hawthorn, and the honeysuckle plants, grown from cuttings of specially richly-coloured plants in the lane, twine upwards vigorously towards the light. A small planting of tutsan expands its yellow buttercup-like flower; I hope it will set good seed, so that I can increase it. The wild sedum known as Orpine or live-long is there too; its flowers, of a deep crimson-pink, come later, towards the end of August. Its pretty tints make quite a display along the roadside hedges, and I hope, soon will in mine.

There are so many other species that I would like to grow in my little length of bank, but unfortunately space runs out. If you look at the best effects in the wild, you will observe that they are made by rather substantial colonies of flowers, particularly when they are next to other colonies of flowers that are in bloom at the same time. So I am resisting the temptation to try and make my bit of bank carry on with a full summer display. I think it is probably better to concentrate on getting really generous drifts of the spring-flowering things going in it. I must look for another site to grow the ox-eye daisies, the feral columbines, the Queen Anne's lace, the sorrel, the buttercups, the foxgloves, the *Geranium pratense*, the ling, the harebells, the betony ... what a rich selection there is to choose from.

My plan for the soggy grey triangle that receives the land drainage below the drive is already being put into operation.

The first thing to do is to cut down the shading trees, and my son Matthew is, as the Welsh say, 'on half' with this. It does seem a pity to cut down healthy trees, but they are irredeemably in the wrong place, and their removal, with the consequent letting in of light and air, is an absolutely necessary first step to anything better. Most of them are rather unremarkable willows, but one is a fine straight alder whose demise I do lament. Unfortunately, it stands squarely to the south-west of my little triangle, and the choice is between it, or the whole of the rest of my scheme. So in the end, there is no contest. But all the same, I'm sorry, Alder.

Once it is cleared, we shall have a triangle with sides of about twenty-five yards long. A rim of grass five feet wide separates it from the drive. Then it drops abruptly, and sinks three or four feet to a ragged mixed boundary hedge. Two or three indeterminate little streams feed into it at different points, covering it with an inch or so of slowly-moving water, which drains out at the lowest point in the hedge to join the river, here passing close beneath it. What we shall have to do after the trees have been removed and the hedge laid is to hire a JCB to dig quite a deep pond at the broad end of the triangle. The spoil can be heaped up on the hedge site to compensate for the natural slope of the land, and a gully made to allow the water to trickle through at the same place as it does now, but higher up. Only time will tell if the springs from the higher land will be sufficient to keep an actual pond going all through the year. As it is constituted at the moment, the triangle tends to become dry enough to walk on, although always muddy, in times of prolonged drought; but a capital sum of water, such as there would be in a pond of three feet deep, might the better be able to stand these occasional depletions.

The long point of the triangle will remain as a bit of sunny marsh or bog. I have written about its winter aspect in another chapter; it will not be less lovely in spring and early summer when it is crowded with kingcups, river mint, water forget-me-knot, yellow iris, codlins-and-cream, loosestrife, ragged robin, brooklime, water germander, meadowsweet and mimulus ... what a list! The mind reels. It is a pity that I dare not add the exquisite white water lily, but the stretch of water will be too small, even if it retains enough depth during the summer, for me to risk introducing such a vigorous spreader. I might try and get a bush or two of bog myrtle or sweet gale, however; and marsh orchids are not unobtainable from friends with ill-drained patches on their farms.

Another beautiful plant association that I should like to introduce here is one that I came across by chance in our lane a year or two ago. It was in July, and the honeysuckle, which is very abundant round here, was at its best. I had used honeysuckle a few days before in a very successful flower arrangement in which it had been associated with some pale pink old-fashioned roses in a wide, flat container, on top of my stripped pine corner cupboard. The solidity of the roses and the airy grace of the trailing honeysuckle sprays, the pinks, ambers, and creams, backed up here and there by the discreet mulberry of flowering cocksfoot, had looked lovely against the honey-coloured wood; I was thinking about it as I drove along, and wondering if I could re-create the effect, perhaps in a smaller and more intimate arrangement. So what was my surprise and pleasure when, on coming to the part of the lane where the honeysuckle grows most thickly, I found that it had been joined by another plant, growing round its feet in a billowing mass of exactly the same pink as my old rose. This turned out, on examination, to be marsh valerian, a reasonably common wild perennial which grows happily enough in wet, boggy places, but was here blooming perfectly obligingly in an ordinary hedgerow. It was lucky for me that I saw it on the day I did, because a day or two later, the Council machine came round and trashed the banks, and though the honeysuckle high in the hedge 'saved', the valerian, in all the glory of its cloud-pink blooming, was dashed away as if it had never been. I must certainly acquire some stock of it, and set it on the further margin of my new pond with the honeysuckle that I hope will soon be festooning that rough old hedge. Safe inside my boundary, the two species can complete their growth cycles unmolested, and spread at will.

Wild flowers growing in their natural habitat are of course very subject to the chance of circumstance. It may be man, it may be animals, it may be the weather that does the damage; but for many species, the year in which they can grow right through and set a big crop of seed is the exceptional one. In my first year here, I saw several wild-flower effects – notably a big stand of musk mallow, and another one of devil's-bit scabious – which have not been repeated, although I have been on the look-out for them. The cattle have happened to be on the rough pastures where these particular wild flowers grow at a different time of year; so that, although individual plants have managed to flower and set seed, there has been no mass display. It was only by the lucky chance of their having a year in which they were left unmolested at a critical time that I realised how beautiful they could be, massed, and how willing they were to grow that way. I wonder how many other wild-flower effects there are that the law of chance is waiting its inscrutable time to reveal.

As far as the actual area of land is concerned, the most important part of Ty Arian is its two little pastures, which, together, probably comprise two out of the three and a half acres. I have written so often of the lovely grassland flowers, yet I never tire of writing their names, and picturing them in my mind. The recital of them is almost a kind of litany, that fills the imagination with their petals and scents. I have them all in my two little fields, growing among the wild and unmanured grasses: primroses, cowslips, buttercups, daisies, white clover, red clover, dog violets, ladysmocks, yellow rattle, tormentil, cinquefoil, lady's mantle, self-heal, bugle, speedwell, bluebells (close to the hedge where the big oak dapples them with the shade of its tawny leaves) – our familiar pasture flowers, the darlings of the spring and early summer; common things all; how unthinkable that we should ever have to live without them. And yet, if it were possible to take an accurate census of their populations, I dare say that many of them would be down already to a mere ten or twenty per cent of what they were in the early years of the nineteenth century. Modern agriculture and the pressing need for food for our big population is driving them from their traditional homelands in the fields. Let me encourage anyone who can spare even two or three square yards in the garden to extend them a welcome there so that they may survive in our country not only for us, but for our descendents to enjoy.

3

Winter Gardening

Strongly addicted gardeners cannot simply turn off their need to garden, and to think about gardening, during the winter months. Fruit and vegetable gardeners, of course, will not even be tempted to do so; pruning, digging, and spraying will keep them out of doors whenever the weather is clement. But I have met plenty of what you might call ornamental gardeners who seem to be capable of putting their hobby to one side from, say, the middle of November till the beginning of March, and ignoring the outdoor world between those dates as if it magically ceased to exist. Such people, it seems to me, miss a lot of the fun; I defend to the death, of course, their right to do so if they wish, but they do deny themselves nearly a third of the year, and a third whose weather often brings us spells of mild and balmy weather as well as the expected snow, frost and fog.

I write, of course, from the point of view of one who lives in a mild area. West Wales comes into the second-mildest climatic belt of this country, being surpassed only by Cornwall, a narrow strip up the west coast of Wales, bits of the West of Scotland, and most of Ireland. My father, when he gardened in industrial Yorkshire, never bothered much about planting things for winter effect; the heavy sootfall of those days of unrestricted coal domestic fires blackened any evergreens into objects of squalor, and the harsh climate, too, was inclined to nip the flowers of even such tough customers as *Jasmine nudiflorum*. But it was probably the soot rather than the cold that made it difficult, because my sister, who lives even further north, near Newcastle-on-Tyne, has arranged a most successful winter scheme in her garden.

It was at the end of November that I saw it, and I thought it was one of the most effective bits of gardening that I had ever seen. Its basis was a tall hedge planted to screen off her garden from an overlooking house, and it must have been ten or fifteen years old at the time I saw it. The backbone of the thing was a row of Scots pines, slender, blue-green adolescents that will probably have to be cut down eventually, as they grow too big, but which make a lovely band of colour now. These are interplanted with beech, loosely trained up as a hedge. This is pruned rather than clipped, and is of fairly open growth, although feathered down to the ground. It keeps its fox-red leaves throughout the winter, and provides both support and noble colour contrast for the next inter-planted thing, which is the dog rose. Somehow my sister must have got hold of a particularly good strain of this simple plant, because, growing through the beech to about six or seven feet high, it had fruited into a positive sheet of scarlet hips. A narrow border along the hedge's foot was planted with seed-raised specimens of *Cineraria maritima*, the variation of growth among the seedlings preventing any suggestion of monotony or over-formality. On sunny mornings following clear nights the whiteness of the hoar-frost on the adjacent lawn exactly matched the silvery *cineraria*; and for the hour or two during which the sun's level rays lit up that hedge, it twinkled and glowed as warmly as any summer border could. It was the sort of thing you had to keep going out to have a look at.

The crowning touch of the scheme though, was not of my sister's devising, and was, it must be acknowledged, evanescent; but, while it lasted, it must have been a strong contender for high spot of the garden year. This was the visit of a flock of waxwings who came several times to feed on the rosehips, choosing, fortunately, times when the hedge was warmly lit by the sun, and lingering long enough to be enjoyed in considerable detail by the enraptured audience at the windows.

This scheme of planting lasted quite well through the whole winter, though of course the bravura touch of the scarlet hips departed with the waxwings, and the *cineraria* would probably have to be pulled up round about Christmas time.

But the Scots pine and the beech would retain their colour until the new leaves came again, and were absolutely hardy and independent of anything that the weather could possibly fling at them. They were also big – a substantial eyeful; my own winter plantings, hellebores, species crocus, and so on, tend to be the sort of things you have to go and pore over rather than things that catch your eye as you glance out of the window. Another bonus was of course that the hedge looked ravishing in April, when daffodils grew thickly along its foot against the new beech leaves, and in June, when the dog roses flowered; and at one flower for each of those thousands of hips, that must have been quite a display.

It is quite a surprise, looking round at gardens generally, to see how little trouble people do take to make winter pictures. My sister's effort demonstrates that you do not need anything difficult or expensive. Yet how often do you see those three things – retained brown leaves, evergreens, and mowed lawn, deliberately composed into a harmonious picture? Not often enough, that is for sure; 'But I don't go out into the garden in winter,' people say. But surely even people who like to keep within doors from November to March must occasionally glance out of the window.

A variant on the simple winter picture scheme was suggested to me by a chance association that I saw in a hedgebank on the road edge at Penllwynplan, the farm I lived at before coming here. In this one, the fox-red element was provided by the dead leaves of a fern – the male fern, I imagine – which contrasted prettily with the pale silvery-buff of dead grass. A stumpy bush of ivy reflected the light most joyously in its broad and brilliant green leaves; and the final note in the composition was the smooth silver trunk of an ash sapling growing up through the middle of it all.

This simple and unplanned association, which blazed into beauty whenever the sun shone on it, throughout the whole winter, suggested a number of variations that might be more suited to a garden – a tame garden, that is. In a wild garden, it would be charming exactly as it was. But ash is perhaps a little crude and, eventually, large, for a suburban setting.

For the russet element, there are a number of possibilities. The fern itself is of course often planted in gardens, and even more often plants itself, being a native, and a willing coloniser. It is beautiful at any time of the year, forming a clump from which the leaves arise in a neat symmetrical circle; and it is not hard to dislodge if it puts itself where you don't want it. It is true that spring frosts do sometimes blacken its too-precocious fronds, and then for a week or two it looks a mess. But you could always cut off the damaged bits if they offended you, and the main plant is perfectly capable of sending up replacements. Alternatively, many of the smaller polygonums die down to a nice mound of bracken-red in winter, and these would give you the extra bonus of pink or red flower spikes in the late summer. A side-note on these is that I find these small polygonum flowers exceedingly long-lasting in flower arrangements. Some of the heathers go rusty in winter, or scarlet, which is even better; the callunas 'Robert Chapman' and 'Golden Feather' are praised for this, though I must acknowledge that I have not yet grown either of them. And if you wish to leave the small scale behind, and go for your russet in a big way, there are other trees besides the beech that retain their dead leaves throughout the winter as long as they are kept in an artificially limited form, as in a hedge: the hornbeam, for example, and the sessile oak. I would always choose the beech myself unless I was unlucky enough to have a soil it wouldn't tolerate; and perhaps it is worth mentioning in this connection that although the beech is usually described as a plant that likes a limy soil, there are plenty of beeches growing around here in a soil whose Ph is low enough to please the most pernickety of calcifuges. In Welwyn Garden City, where I once lived, there are splendid beech hedges, in full maturity, all round the town centre, and the sight of those full, brilliant strokes of colour in the winter sun is as warming as a cup of hot tomato soup. If you are in the extremely unusual position of gardening on a real land-scape scale, of course, you can introduce bracken-covered hillsides, or great plantations of Japanese larch. But few of us can hope ever to garden on this Homeric scale. One or two coniferous trees give a good colour for the early part of the winter, notably the Swamp Cypress, and *Cryptomeria japonica*, although on some soils the latter may turn purplish rather than red.

The silver part of the picture can be presented either as bark or as leaves. Silver birches seem to offer the palest bark, and a birch tree is an adornment to any garden. I read somewhere years ago that it was important in acquiring one to make sure that it was *Betula verrucosa*, because these were the only ones that coloured up reliably in the autumn. Photographs of birches of this kind round Glen Afric in Scotland certainly make one long to grow it; they appear in the October sun as pure gold, rather like the Mallorns of Tolkein's imagination. But when I did buy a birch, and went to some trouble to make sure that it was verrucosa, it rewarded me by instantly developing a kind of witch's broom infection, and virtually dying on its feet. I say virtually, not quite, because it does still maintain about ten per cent of living tissue, and, when I saw it this summer, had surely two hundred green leaves on its gaunt and blackened twigs. But it can hardly be described as an ornament to the garden and, if it were still mine, would certainly go for the chop.

The other common birch, *Betula pubescens*, is presumably the one you are supposed to guard against getting by mistake. All I can say is that some friends of mine once went on a picnic and arrived at my house the next day bearing a seedling of this birch; and that when I planted it out in the garden, it took and flourished, and grew, and continued to do so; and that every autumn it turns as yellow as a hatful of golden guineas; and that on my own experience, if I were given a choice between it and *verrucosa*, I would opt for it every time. But an experience based only on the behaviour of two individuals can hardly form the basis for generalising; and if you want a pretty silver trunk, your chance of reward is probably as good planting the one as the other.

An alternative to the silver bark of birch, beech, or juvenile oak is an evergreen shrub, and the one that comes most readily to mind is *Senecio laxifoliis*. This is a shrub that I hate to be without; and considering how easy it is to strike cuttings from it there is never any need to be in this unhappy position. It is supposed to be slightly tender, and presumably one day it will up and teach me that it is; but as yet the only way I have ever lost it is by selling it in the garden that it is growing in. Further, I remember a plant of it in Hertfordshire coming completely unruffled through the dreadful winter of 1962–3, when the diesel froze in the buses as they stood in their garages, and the milk habitually appeared for weeks with its gold and silver tops pushed up on cunning little iced cream mushrooms which demonstrated most nattily that liquids expand on freezing. The *senecio* makes a rounded bush that will grow up to four feet high and a good deal more across, but which can also be kept smaller by judicious pruning. Its leaves and shoots are at their whitest when new, in the summer, but it maintains a neat, pewtery presence throughout any winter that I have ever experienced, and would most admirably fulfil the middle place in such a red, silver and evergreen planting as I have in mind. In summer it will pay its rent with truly beautiful bunches of white buds which eventually expand into yellow flowers not unlike those of the ragwort. And if this causes you to wrinkle your face with instinctive scorn and distaste, let me beg you to reconsider the matter. After all, it is not the appearance of its flowers that makes us hate the ragwort, but the fact that its poisonous juices kill stock. Looked at dispassionately, it is actually rather a pretty flower, and I have often used it effectively in large-scale autumn flower arrangements in a big salt-glazed jug with such other villains as seeded dock, bracken, and, ultimate poisoner, tubular water dropwort.

Anybody who possessed an experimental mind, and lived in a clean area, might like to take the somewhat Japanese course of introducing a shapely pale-coloured boulder into the middle of their red/silver/green winter planting, and encourage it to cover itself with silver-green lichen. It might look absolutely lovely; it might look merely ludicrous and affected. It depends on the kind of geological situation you live in, and on your artistry in arranging things.

For small schemes which are designed to make a tiny focus of attention, perhaps to be looked at from a particular window, there are various other ever-grey or silver plants that can fill the bill. *Stachys lanata*, though it can look rather tatty in a hard winter, provides a good splash of white if it is trimmed back early enough – say in August – to have covered itself with a nice suit of tidy young leaves. This means cutting off the flower spikes almost as soon as they appear, but at least there is the bonus that you can preserve them then, at their best, for use in winter arrangements of dried flowers. Lavender, well trimmed back to keep it bushy, gives a year-round silvery-pewter effect; and the foliage of pinks is a winner, though the effect here, it must be admitted, is perhaps bluish rather than silvery. My sister's friend, *Cineraria maritima*, is another strong silver that will sometimes stand the winter, though I would never feel tempted to rely on it for a winter scheme anywhere very chilly.

The third ingredient of the picture, which is shining green leaves, offers a lot of scope. Ordinary wild ivy takes a lot of beating, and once it has reached maturity it will crown itself with flowers and berries that are lovely to pick and that will please both insects and birds in due season if you leave any behind. Holly is another stalwart, the hermaphrodite variety 'Van Thol' being the best bet if you want both berries and a dark, shining leaf. Gardeners on a lime-free soil might choose to try a camellia or a pieris; less favoured localities could use one of the mahonias, or *choisya ternata*. Laurels have wonderfully brilliant winter leaves, and grow anywhere, but here again we are venturing into large-scale gardening, for a laurel's nature is to be expansive, and a laurel pruned is for my money a laurel spoiled.

There is a certain pleasure in remembering the moment when a particular plant made its impact on us, and I do recall exactly when I first realised what a lovely creature the uninhibited laurel was. It was in February, and I had to go by train to Swansea, for some reason. This is a most beautiful stretch of railway, hugging as it does the left bank of the tidal river Towy all down its estuary, and then following the coast round for a long way. It was no less beautiful than usual on that sunny February day. Heavy rain had been falling for weeks, and there was a lot of what golfers call 'occasional water' standing about, which reflected the low-angled sunlight into a wonderful refractive crystal brilliance. In this prismatic radiance, the laurels stood supreme. Big, abundant, untrammelled, they grew here and there along the railway banks, the plainness of their simple rounded outlines most exquisitely complemented by the formality of their symmetrically-arranged leaves. And how they took the light! Those brilliant varnished surfaces splashed out great flakes of light, white, yellow, pale blue; the effect was as gay as a bank of flowers, but the month was February, and the plants in question were as tough as an old boot. I determined then and there that I would grow laurels in this way if I ever had the room; and I have not forgotten that promise to myself, even though I have not yet put it into effect. To recreate the picture, I must obviously site them somewhere spacious and sunny, and, occasional water being *but* occasional, perhaps my laurels had better be set to grow near a sheet of permanent water, whose twinkling ripples can reflect the light in brilliant flashes off those noble varnished leaves. Then if I back my laurels with half a dozen silver birches, and arrange a band of bracken in front of them, I have my classic winter picture ready made. Wild daffodils, it has not escaped anyone's attention, love to grow 'beside the lake, beneath the trees'; it could be a lovely feature.

Such a sheet of water, a pond, really – which among us can expect to garden with a lake? – offers a complementary opportunity for the growing of plants whose big gun is the colour of their winter bark. My own favourite is the brilliant, sealing-wax-red 'Cornus Alba Westonbirt' variety, and I remember all too well my first introduction to this plant, it having obtruded itself into my consciousness during an interview which was, to say the least of it, getting sticky.

It was at St Hilda's College, Oxford, where I was being interviewed for a place in the school of English Language and Literature. The thing had started inauspiciously. Knowing that I had to present myself outside the door of one Miss Whitelock at 10 a.m., I had set out at about five to to find her room, only to be told that it was not in the main building at all, but in the South Building, some way down the road. I asked directions from a white-haired woman in a tweed coat who was just leaving the college, and when she pointed it out to me, we proceeded down the road towards it more or less together, at an anxious jog-trot. She seemed to be in as great a hurry as I was. Being younger and spryer, I actually got to the building before her, but she got her nose in front again when I had to stop and ask for further directions. She was, of course, Miss Whitelock, and we arrived, simultaneously, gasping for breath, outside her door at about five past ten, in a lamentable atmosphere of farce which we both tried to ignore, but which coloured all the first part of the interview – conducted, perforce, in very short sentences.

After a few minutes the door opened and another don came in. Her presence only added to my awe, for she was Helen

Gardner, a scholar of wide repute, whose books, as well as those of Miss Whitelock, were familiar to me. But whatever my opinion of her might have been, I could tell that she didn't think much of me, for she was frowning as she riffled through my entrance papers.

'Whatever made you write about Euphues?' she enquired, disapprovingly; and I was much too timid and inexperienced to reply 'A desire to show off', though that would have been the truth. Instead, I murmured something inaudible, and looked out of the window for inspiration. And inspiration there was of a sort, though not of the right sort to get me a place at St Hildas. For down in the frosty meadows by the River Cherwell I saw a great thicket of what I instantly realised must be 'Cornus Alba Westonbirt' variety, a splendid block of scarlet in the morning sun; and it has inspired me to plant it wherever I have gardened ever since, although I have never achieved a hundredth part of that display yet.

I suspect that there are two reasons why my plantings have never been as good as that one down by the Cherwell. The first is simply time. What I saw there was a real thicket, which must have been established for many years, and presumably cut back regularly to keep up a plentiful production of the young shoots which of course show the brightest bark. The other reason is situation. Dogwoods like damp; our native dogwood, with its duller crimson shoots shows this by the places it chooses for itself, lining the banks of canals or hanging over its ruddy reflection in mild ponds. The Oxford dogwood was growing in flat ground right down by the river, so presumably the water table would have been high, and its roots would not have had any difficulty in getting into the soggy stuff that sets a dogwood full ahead. My much sparser plants had to do the best they could with ordinary garden soil—indeed, in my Hertfordshire garden, with a rather gravelly soil, and a Thames Valley rainfall, which is one of the lowest in England. Here at Ty Arian I have a little triangle of swampy land on one side of my drive which seems admirably suited to a dogwood thicket, and I intend to have one there. The optimal position for plants whose main effect is in their winter bark, is where they can be illumined by the level rays of the setting or rising sun; it doesn't much matter which – both come within the normal out-of-bed period of most people during the time when the leaves are off the trees. The horizontal light of hail and farewell is always redder than the midday sun, and reflects off the brilliant bark in a glow of astonishing intensity. If the orange-barked willow, *Salix britzensis*, can be planted just behind the dogwood, and pollarded so that its vivid young shoots overtop it, you have a wonderful bit of winter colour. Considering how easy both the constituent parts are, it is odd that it is not more often planted. I have read that this particular dogwood will not grow from cuttings, and that increase consequently has to be from layers. Bearing this in mind, it might be a good idea to plant the first, bought plant or plants obliquely, so that several twigs can be layered from the word go, to get your thicket off to a good start. The willow, of course, will grow like magic from any shoot stuck into reasonably damp ground.

It might be possible to diversify this scheme of bright winter colour further by introducing a splendid little thing which is one of the few things I found on the credit side, in gardening terms, when I came to Ty Arian.

I saw it first one day in January, when I had made an offer for the place but had not yet signed a contract – a nerve-racking, dreary time, when I used to drive over and prowl around the deserted holding, wanting it very badly for my own, but terribly afraid that something might go wrong with the negotiations – torturing myself, in fact, a silly but irresistible thing to do. I used to leave my car at the bottom of the steep, stony, curved drive, and wander round, getting thoroughly cold, and wondering how it would feel to be able to open that blank closed door, and go in, and light a fire, and make a cup of tea. And then when I was too cold to put it off any longer, I would go home.

It was on one of these visits that, as I hurried down the drive to my patient Mini waiting at the gate my eye was caught by a scrap of scarlet away to the right amongst the straggling undergrowth. Thinking to myself, 'Another bit of blown-around rubbish from the yard' I turned aside to investigate – and to my amazement discovered that it was no rubbish, but a fungus; and not just one, once I had my eye in for it, but a whole family. Growing both singly and in clusters, they formed a series of smallish cups, anything from half an inch to two inches in diameter; and although their outsides were an inconspicuous bluey-white in colour, their lining, which was what you saw most of, was a vivid red – blood-red rather than scarlet, perhaps; it reminded me very much of the wrapper of a bar of Bournville chocolate, which is what I thought I was going to tidy away when I first saw it. The texture was suede-like, and the plants seemed perfectly indifferent to the icy east wind which blew around them, ruffling the dead bracken and the forlorn leaves of hart's-tongue fern which curled around the mossy fallen branches upon which they grew.

The bottom of the drive was flanked on both sides by sparse and scrubby trees which had shed lots of branches over the years; and as it was a place also which by its configuration received all the natural drainage and run-off water of the little estate, it was also pretty wet. Part of it was a disagreeable slimy mud, but round the edges, the ground and the dead branches were coated with a pale-green feathery moss, and it was against this background that the blood-red cups of the fungus displayed themselves. I have learned to distrust my mind's eye when I remember things, because it is inclined to gild the lily; so I will not describe what I saw as a blaze of scarlet like a field of poppies or a flaming sunset; nor will I pretend that the fungi met, edge to edge, to cover all the available space with their jewelled carpet. But they did make a display. Pure, vivid red is not the sort of colour you expect to find in the greyest months of the year; and, as with chile powder in cooking, a little goes a long way. It is winter again as I write this, late February, two years on from the time I first noticed the red cups; and as they are in their full glory there is no difficulty in making an accurate report of the square footage of colour that they make. So I have braved the belly-shrivelling wind to the extent of walking down to the bottom of the drive, and I am now in a position to report that the fungus occurs in two pieces of ground each measuring perhaps six yards by two; that the richest concentration was on one particular bit of dead wood about three feet long and as thick as my upper arm and which bore thirty-seven cups of various sizes; and that my estimate of the total number of cups visible, without looking for them by burrowing down among the dead grasses and brambles, was about two hundred. It is a poor day for colour in this bitter east wind, the sky bleached, shrunken and withdrawn to the extent that even the bracken has faded to a mere dead-leaf brown, but even in this light, the red fungus glows. In bright sunlight, it shouts.

Like a true gardener, I am seldom content to leave anything exactly as I find it, so I intend, in the next few weeks, to divide some snowdrops that I want to move, and to plant them down in the fungus area so that next year the colours can complement one another, blood red and snow white, as in the old fairy story; I shall also, tentatively, make a start on clearing away some of the concealing brambles that infest a certain proportion of the area; but here I shall have to be careful, lest it turn out that it is only their shelter and protection that enables my little red darling so easily to put up with these seasonable but bitter blasts. It may seem that I am making rather a lot of a small matter in writing so much about this chance discovery; but the truth is that I have neither seen it nor read about it anywhere else before, although I have been passionately interested in outdoor winter gardening for about thirty years now. Assuming, that is, that one acknowledges the deliberate cultivation of fungi to be a legitimate branch of gardening – and why should one not? The name of my great discovery appears, insofar as I can trust my fungus book, to be *Peziza (Sarcoscypha) Coccinea.*

In a mild spell in mid February, I transported a convenient branch well studded with red cups to the edge of a flower bed where there was a cheerful display of crocuses and double daisies. The *peziza* survived for a few days, playing to some extent the part that will be taken over later, even more brilliantly, by little scarlet species tulips; but it did not last. It became tattered and 'sought-into' looking, and I kept finding large bits of it broken off. I suppose the birds found it too noticeable to ignore. So in the end, I just broke up the rotten branch and used it for kindling. Only time will tell if the *peziza* can indeed be introduced, with its attendant snowdrops, into the foreground of a dogwood-willow planting; but who knows? It may work out; and until I know, I can at least dream.

Another dream that I have embroidered on nights (fortunately rare) when I have found it difficult to get to sleep, concerns the design of an ideal winter garden. This is a flower garden rather than simply a winter *effects* garden, and, given the right situation and a prodigious amount of money, shouldn't be too hard to achieve.

As it is only a dream away, I allow myself an absolutely perfect site, which is backed by a shallow semi-circle cut into the south side of a hill, like a quarry. But instead of being rough like a quarry, the back wall of this winter garden is faced with smooth sandstone blocks, and towers up to a protective ten feet. Most of the ground in front of it is bed, but a broad cross of paving in the same stone provides dry access and forms a firm footing for a comfortable slatted wooden seat placed squarely in the middle, under the wall, where it will receive any sun there may be. In my imagination, I often sit there in the winter months drinking my morning coffee and gazing around at the flowers which grow in the four beds formed by the angles of the flagged paths. The sheltering effect of the arc of retaining wall is extended by some quite large trees and shrubs planted at the extremities of the crescent, themselves enjoying the warm south-facing situation, and protected in their turn by such evergreen toughs as holly and evergreen oak, that flank them to their north-east and north-west sides. Wintersweet might grow here, and witch hazel; Rhododendrons *nobleanum, venustum, praecox*, and various others, could be tucked in on the eastern side where the boscage behind them would keep the destructive morning sun off their blossoms after cold nights. This would be the place too for early camellias, particularly if matters could be so arranged that the shade of some deciduous trees, planted some way in front of them, fell upon them in summer, and protected them from excessive sun.

Over the tall wall at the back would trail various lovely things planted into the soil at the top, and allowed to hang down like a curtain. *Jasmine nudiflorum* would be enchanting grown like this, though admittedly a south wall is more than it needs; *Forsythia suspensa* also is quite happy to trail, and would keep up the succession of yellow with its flowers that are so much paler and prettier than those of its more popular sister, *Intermedia spectabilis. Clematis balearica* gives its yellowish-white cupped flowers bloom in February, and could also hang down prettily behind the seat; and the shelter of such a warm wall would keep the handsome variegated ivy 'Gloire de Marengo' safe from the frost-burn that makes such a mess of its leaves in positions where the north wind can get at it.

Scent, on those balmy days that do so often occur in our much-maligned winter, should be quite a feature of this little garden. Winter flowers of poignant sweetness are the *Loniceras*, *fragrantissima* and *purpusii; Mahonia bealii; Viburnum fragrans*, or its improved hybrid, *Bodnantense*; the charming *Prunus sub-hirtella autumnalis*; and, most seductive of all, the winter-flowering *Daphnes*, a team which consists of the well-known *mezereum*, and the even more wonderful *D. indica*. The gold-variegated form of the latter, *Aureo-marginata*, is said to be hardier than the type, and I knew a bush of it that grew happily enough in a border under the south wall of a house in Rickmansworth. I would try to fit all these shrubs into my ideal winter garden, as well as such stalwart, albeit scentless, favourites as *Virburnum tinus*.

There are some berrying shrubs too that give a display right through the winter, and these I would certainly include. Both skimmias, in red, and, pernettyas, in pink, lilac, crimson and white, seem to have berries that birds don't like. But both also need husbands, being dioecious; so you have to have at least one male plant of each, if you are to get your display of berries. The pernettya insists on an acid soil, but the skimmia is less pernickety; either will keep up a bold presence, whatever the weather may do.

No winter garden would be complete without some plants of the hardy and aimiable heather *Erica carnea*, and as this is one of the few members of its family that is indifferent to the presence of lime in the soil, anyone can grow it. Any good nurseryman's catalogue will give a choice of varieties, but I would advise you to look before you leap if it is at all possible, for their descriptions of these heathers often seem to me to owe more to artistic imagination than to scrupulous observation. 'King George', for example – perhaps the most popular and widely-grown variety – is described by most nurserymen as 'Bright Rose Pink'. In my experience, it is quite a faded, subfusc, purplish sort of pink – not in any way nasty, and welcome indeed at that particular time of the year; but not bright. It does, however, make a hearty and obliging plant. Varieties I have seen in other people's gardens that have struck me as really vivid have been 'Vivelli' and 'Winter

Beauty'; and the well-known 'Springwood White' is a lovely thing.

In this garden of the imagination, money being no object, I would not stint myself of hellebores. As a family, they seem to have a leaning towards winter flowering, and if you sat whenever you could in your garden, from December through to the spring, you could revel in *H. niger*, the Christmas rose, *H. orientalis*, the Lenten rose, *H. foetidus* (you needn't smell it, after all), and *H. corsicus*, in turn. All the hellebores have the quality of firm shapeliness usually referred to by gardening writers as 'good drawing'; and in my experience of them, which has been sad, all are subject to extinction by a kind of fungal infection that covers their leaves with black blotches, and eventually kills them.

But, happy as I would be to revel in drifts of hellebores kept healthy by judicious spraying, it would be in the bulb order that I would really make the money fly. There are so many little things – they all seem to be little, the better to cower behind stones and folds in the ground, perhaps – that bring us their flowers in these darkest months of the year, that choice could be quite difficult. But in a garden like this, where both the beds and the cheque-book are infinitely elastic, the problem dissolves. I would have them all. In they would all cram, tightly together – species crocuses, tiny brilliant tulips, miniature cyclamen, early Cambridge-blue muscari, a wonderful variety of irises, a profusion of delicate daffodils, scillas, anemones, hepaticas, chionodoxae, snowdrops, aconites; the imagination paints a picture so full of superlatives that, as Othello might have remarked, 'The sense aches at it.' And, in spite of the gloomy prognostications of the gardening Jeremiahs, I have had enough success with the various constituent parts of such a planting to know for sure that it would work. They really do flower in winter; when the sun shines upon them, they open up widely and look extremely brilliant.

There is one small point in the arrangement of my winter garden in which I would differ from any other writer whose works I have read. And that is in the deployment of my yellow crocuses. Most of the crocuses so described are of a brilliant, vivid, blackbird's-bill colour that is really more of an orange-gold than a yellow; and again and again it is recommended that they be planted in association with the winter-flowering heathers, with Daphne *mezereum*, or even with Rhododendron *praecox*, all of which have flowers in the purplish-pink range. I think this colour chord is absolutely beastly; and although I know that taste is an individual matter, and that '*de gustibus non est disputandum*', I shall guard against it most sedulously. In my garden, the crocuses that grow near enough to the pinkish things to come into the same eyeful (or '*coup d'oueil*' as the French more elegantly phrase it) will be the purples, the violets, and the whites, which will be delightful. *Primula wanda*, too, will take her place with this bit of planting, the sheer depth of her vivid magenta giving richness to the lighter colours. And in the complementary planting, which I envisage on the other side of the broad flagged central path, I shall have all the colours of the crocuses including the yellows mixed together round the white form of Daphne *mezereum,* and drifts of the lovely *Erica carnea* 'Springwood White'. So there.

As a final touch to this winter garden of mine (I am getting expansive I know, but think what Bacon allowed himself), I would like it to overlook a view of trim parkland, in which noble oaks, ilexes, and a dark, pointed, brilliantly-berried holly or two diversified the middle distance. Further away a curve of august rhododendrons would melt into a receding haze of plum-twigged birches, leading to a folding of distant hills, scarfed with larch and spruce. I could easily go on landscaping it as far away as the county boundary. What does it matter that I know I never will? What, after all, are dreams for?

4

A Pride of Peacocks

My house stands on a shelf cut into the side of a hill which projects in front of it in a feature which could, flatteringly, be described as a terrace. It was Lord Peter Wimsey who observed that peacocks need a terrace; my friends Ruth and John believe that the natural corollary of this is that a terrace needs peacocks. Of their boundless generosity, they decided to give me some.

Diligent enquiry located a place in Angle where peacocks were bred. Yes, they would obligingly 'spare' us some (a curious Welsh usage which, by putting the buyer into the position of one who is receiving a favour, gives the vendor a good foundation for bargaining). So in September, when they were old enough, we went down to collect them.

It was a golden day. We ate our sandwiches down by the yacht moorings, where the pellucid water dashed itself gently to and fro over the rocks, while the flat sea emphasised its level against the sunlit, rounded cornfields. There is a big oil refinery at Angle, so you have to be careful which way you face when you sit down to eat a picnic. Twenty degrees too far round, and you might be forgiven for imagining yourself in the outskirts of Leeds or Doncaster. But it is all fairly local, and once you have got yourself into position with your back to the smoking chimneys and vast squat storage tanks, you can think yourself back into the Pembrokeshire of your early days, but with the pleasant additional entertainment of watching the big oil tankers coming in to their moorings, or setting off casually, in ballast, for the return journey to the other side of the world. We basked, watching the little sailing boats trying to pretend that there was enough wind to stretch their flapping canvas; we flung our apple cores to the somnolent gulls rocking on the twinkling ripples of the incoming tide; we nearly went to sleep. Then, the hour of our appointment with the gamekeeper being now at hand, we pulled ourselves together and went off to attend to the real business of the day.

It was an impressive estate upon which our peacocks got their first blink of day. A long drive, flanked by young walnut trees, wound between acres of lawn; woodland and wild boscage were marked off from the more sophisticated area by a splendid rampart of hydrangeas, now in full flower, in all their glory of purple, crimson and pink. A trelissed arch, ramped over by a hip-laden rose, led into the rearing field, where, on a lawn of somewhat shaggier green, coops stood dotted around, and where a row of tall trees on the seaward side provided shelter from the prevailing wind as well as perches for about forty peafowl, who came and went as they pleased.

'Don't they ever wander away?' we asked the gamekeeper.

'No, they know where they live. They come to be fed every morning and evening, and in between times they're about the place. Look, there's one of them displaying in the garden now.'

And sure enough, as we looked back through the arch, there was one of the big male birds spreading his tail and rattling his feathers on the shaven lawn in front of the hydrangeas in a glory of colour that would have taxed the palette of even Matthew Smith.

Geese, ducks and miscellaneous poultry pecked about the field, and in various wire-netting runs broods of mallard, chickens, and even a few late pheasants clucked, quacked, and preened. Feathers lay everywhere, from the downy curled breast feather of a goose to the great eyed plume discarded from the tail of one of the peacocks. We were shown our purchase – a peahen with two young in a long run, and we bombarded the gamekeeper with questions.

'Food? Oh, anything! Anything at all for peafowl. Pellets – laying, rearing, they'll eat either. Yes, mixed poultry corn, perfectly all right. Just keep them fastened up in a run somewhere for three or four weeks or so, until they begin to feel at home. Then let her out first, by herself. Leave the young ones in the pen, and she won't go far away from them. Then they can all go out together. They won't wander away.'

'What about foxes?' we asked. 'Do you ever lose any?'

'Well, maybe we do sometimes lose a sitting hen. I'm not quite sure. We don't really know how many we've got. I expect we do, from time to time. But they fly up into the trees to roost, you know. No fox could get them there.'

'How do you manage about breeding?' we wanted to know. 'Do you have to put them in broody coops?'

'No, they make their own nests, and you only realise they've done it when they come back with some young ones. But it's then you have to watch out. *Then* you have to catch them and put them in a run, the young ones and the mother, like those ones of yours are, otherwise the other ones would kill them, the older ones, you know. Then when they're big enough, they can come out.'

'How long have those been in the pen?'

'Oh, six or eight week, surely.'

'What sex are the young ones?'

'Well, you can't really tell yet. They look much the same till six months or so. But *I* think you've probably got one of each there. *He* thinks (indicating an elderly man, perfectly silent, who seemed to be his assistant) that you've got two hens. But I'll tell you what we'll do for you. If it does turn out you haven't got a male, bring one back, and we'll swap you, so you're certain to be all right in the end. How's that for you?'

We thought it was generous and good. But there were still a few more things we wanted to know.

'What about the garden? Do they much scratch things up?'

The gamekeeper laughed ironically. 'Oh no, not really,' he replied. 'Though the gardener says that they do. He's a bit inclined to curse 'em.' ('Bit of old needle there,' commented John afterwards.)

'And what about noise? Do people complain?'

'Well, they do make a noise, you have to admit it. But there's nobody very near us here, of course, and of course we're all used to it. We don't even hear it any more. But there's no denying, peacocks do make a noise. But I suppose if you minded all that much about a bit of noise, you wouldn't be wanting peacocks.'

This logic seeming to all of us irrefutable, we fetched the travelling crates from the van, and set about trying to get the peafowl into them. It was far from easy. The mother came fairly readily to hand, but the two babies were much more slippy and, dashing like quicksilver to the end of the long narrow run, lurked, tight against the netting, hopelessly and infuriatingly out of reach. It was here that I made a big mistake. Seeing the gamekeeper and his mate crouching over the other end, the first poised for action, and the second with his hands on the removeable lid panel of wire netting that formed the access to the run, I banged with my fist on the end where the babies were cowering, to make them run up to the other end, which they did. Only, at that moment, the assistant unluckily moving the lid so that the gamekeeper could reach in, one of them abruptly took flight. Before anyone could stop it, it had soared up out of the run, and flown into the air, only coming to rest on the lowest branch of one of the boundary trees where it clung, frightened and panting, while I hung my head in shame, and expressions of polite blankness formed themselves on the countenances of all the others.

'I was afraid that might happen,' remarked the gamekeeper, with self-control. 'Now how the hell we're going to get it is anybody's business.'

'Let's try and get it down from there anyway, before it decides to go higher up,' said John. Looking round, he found a blown-down branch about eight feet long and, scrambling up the bank and the fence post into the stumpy lower growth of the neighbouring tree, he managed at the full stretch of his arm to poke the peacock, which was about fifteen feet off the ground. To our unspeakable relief, it took wing again and disappeared over the hedge into the garden in a long flapping glide. We all rushed after it.

'Hold back! Hold back!' cried the gamekeeper, as we pounded through the arch. 'Look! There she is! Look, there, on the floor, beside the walnut! Now the question is, will she let me go up to her?' But after that it all came right, and the peacock remained, crouching, until he grabbed it and restored it to its sibling in the travelling box, unharmed except for the loss of a few feathers.

'Oh! There's lucky we were!' exclaimed the gamekeeper. 'She must have been a bit dazed, not being used to flying.'

Indeed, we were all rather amazed that the little creature could fly so well, it having spent all its young life so far in a coop about two feet high where even the rudiments of that art could scarcely have been being developed.

The remainder of the peacocks' journey passed without incident, and that evening saw them installed in one of the enclosed dog kennels, with closeable inner room and wired run, which my predecessors, the Smiths, had so thoughtfully left me. We wired in the top, erected perches, provided food and water, and left them to get acquainted with their new premises, knowing that for the moment at least they were as safe from foxes or any other dangers as they had been in their ancestral home.

It was raining in the morning, and when I went out I found them sitting on one of the perches, the hen between the two young ones, with one wing spread protectively over each. When they saw me they quickly hopped down and ran into the inner chamber. With soothing murmurs, I replenished their food and water supplies, then waited, very still, until they worked up enough confidence to come out and feed so that I could get a good look at them. They were all very similar. The hen, who was about twice as big as the babies, was the size of a fair turkey, but on much longer legs. They all had crests, and aristocratic striped faces with large expressive grey-brown eyes. Plump cheeks tucked into the corners of their beaks gave them a pleasant expression, with the look of people politely trying to suppress almost uncontrollable giggles. Their necks were long and faintly iridescent, gleaming in a colour which varied between the spring and autumn aspects of the beech tree – yellowy green and tawny copper; and at the top, just below the head, there was a curious little constriction, barely an inch wide. I became aware that the angle of their neck feathers was an index of their feelings; they raised and lowered them a dozen times a minute. Feathers fluffed out indicated emotion – fear, greed, aggression; feathers sleeked down meant 'All's well'. Their breasts were a pale ash grey, their backs delicately patterned in a subtle dead-leaf brown and black, and chestnut flight feathers peeped out at the bottom of their folded wings. They had tails and trains, but nothing compared with the ornament of the mature cock birds. Ours had tails about a foot long, with a downward sweep, but not long enough to touch the floor.

'The hen bird ought to get tame enough to feed from your hand in a bit,' the gamekeeper had said; but actually it was one of the babies that first plucked up courage to snatch a piece of proffered bread. This feat of daring obviously caused him immense agitation; he not only raised his neck feathers until they stood out at right angles, but he also flattened his crest back so that he looked like a cheeky pony with its ears laid back. Gradually the others acquired confidence, and soon all three would share a bit of bread, which seemed to be accounted a great treat. The first baby always retained the edge in daring, and indeed, this was the only thing that at all enabled me to tell them apart. We named the bold one Pyramus, the timid one Pelleus, and the mother Thisbe. It was drawing a bow at a venture to give the babies male names, but in due course as the weeks passed and their necks began to show more and more of the characteristic green, blue and purple of the cock bird, we realised that we had chosen correctly – we had been lucky enough to get two cock birds.

After about three weeks, we let Thisbe out. We manoeuvred her out of the pen and clapped the door to in the faces of the eager young ones, then stood back to see what would happen. Everybody's neck feathers stood out at the highest possible angle, and everybody made his or her alarm call. For the young ones, this consisted merely of the most feeble and lisping piping note, strangely incongruous from two already big hearty birds; but Thisbe produced a great brazen goose-like honk, that came out sometimes on one note, and sometimes on two, in a major third, which sounded just like the call of an agitated diesel train.

Honking anxiously, she paced up and down the strip of faded autumn grass outside the pen, then stopped, cocked her head on one side and looked at something. Her eye had been caught by something that was lying on the ground. Stooping, she quizzed it yet more narrowly, then picked it up in her beak. It was a large dead sycamore leaf. What could she be intending to do with it? Cleverly, she turned it round, as a kingfisher does a minnow, until she had it by its stalk. Then, to my utter amazement, with a couple of choking gobbles, she swallowed it! I looked at her in horror. How that big coarse leaf had gone so quickly down that tiny narrow constricted little gullet I should never know. And did she know what she was doing? Was she in the process of committing suicide by choking herself to death? Apparently not. Blinking with what looked like satisfaction, she stalked off, pausing only to nip the end from a blade of grass from time to time. The babies, left alone in their pen, peeped disconsolately.

In the evening I shepherded her back into the pen without much difficulty while the young ones were feeding, and after a few more days I took to letting them all out together. At first I tried to put them away in their house every evening, but before long they pre-empted me by flying up to roost high in one of the big sycamore trees by the drive. As I had already discovered that they were utterly indifferent to rain and storm, choosing to sleep on the outside perch on the most horrible nights even though the inner perch, in shelter, was only four feet away, I did not feel called upon to try to do anything to prevent it.

Their night-times were thus arranged to our common satisfaction, but their daytime behaviour was something of a puzzle and a disappointment. One keeps peacocks, after all, for their decorative qualities, to strut on one's lawn, or at any rate, somewhere where their decorative feathers can be seen and admired. Most people's peacocks seem to understand this, and do their meed of showing off as per schedule. Not so mine. Very early in the mornings they would descend from their tree, commenting hysterically on the hazards of the long planing flight down from there in wild variants of the diesel alarm note; then, having pecked around for half an hour or so before anybody was up, they would betake themselves to the beams of the cowshed and would spend the whole of the day couched up in the shadows right under the pitch of the roof. At dusk they would come out again, and you might, if you were lucky, see them on top of the cowshed roof, which they used as a staging post on their way to the sycamore. They looked particularly pleasing at that time, their crests silhouetted against the fading rose of the sunset west. When I put corn in their hopper, they would descend briefly; if I offered bread, they would cautiously accept it; but as for strutting, posing, and showing off, they just didn't go in for it. Perhaps they felt that my lawns didn't deserve it; and indeed, casting my mind back to the shaven acres of their ancestral home, I could not but admit that they had something of a point.

With the spring, things got rather better. As the light lengthened, so they spent less and less time roosting in the tree. The boys were as big as their mother now, and their necks gleamed with enamelled brilliance. They would be waiting on the ground when I went out after breakfast to feed them; and one day one of them, startled by the dog, faced abruptly round and displayed at him. It was quite an impressive sight. Although he had none of the long eye-marked feathers of the mature male, he managed to spread his tail coverts into quite a big round fan, and he tucked in his chin and rattled his plumes in the most authentic way. In another week or so, his brother had picked up the idea too, and they took to spending a considerable time every day in practice. Their chosen area was outside the coal shed, and there they would work away, spreading themselves out laterally and compressing themselves fore-and-aft with all the dedication of yoga experts striving for one of their supremely unnatural postures. From the front, as I say, it all looked quite impressive. From the side, it looked strange. But from behind, it was a sight of such pathos that it went fair to tear the heart out of your body, so much did it speak of the tears that are implicit in the condition of the unconsciously ridiculous. For if from the front they were heroes, and from the side, at least professionals, from the back they were clowns, and unintentional clowns, which are the saddest sort. In the display, the tail feathers are braced forward, supporting the brilliant covers, and the bird squats slightly down, quivering its drooping wings. So at the back, nothing is covered up, and the view is of a couple of thin, bent legs, grey, as if wearing old lisle stockings, and of a pointed downy bum, sticking out all defenceless and ludicrous. Medieval bestiaries propounded the theory that the peacock is ashamed of its legs. It has no need to be, in my book, because it has quite nice legs really, slender and functional, even if perhaps a little dull in colour. Any shame it has going, it would be much better advised to apply to its bottom. But I suppose too keen a sense of the ridiculous is an inhibiting thing to have, even for a peacock.

The noise that we had been led to expect from our peacocks took some considerable time to develop. To begin with, the boys just peeped, like very young chickens, and all the honking and dieseling came from their mother. By about February, their voices were beginning to show signs of breaking, and from time to time they uttered lamentable adolescent croaks, like schoolboys. But it was not until April that we heard the true peacock scream, and then, oddly enough, it was in the middle of the night.

It was a black and rainy night, and our young cat, for the first time in her life, had elected to spend the night out. This we did not mind, knowing cats to be well able to take care of themselves in normal circumstances. But when I was abruptly awakened from profound sleep at about 3.30 a.m. by a series of homeric caterwauling screams, I rushed downstairs to the front door, convinced that the worst had happened, my sleep-fuddled mind flooded with ghastly pictures of a little black figure dragging itself, wounded, up the drive. Hideously wounded by what? Fox? Badger? Dog? Passing car? By the time I had wrestled the door open, the terrible crying had stopped, so 'Puss, puss, puss!' I called into the black and unresponsive night. 'Here I am,' replied a little black figure with a purring meow, as, tail erect, furry, dry, and perfectly all right, she doubled in round my ankles; and then the night was split once again by a dreadful double banshee wail from the tree, and I realised that both boys had suddenly come of age, and wanted everybody to know about it as soon as possible. It was really quite embarrassing. Every dog in the neighbourhood started to bark; you could hear the tidings being passed from farm to farm all the way up the three valleys; and I cringed as I pictured disturbed and angry neighbours leaning out of their windows to see what all the bother was about, or pulling their pillows over their heads in sullen despair.

After that, the boys used to have a brief call almost every night. They would always perform together, one starting, and the other overlapping his cry, so that the two voices rang out in a dolorous chime. After about ten screams, they would be silent for the rest of the night, though they usually managed a brief *aubade* when dawn was grey, which was, of course, rather uncomfortably early in the morning. Fortunately, the local dogs soon got used to the noise and ceased to comment on it, and as our nearest neighbours are five hundred yards away at least, and sleep round the other side of their house anyway, the screams came to their ears no louder than the hooting of a distant owl. Peacocks are supposed to foretell rain by their screaming – indeed, the Welsh say that the word they utter is 'Glaw! Glaw', which is the Welsh for rain. It may well have been so. Certainly the spring and early summer of our peacocks' adolescence were among the wettest ever recorded, though it did seem a little gratuitous of them to save their weather forecasting entirely for the hours of darkness. I never heard them venturing on any meteorological predictions in the daytime. In point of cold, scientific fact, it seems more probable that the calling is a spring phenomenon, and has something to do with the breeding cycle, because by late July the birds had entirely stopped doing it, and could not be tempted into their yowls however imminent the rain.

As gardeners, the peacocks pretty well lived up to the gamekeeper's prophecy too. When the first daffodils were bending their necks and swelling their buds there was a destructive sally, and six or eight buds were pecked to pieces in a rather un-called-for way; but after that, I put protective netting over anything too tempting-looking and, as the spring strengthened, sheer weight of numbers came to the rescue. It is easy, and probably fun, from a peacock's point of view, to peck the heads of a couple of dozen 'February Gold', but like vandals they shrink from too much exertion and when the early daffodils were overtaken by the many hundreds of March, they found it too much trouble, and left them alone. Occasionally they would nip off a head here and there, but they looked so beautiful while doing it that I was more than half inclined to forgive them anyway. To see Pyramus, glorious neck flashing its jewelled richness in the level rays of the evening sun, pause, delicately savouring a spray of azure forget-me-nots that he held in his beak was a wonderful experience. After all, there were plenty of forget-me-nots left.

Really, the peacocks did more damage in the garden with their feet than with their beaks, and their heedless tramping to and from across the beds did put paid to some of the more slender and delicate things. They killed a peony and quite a large bearded iris, too; they also grazed, very selectively, a nice braird of annuals, leaving the *gypsophila*, but completely clearing some good hearty seedlings of *nemophila* and *phacelia campanularia*; an odd nicety of taste. In the end we arrived at a *modus vivendi*, with wire protectors over the things I was determined to save from them, and a tendency on their part developing to go round rather than across as the increasing growth of the tougher perennials blocked up their trackways. But it was not an entirely satisfactory solution from my point of view, and next year I intend to try the effect of a system of thin wires, fixed in a foot-square grid, about ten inches above the ground. It should make it awkward for them to walk, or indeed, even alight; it will cost me nothing, as I have plenty of electric fencing wire left over from farming days; and, all being well, the plants, unpecked and untrampled should soon grow up tall enough to hide it. Of course, time is on our side in the matter of the peacocks and the garden. When you think of the classic garden in which these lovely creatures are to be found, you realise that it is a mature one. They don't seem to bother with shrubs more than three feet high; established drifts of flowers, too, they retire from, daunted. So the problem of co-existence shrinks to the easily contemplated one of simply keeping them at bay for a few years, while the garden has a chance to establish itself. I am quite hopeful of success in the long run.

Shortly before Christmas, my career as a keeper of fancy fowl received a further impetus when I was given a pair of guinea fowl, originally intended for Christmas dinner, but safe enough, had they but known it, from having their necks wrung by me. I put them in the peacocks' now-vacated enclosure, and they skulked, miserably terrified, in the deepest corner of the inner chamber, venturing out occasionally to pick at their corn but scuttling back again at the merest shadow of any movement in their vicinity.

'Perhaps they'll feel more relaxed when Christmas is over!' remarked my son Matthew ironically; and sure enough, when a bought turkey had stood in for them on the sacrificial dish, they did seem to acquire more confidence, and in a month or so became tame enough to be let out to live free about the place with the peacocks.

There was no difficulty about naming them. Years ago, we had had some friends who had cherished on their farm a single male guinea fowl which their son, who thought it had an Egyptian look, had christened Amenhotep. During the course of the creature's life, a rather simple-minded local boy came to work for them, and he, never having seen a guinea fowl before, jumped to the conclusion that 'Amenhotep' was a generic rather than a personal soubriquet, and used to puzzle chance visitors to the farm by asking them such questions as 'Do you have Amenhoteps at your place?' 'Or have you ever eaten an Amenhotep's egg?'

So 'The Amenhotep' our guinea fowl became; and as time went by and the skinny, frightened waifs developed into maturity, it became apparent that we had luckily acquired one of each – a cock and a hen. The male became '*The* Amenhotep', rather as the head of a Scottish clan is The MacArthur, or The Douglas; and the female, after a period of being known awkwardly as 'The female Amenhotep' was metamorphosed, in a moment of execrable punning, into 'The Am-*hen* – otep'.

They were frightfully ugly. The male, in particular, with his bare, skinny white neck, sparsely maned with grey hairs, his little red wattles, and the disgusting dark lump like a boil on the back of his bald pate, looked as if he had been created as the winning entry in an ugliness competition. His wife, although smaller and discreet, less in every feature, as you might say, was not much better.

It is true that their feathers were nice. The Am-hen was quiet and discreet in Quaker grey, with white wingtips, but the clan leader himself was dazzlingly attired in white spots on a slate grey ground. Both kept themselves as neat as new pins and appeared perfectly waterproof, whatever the weather threw at them.

They had rather dear little legs, too. I noticed a curious phenomenon about these. The fronts of their legs were a brilliant pink, whereas the backs, and the soles of their feet, were orange; so they presented a different colour from the hock to the ground, according to whether they were coming, or going.

They took to roosting every night in the same tree as the peacocks, but much lower down. There you would see them, perched head to tail in the gathering dusk, quietly exchanging little purring remarks – pillow-talk, as it were – and there they would stay, safely out of reach of the prowling fox, until morning. But there their association with the peacocks ended. For with the coming of the daylight, the Amenhoteps would set out on their travels, and there was no knowing how many miles they would have covered before you saw them again.

They seemed to walk, not fly, although they must have taken wing briefly to cross the river, which they often did. But whenever you saw them, dots a quarter of a mile away, or met them in some distant field, to which you had penetrated in the course of walking the dog, there they would be on foot, trudging along in single file, he leading, she about a yard behind; and both looking as demure and unruffled as if they were simply plodding across the farmyard, in the perfect safety of their own home. With their downcast eyes and plain, dark feathers, they rather gave the impression of a couple of Victorian missionaries, conscientiously bringing civilisation to outlandish parts.

As the spring declared itself and the first heady indication of maturity began to work in his blood, the Amenhotep became quite aggressive. He began to attack the peafowl, getting no change at all out of Thisbe, who simply faced round at him and received all his charges with outspread wings and a determined mien, but regularly frightening the boys into the screaming hab-dabs. Sometimes he pursued them remorselessly for two or three minutes at a time, running after them on the ground, and even taking wing to continue the engagement when desperation sent them looking for escape in the upper air. The battle would be terminated with a burst of feathers blowing away on the breeze, fearful honks and screams from the victim, and a ten-minute diplay of harsh crowing from the victor who would perch in triumph on the cowshed roof, or on top of the dog pens.

When he was chasing the peacocks on the ground, the Amenhotep used to adopt a particular attitude, arching his wings up over his back and deepening himself so that in profile he looked much deeper than usual, whereas from the fore-and-aft aspect he became very narrow indeed. When he shaped his body into this curious flattened plane, with his high arched back and down-drooping tail, he always reminded me of something, and the image nagged away unplaced in my mind for several weeks before it managed to drag itself free from the tangles of my subconscious. The thing he resembled was, of course, a flea. Successful aggression and freedom lent a new lustre to his whole being, and an area of iridescent lavender plumage all round his neck enabled us to remark that 'In the spring a livelier iris changes on the burnished Amenhotep', a statement that may or may not have been worth making. His dark, demure little wife, who looked as if she was always, in spirit at least, carrying a prayer-book and a reticule, took very little notice of his battles and drew attention to herself only in the most characteristically negative way, by disappearing. So discreetly, indeed, did she withdraw from society that I couldn't remember, when I noticed that she had gone, when I had last seen her. I eventually realised that she had stopped accompanying her noisy spouse on his food-gathering forays, or roosting with him in the sycamore, but couldn't say when. Such is unobtrusiveness.

But, having undertaken the ownership of fancy fowl in the first place with no illusions about their popularity with foxes, I was resigned in advance to losing them if that was the way it was going to turn out; and, the Amenhotep himself showing no sign of grieving, I didn't feel called upon to do so either. So I didn't. The more, then, was the pleasure when, early one morning I heard a decidedly antiphonal burst of ancient Egyptian in the yard. I looked out of the window, and there the lady was. She was looking a little thin and bedraggled, but was lively enough, and decidedly vociferous, pecking away at the empty food hopper and declaring that the service in this place was becoming really too, too terrible. I hastened out and replenished the supply, and she ate briskly for a few minutes before fading discreetly out of view while my back was turned. It seemed obvious that she had made a nest somewhere, and when her husband took to standing up at the top of the field and making his harsh noise near a big overgrown bank of blackthorn suckers, we assumed that the nest was somewhere in there. But we never found it, and when, some weeks later, she came back to live with him in the yard, it seemed clear that some ill had befallen the eggs. Perhaps a rat or a fox found the nest; perhaps the male bird was just not old enough to be a fertile parent. It didn't really seem to matter, and the female reverted to her original life style without any appearance of loss – at least as far as one could tell, through the habitually cross-grained expression that Nature had painted on her pinched countenance.

I thought that the guinea fowl might possibly breed successfully later in the year, but it was not to be. Very shortly after rejoining her husband on his evangelising trips around the countryside, the Am-hen-otep disappeared again. This time it was the end. Presumably a fox must have nipped out when the birds were incautiously walking too near to his lying-out place, and have acquired that Christmas dinner that was supposed to be mine. I never found any dark grey feathers to tell the tale, but I hardly expected to. The Amenhoteps' range was always more far-reaching than mine, and besides, foxes often enough take their prey into their earths to eat, particularly if they have cubs.

The Amenhotep has remained a widower, and seems none the worse for it. Having nobody but the peacocks to associate with, he now sticks close to them all day and all night, and has quite given up his bullying attacks on them. Perhaps it was only the sexual stimulus that the presence of his female gave him that made him so nasty. Perhaps it was just adolescent spleen...

The strangest development in my life as a bird-fancier came about entirely by chance, and I still find it hard to believe that it happened.

I was walking back one Sunday afternoon after having lunch with Ruth and John when, as I approached my own gate, my eye was caught by a flash of brilliant colour moving across the yard. Intrigued, I hurried up, and was absolutely confounded to see a cock golden pheasant, in perfect plumage, slip furtively across the open space and into the long grass at the opposite side.

It seemed too dramatic to be true, and I literally pinched myself to see if I was dreaming, and cast my mind back over my lunch-time potations in case I could possibly be drunk. But there was no doubt of it, I was both sober and awake; and there was the pheasant's golden head gleaming out of the tall grass to prove him real and no illusion. I dashed into the house for a bowl of corn to try to tempt him to stay, but alas! by the time I had got it, he had disappeared.

How on earth a bird as exotic as a golden pheasant should have walked into my life was a puzzle. Nobody anywhere in the neighbourhood owned or bred them; and indeed, nobody but me having seen him, people were just a little sceptical of his existence, and clearly wondered if I was working my way round to some elaborate practical joke. But I knew he was real; I had seen him, clearly, if fleetingly; and from then on I kept a good lookout for him, in case he should be lurking anywhere in the rough grazing, or down in the reedy undergrowth by the river.

And in due course my optimism turned out to have been justified. He appeared again, and this time I saw which way he went, and was able to discover the thicket he had chosen for his home. I went up there with corn and, although he was very shy for the first few days, his confidence gradually increased, until it became clear that he was waiting for his hand-out, and was willing to come and peck it up from the earth within a few inches of my feet.

The big puzzle was what to do with him. He was a beautiful bird. Rich golden feathers covered his head, sweeping backwards like a continental man's haircut without a parting. His neck was covered with a cape of orange feathers, each one outlined in black; and a mantle of dark green covered his back, between his wings. The wings themselves were of a rich prussian blue, and his tail was immensely long, and delicately mottled in brown and black. But the chief glory of his plumage, and the feature that made him not merely bright but absolutely gaudy was his breast and belly, which were covered in feathers of the most brilliant red. But this lustrous beauty, so striking and unusual, had to be his worst enemy in a wild situation. A ground-running bird – I never saw him fly properly; indeed, I used at one time to wonder if he'd been pinioned – he needed the camouflage of the ordinary pheasant, or the snipe. or the woodcock, to escape the attentions of predators. Even lurking in the depths of his blackthorn thicket he showed up like a piece of jewelled enamel-work; and I trembled when I thought of the shooting parties that sometimes tramped over the rough grazing in the winter.

At the same time, he had obviously managed all right up to this time. He was rather a small bird, it is true, and a certain weakness in his legs led me to wonder if he had had every advantage in upbringing, or had had to look after himself in a tough world from a very early age; on the other hand, his plumage was magnificent, glowing and shining, and with every feather in place. One way and another, he had managed; though it seemed fair to assume, from his tameness, and his appetite for the mixed poultry corn also relished by the peacocks and the Amenhoteps, that he was no stranger to mankind, and its aviaries. It was, of course, summer, when the living is notoriously easy, with reasonably warm weather, and a handsome supply of insect food readily available to the sharp beak and the scanning primrose eye. How would he make out in winter, I wondered? When food for every creature would be shorter, and when, in addition to the trigger-happy sportsmen, he would have to face the risks of hungrier, more desperate foxes? Another consideration was that he was alone, and presumably lonely. If I caught him (leaving aside for the moment the question of how), perhaps I could manage to get him a wife from somewhere; and indeed, perhaps the two of them, properly introduced and domiciled, could live free about the place like the other birds did – coming every day to be fed, but at liberty to chose for themselves how they would spend their time – and where.

In the end, my mind was made up for me. I had formed the habit of taking him up his corn late in the afternoon, and of talking to him while he ate it, pecking cautiously round my feet. Then one day he was not there. I called, and searched, but in vain. Nor did he show up the next day, and I assumed that a fox had got him, more particularly when I found one of his two-foot-long tail feathers lying on the ground under his favourite perching place. I hardly expected to see him the next day; indeed, so sure was I that the brilliant presence would visit my life no more that I actually took Tip with me when I went up that afternoon, and, finding the covert still gloomily bare, he and I continued past it for a proper walk. But on the way back, impelled by some freak of fancy, I just turned aside from the path and glanced up under the bushes – and there he was! I took Tip home, and came straight back with the corn.

But one glance was enough to show me that things were not as they should be. He must have had a brush with something – fox, badger, or possibly even feral domestic cat. For his magnificent orange and black cape was almost all ravished away; his tail was a shadow of its former glory; and all the confidence had gone from his manner, which was now miserably nervous. He did venture to peck up some of the corn, but only after I had thrown it a good distance away from myself. After pecking a few grains, he stood still, in a hunched attitude, blinking like a sick man; the pupils of his yellow eyes rapidly contracted and dilated several times. When I moved, to throw more corn, he scuttled fearfully away under the dense blackthorn thickets. He looked far from well. I longed to take him under my protection and keep him in safety, at least until he could have a chance to recover his verve, but how on earth was I to catch him? The place where he lived and fed was a thicket formed by twenty years of suckering by a blackthorn hedge; the original bank, with a few half-derelict old ash stumps still growing in it, ran up the middle of it like a spine; wandering paths, trodden out by the cattle, threaded it; but the bulk of it was completely impenetrable scrub, thorny, and giving access only to someone who, like a fox or a pheasant, could get along in the foot or so of space between the lowest branches and the ground.

I considered nets. But there were difficulties. I had not got any nets myself, and I did not want to borrow any, as that would have meant giving reasons, and I was loth to publicise his presence, lest trigger-happy cowboys might come gunning for him as a trophy. Besides, he was a nervous creature, and I felt that there was no way I could ever manage to work my way round so as to be able to set the net between him and the thicket. He would have darted away at the first movement, and then I would have lost him, not only for that time, but quite possibly for ever. A failed effort at capture would presumably alert him to the possibility of danger from me and ensure that even if he still came out to eat the corn, he would in future give me a wide berth.

In the end I just picked him up. He was pecking away quite busily about eighteen inches away from my feet with his back to me. The Amenhotep, who happened to be present, was eating corn too. Maybe the pheasant felt that there was safety in numbers, and relaxed the cultivated alertness of the feral creature; maybe (oh, dreadful thought) he trusted me. At any rate, when I suddenly made up my mind to try, leaned down and grasped his tail, and hastily got my other hand on to his wildly scrabbling legs, he was not quick enough to get away. His prussian-blue wings beat the air in vain. His flame-coloured, blood-coloured breast lay in my hand. He was my prisoner.

I am certain, from the way he behaved on the way back to the farm, that he must have been aviary reared. He gave two or three struggles; he glared at me, wild and tragic, out of his primrose eye. But for most of the time he just lay there, wings drooping, unwilling, but resigned. And, murmuring the soothing nonsense with which I had been in the habit of enlivening his feeding sessions, I carried him gently back, while all the time my conscience pricked me more and more deeply.

For after all, what had I done? I had betrayed a trust. I had built up his confidence in me, week by week, and seduced him from his natural wariness with gifts of food. I had assured him many times (in words which I understood, even though he didn't) that I meant him no harm. I had led him on. And then I had pounced. I had hard work to rationalise my actions as I bore him away into a captivity he didn't want, and felt his heart beat fast with fear against my hand. I reminded myself that to some extent I was only taking him into protective custody. I promised to try to find him a wife to ease his solitude. And, conscience still not being entirely happy that my motivations in picking him up had been a hundred per cent altruistic, I finally bought it off with an inner promise that I would eventually set him free again, come what might; though I did not at that particular moment actually fix a date for it.

It was even more distressing when I released him into his pen. It was quite a big pen, say eight feet by four, and tall enough for me to stand upright in, and it communicated by a propped-open door with an inner chamber of the same width and height, but only half the depth. We had wedged branches across it here and there as perches when we had originally prepared it for the peacocks, and feed and water hoppers stood on the floor. It was really not a bad pen as pens go. But to him it was dreadful. As soon as I let him go, he flew up in a panic, and banged himself again and again on the wire. Feathers, knocked out of his head and breast, floated down to the ground. I got out of the pen as quickly as I could, and stood some distance away, but the poor bird continued to rush hither and thither, measuring the confines of his prison, now running, now flying, until at last, after two or three minutes that seemed a lot longer, he noticed the dark place in the corner under the support of the inner perch and, crouching down there, quiet at last, began to take stock of his situation.

By the next day he was calmer, and I never again saw the awful panic flight of his first traumatic moments of captivity. He still ran into his inner sanctum whenever anybody passed near his pen, but I used to see him when I looked out of the window early in the morning out on his perch, preening himself, or pecking about on the floor looking for corn or for insects among the grass and leaves that I used to strew for him. He did not appear to pine. I supposed that to some extent he missed his freedom, but as far as I had been able to tell, even when he had lived in the wild he had not moved around much, always being found doing nothing on a branch, within a radius of five yards, at whatever hour of the day one chose to visit him. But whether from the trauma of his capture or from the change of diet I don't know, within two or three weeks he began to moult. This of course made it essential for me to keep him for the time being. I could hardly have let him go back to the wild situation only half feathered.

I made enquiries about a possible mate for him, but learned from the experienced pheasant-keepers whom I consulted that getting him one would not after all be doing him so very much of a favour. 'Pheasants and things don't hang about together like ducks, or peacocks,' my informant told me. 'Oh, yes, they'd breed, probably, but you'd have to keep them in a pen. If you let them go free, they'd probably just wander away. I don't think you could rely on having them living free about the place, like your peacocks do.'

He told me, too, that pheasants sleep on the ground, thus putting themselves in particular danger from such predators as cats and foxes. I remembered the bit in *Tess of the d'Urbervilles* when, benighted in the wood, she keeps hearing the thud! of the roosting pheasants who, having been injured in the day's shoot, fall to the ground as their wounds overcome them; but it seemed impolite to contradict him, so I held my peace. But I did decide that I was not going to risk fifteen pounds on a hen bird just to have it wander away; and nor did I want to keep either it or him permanently penned up.

To set my golden boy free again, then, was the obvious answer. It would be only proper to wait until he had regained a good cover of feathers; but at the same time, it was important to let him re-accustom himself to the outdoor, and perhaps self-sufficient life while we were still in the warm and easy months of summer. We fed him with as wide a variety of foodstuffs as we could command; we gave him layers' and growers' pellets as well as corn; we brought him what we could capture in the way of insects; we put greenstuffs and cut branches from the kinds of bushes that used to surround his favourite roosting-place into his pen. He picked at it all. Presumably he ate the swatted flies, the occasional caterpillars, that we laid on a flat stone in front of him; he certainly nibbled at leaves and scratched over pellets. Anyway, he refeathered surprisingly quickly, and there came a day, about five weeks after his capture, when I deemed him to be in good enough plumage to face the world again, and decided to set him free.

I can hardly bear to write the end of this story. It did not turn out well. After breakfast, I opened the door of his pen, and laid a trail of corn that would have taken him out, over the low threshold, into the big world again. Then I told everybody to keep well away, and to let him take his own time coming out. The dogs (we had a visiting dog, an elderly golden labrador, as well as our own Jack Russell) had never taken a scrap of notice of him in his pen, being well accustomed to the peafowl and the Amenhoteps around the place, but, nevertheless, we shut them up out of the way in the kitchen. And then we went about our own various avocations and left him to find his way out. The morning passed.

After lunch I went down to the river to fill a can of water to water my cuttings bed, and presumably I didn't take adequate care to close the kitchen door behind me and keep the dogs in. At any rate, when I came up with the water, and bethought me to slip into his pen and just check that he had indeed gone out, there was a red feather from the underneath of his tail on the floor. A red feather – and it was red at both ends... A bead of blood on the quill end brought my heart into my mouth, and I ran quickly out of the place, fearing the worst. And sure enough, when I got round the corner, there were the two dogs, standing shoulder to shoulder, eyes bright, and tails wagging, pleased ... and in Tip's mouth was the body of the golden pheasant, eyes closed, wings flopping, dead, dead, dead.

'Put it behind you,' said John. 'Forget it, it's all you can do,' said Mick. But I still feel very bad about it. Because after all, if I hadn't interfered, the little creature would probably have been still living free and happy in his chosen territory, up on the rough grazing. And as I laid the small bright body in its grave, I resolved that for the future I would try to eschew greed, possessiveness, call it what you will; and would let alone other forms of life, and not pretend that my covetousness was a disinterested wish to protect them. Poor golden pheasant. It was sad, for him, that he was created so bright.

5

Getting into Wild Flowers

People often ask me about getting into wild flower gardening. Often they have had the sad and guilt-inducing experience of digging up plants in the country, and having them die when planted at home. Naturally, nobody wants to be responsible for the death of even the commonest weed, if it is worth the trouble of collecting. So they ask me where they went wrong, and what they should do in future.

The first thing I always tell them about is the law. Because nowadays it simply isn't allowed to go out and dig up wild flowers, just like that, from fields, or commons, or road verges. To collect a plant, you must have the consent of the owner of the land on which it is growing. There is also a list of plants that must not in any circumstances be molested – dug up, or picked, or have their seed collected; these are the Alpine gentian, Alpine sowthistle, Alpine woodsia, Blue heath, Cheddar pink, Diapensia, Drooping saxifrage, Ghost orchid, Killarney fern, Lady's slipper, Mezereon, Military orchid, Monkey orchid, Oblong woodsia, Red helleborine, Snowdon lily, Spiked speedwell, Spring gentian, Teesdale sandwort, Tufted saxifrage, and Wild gladiolus; and of them I do not speak. My interest is specifically in *common* wild flowers. I have not the expertise to attempt the really threatened varieties, even those that can be obtained, cultivated, from nurseries. So I leave them alone. And as a general rule, the moral of the would-be cultivator of wild plants, as far as collecting seed or seeking permission to dig up, is concerned, should be – if in doubt, don't. If you want to acquire a stock of some widely-distributed thing, like sheep's-bit scabious, say, or bird's-foot trefoil, pluck up your courage and go to ask the farmer. You may be unlucky; he may be suspicious of your intentions, particularly if he lives near a densely-populated area and suffers a lot from the depredations of tiresome town dwellers; alternatively, he may think you are mad. An astonished stare and 'Take the whole ruddy lot if you want to' is the response I have usually found; but I do realise that I am lucky in that I live in the deep country, and besides, I never look to take a rooted plant if any other means will do. Seeds or cuttings do less damage to natural stocks. Even if you do need to take actual plants, and the farmer has given you carte blanche to do so, you should not be greedy. You do need more than one individual, because some plants can only set seed when they are cross-fertilised; and I suppose you have to make some allowance for possible mortality, but really, three specimens are plenty. If you are so uncertain of success that you feel you need many more, you shouldn't be collecting them at all until you have improved your general gardening skills. What you acquire from nature should be regarded as the basis for your display, not for the whole display itself. Collected plants are stock plants, from which others are to be raised, and only by looking at the matter in this light can you be said to justify yourself as a conservationist. You should make sure that there is a net increase, not a decrease, in the amount of that particular plant in this country as a result of your efforts; otherwise, you are on the wrong side.

The next thing I utter into the ears of anybody who asks my advice on the subject of growing wild flowers in their garden is the simple and conventional phrase 'horses for courses.' It is such an obvious consideration that I sometimes feel almost ashamed to make such a point of it; but experience does show that people will insist on trying to grow wild flowers in surroundings that are totally unsuited to them on the grounds that 'they are only weeds, after all – they ought to be able to grow here, if proper flowers can.' Certainly there are some weeds which are absolutely ubiquitous – the dandelion, the lawn daisy, the nettle, the creeping buttercup, and so on. But most wild plants have at least a preference for a particular kind of habitat, and you might just as well take account of it as not. There are so many lovely species available for growing, naturally and happily, on any kind of soil that it seems pointlessly bloody-minded to waste your time struggling with ones that are out of their element. It is not always easy for people who garden in the middle of large towns, or in the vast built-up areas of suburbia, to know what were the particular wild flowers that were native to their area before civilisation changed its nature. But it is not difficult, with a little thought, to find out. Any gardener must of necessity know roughly what kind of soil he has in his garden, whether it is loamy, stodgy, sandy, gravelly, or what-have-you; and a very simple test with a little kit available from chemists or garden shops will tell him its degree of acidity or alkalinity. Armed with this knowledge, he can consult any reference book of wild flowers worth its salt, and at least be saved from the grosser mistakes. But really, the amount of knowledge needed to grow most wild flowers successfully is not very daunting, and most people who are ordinarily competent gardeners should not find them difficult at all.

For the person who owns an average smallish garden, I think it is a good idea first to allocate a bit of ground and then to decide what wild flowers will suit it, rather than to proceed the other way round. You are only building up trouble for yourself if you set your heart on growing sun-loving arable weeds when the only place available is in the deepest shade. If the bit of ground you can spare happens to be under the shade of the only big tree in your garden, let this fact be the first consideration. It is shady, it is sheltered; what natural habitat does it resemble? Then you can set about collecting the sorts of plants that will be appropriate to such a situation – natural woodlanders; primroses, bluebells, sweet violets, celandines, Solomon's seal, wood goldilocks, and so on. They should grow away there very happily. Whereas if you had decided at the beginning that you had wanted to grow harebells, pasque flowers, wild thyme, and cinquefoil, and had attempted to do so in that shady situation, you would have been disappointed, and the plants would have been at best unthrifty, and at worst dead. On the other hand, if the piece you are going to allocate is a free-draining bit of gravel in full sun all day, it will be no use yearning for shade-loving woodland plants. I seem to labour this point, I know; but people are so inclined to conceive a great desire for some wild flower that has, perhaps, nostalgic associations for them, that they acquire a stock of it by hook or by crook, stuff it into the first bit of garden that offers itself, and then become quite plaintive when, grossly unsuited by the situation, it quite naturally up and dies on them.

When you have set aside a part of your garden for a patch of wild flowers, you must make sure that the soil in it is in a suitable condition for them. This does not mean necessarily enriched, because most wildlings are accustomed to a fairly sparse diet, but it does mean appropriate in kind. Thus, obviously, woodland plants are going to want a soft, leafy soil, and if the ground under your big tree has got beaten down and impoverished by years of having the leaves swept up in the autumn, you must dig it through and add the missing humus in the form of peat for the time being, and resolve to let the natural leaf-fall lie there in future. Road-verge or pasture plants will want a loam, and will probably like it to be fairly firm. Plants like stonecrop and valerian, which are at home in walls, will want pretty sharp drainage; and deep rooters like comfrey will want a reasonable depth of soil to get their fangs into. Another thing always worth bearing in mind in a long-cultivated garden is that the Ph, or measure of acidity, of the soil may have been raised by injudicious liming in the past; if you want to grow lime-hating plants, it is always worth checking this point before you acquire them.

Everything being ready, the next problem is to acquire the stock. It is a lot easier to get seed of wild flowers now than it was even five years ago; I have written in another chapter about the splendid Seed Exchange scheme, and mentioned one or two firms that supply wild flower seeds commercially. Compared with the price of garden seeds, wild ones strike me as remarkably cheap, and if you can, I certainly think you should raise your plants from seed. Apart from the moral and legal aspects of collecting actual plants, there are other advantages in having home-grown seedlings. You get a good genetic spread for one thing. A large number of plants grown from seed must obviously have an advantage in this way over a similar number raised from cuttings or divisions. Also, you can plant them out into their flowering positions at the best time, when they are small, and are growing strongly; you can in some cases even sow them direct, which gives them a much better chance of settling down than being transplanted as adults. Most seed packets have directions on them about the culture of their contents; and there is nothing particularly difficult about wild seeds as opposed to tame ones.

Many people, though, prefer collecting their seed to buying it, and with the kinds of common plants that I like and recommend, there can be no possible objection to this. A few simple rules should be observed. First, it is not often much good harvesting seeds while they are thoroughly unripe. This statement needs a bit of qualifying, for in some cases when the seed-pod is completely formed and has attained its full size, the plant can manage the last bit of the maturation process with the whole stem cut off, and kept in a jug of water on a sunny window sill. But in my experience, picking seeds where the pod has not grown to its full size is a waste of time. I have never known them to germinate.

Secondly, the seed should be dried before storing. This should *not* be done by heat. It is surprising how many people dry seeds over the Aga, or in the airing cupboards, and are puzzled at the low rate of germination that they get with them. Dry your seeds cool. Again, the window sill is the place. Put your seeds, as soon as you get home, on a saucer, pods and all, just as they are, and leave them in a dry and reasonably cool room for several weeks if necessary, getting what sun there may be, until the pods are crisp and thoroughly dry. Then you can easily rub the seeds out of them, and get on with the next process.

I hardly ever commit a whole batch of seeds at one time. They come to hand, in the natural course of events, in the summer and the autumn; and what I do myself is nearly always to sow half of them straight away, and keep the other half in reserve for a spring sowing in case the first one fails. This belt-and-braces policy follows what happens in nature, really, when seeds fall arbitrarily to the ground, and germinate over a long period of time. If the autumn sowing survives the winter, well and good; one is that much further on. But if it fails, there is still a modicum of shot left in the locker, and all is not lost. I usually do up my seeds in little flat packets of paper, with the name written on them, and a fastening of sellotape; then I put them, absolutely dry, into some fair-sized container like a Nescafé jar, and seal the lid on with more sellotape; and after that, they go out into the stable for the winter. Getting frozen doesn't matter at all to dry seeds of native species. The two important things are to keep them cool and dry – and, of course, identified.

Collecting your seeds from the wild is a constant source of pleasure, and the few difficulties it presents are easily overcome by a bit of experience and sensible anticipation. It is easy to get into the habit of slipping into your pocket a few little bits of equipment – if you are lucky enough to *have* a pocket, that is. Women's trousers always seem to be made without them for some reason or other, which is all right if one is wearing a jacket, but a bore in hot weather. One can carry some kind of bag, but it is pleasanter to have one's hands unencumbered. Almost anything does to collect seed in – an old envelope or two, a little plastic bag, a typewriter ribbon tin – even the corner of one's handkerchief; but it is important to keep the various kinds separated, particularly if you are collecting the seeds of similar species on the same day. As to the amount you harvest, good sense and a conservator's conscience must be your guides. If you think the plant you are after is rare, even merely rare in that locality, it behoves you to be very sparing indeed. And another thing to remember is that many small birds eat the seeds of common wild flowers, so there is no point in taking away more, even of the commonest sorts, than you can hope to use, and thus depriving them of a useful part of their diet.

Seeds that you can cull from places near enough to your own home to be visited regularly can be taken at the moment of perfection, but ones from more outlying places pose their own problems. Perhaps you are staying away from home, or are out for a walk in an area well away from your usual beat when you see a fine stand of something you have been looking for for years. It is in full flower, with not a seedpod in sight; what are you to do? The first thing is to make a really thorough inspection of it, just to make absolutely sure that there are no pods nearly enough ripe to be worth culling. Often enough there are individuals in a drift of plants that are either unnaturally precocious, or unnaturally tardy, and these may show up on a closer inspection although they may be concealed to the casual eye by the open flowers of their more regular neighbours. But if the narrowest search fails to find what you want, do not despair; you must mark the place, and come back again. Of course, if you are on your holidays a hundred miles away from home, this may not be possible, but even then, if you can identify the place adequately, you may be able to find some local enthusiast who will collect the seed in due course and send it on to you, perhaps in return for a swap of something choice that you have in your own locality. The thing to do is to mark the place in such a way that you can be sure of finding it again, and yet not do any damage, or create such an obvious blot on the landscape that some passer-by, or the land's owner, will tidy it up before you have a chance to return. I have often made a note of the site of a desired plant by a simple system of taking bearings. 'Crown vetch – Gareth's second hayfield – flat-topped holly in line with silo tower – seventeen paces in from hedge' is the kind of note I make, and it enables me to find the plant again nine times out of ten without leaving any mark of my visit at all.

If you can't see any suitable feature in the landscape to take these rough bearings on, there are one or two unobtrusive ways of putting a mark down so that you can find the place again without drawing everybody's attention to it. For a plant growing out in a field, a brightly-coloured golf tee, pushed in right to its neck is useful, as long as you expect to come back to collect your seed fairly soon. Of course, if you have a couple of months to wait, such a mark could get so grown over as to be useless. In a hedge, a small and discreet bow of the sort of coloured plastic string that we use for tying up bales with can be your leading light; but it must *be* small, or the farmer may remove it to use the string for some temporary fencing repair! You should certainly never cut blazes as marks on other people's hedges or trees; similarly, it is unpardonable, in trying to get at awkwardly situated seed-heads, to break or bend or in any way damage a hedge. We must always remember that people farm for a living, whereas we only grow wild flowers for pleasure. By the same token, it is no use getting all uptight if, when you come back in the hope of collecting your seed, you find that in the meantime stock have been turned into the field and have eaten all the plants up. Go home and get out your wild-seed catalogues; the chances are that you will be able to get a starter of your chosen seed from one source or another, even though you may have to pay for it.

As a last resort, if you find something you desperately want, and the seed is simply not ripe enough to collect with any hope of its maturation, you can sometimes get away with digging up one of the seed-bearing plants and re-planting it in a favoured spot in your own garden, there to finish its job. It will almost certainly die itself from a move at so unpropitious a time, but a plant well on with seeding can often direct its last failing energies into hurrying on the maturation of its seeds – a habit which is obviously biologically advantageous to it, and which you can make use of. But I cannot emphasise too strongly that you should never dig up anything that is at all rare, and that you must never dig up anything without the permission of the owner of the land.

Many of the seeds one collects can be grown, as I have said, like any other seeds – sown in boxes, or in drills in the open ground, for later transplanting, or, in the case of annuals like the corn poppy, sown *in situ;* but the seeds of most of the berry-bearing plants call for a rather different technique. These must be stratified, which means that they must be buried in sand, and left out of doors through a winter, unprotected from the weather, for the fleshy outer part of the berry to rot off, and for the stimulus of the cold weather to start the process of germination. Some seeds with fleshy coatings actually have a hormone in the flesh which inhibits germination; many are biologically arranged so that they can pass unharmed through the digestive system of a bird, and germinate when they are voided in its droppings – nature's provision of pelleted seed. But, not having control of the bowels of suitable birds, we are forced to fall back on stratification, and it seems to work quite well. You should wrap a bit of fine-mesh wire netting round your pots or boxes of stratifying seed, to protect them from the depredations of mice, who love such things as cherry stones; and in spring, you sort the seed out of the sand, rub away any remaining fleshy material, and sow it in the ordinary way. Then you may have to wait for quite a long time before anything happens. I am sure that I have often thrown away pots of perfectly viable seed simply because nothing has shown up in, say, six months. of my having sowed the stratified seed. I am more inclined to leave it for eighteen months or two years nowadays. Even when you do decide that nothing is going to happen after all, and that you would like the seed-pans back in use again, there is something to be said for decanting the lump of compost carefully, right way up, into a damp and shady spot where it can remain undisturbed for another year or two. Germination is a freakish thing, and particularly with hard seeds, you can get unexpected surprises. Some seeds, likewise, will germinate, but will make only root growth in their first year – notably peonies and certain lilies. Again, I grieve to think of the pans of probably perfectly good lily seeds that I have heedlessly tossed on to the compost heap in years gone by. But never mind. One of the nicest things about gardening is that you can always try again.

People tend for some reason to overlook the fact that many plants can be easily raised from cuttings. Soft, or tip cuttings can be taken at any time when a plant is in active growth; detailed directions for this process, which is not a bit difficult, can be found in many garden handbooks; the clearest exposition I have read is Christopher Lloyd's, in *The Well-Tempered Garden*. Cuttings of woody subjects are best taken when they are half ripe, between July and October, though I have often had success with suitable twigs stuck in as late as January. I usually take quite small twigs, stripping them off where they join on to the next stem, choosing ones that are going to be between six inches and a foot in length. I remove all the foliage from the bottom half of each twig, and the end halves of the remaining leaves if they are of a big or floppy kind. Then I dust the raw end of the twig in hormone rooting powder, and stick it into the ground for at least half its length. I tread the ground tightly around it, and make sure that it is kept constantly watered – daily in hot weather – and shaded from the sun. If you can stick it in under a north wall, you won't have to bother about shading it. And then I wait; and more than half of the twigs so casually treated turn into nice little rooted plants. Some things seem to be incapable of rooting from cuttings, but you can only find out which by experimenting and as there is no money at all involved, the disappointment of occasional failure is not intolerably severe. Again, it is obvious that you should only take cutting material from a stock plant that is well able to stand the loss. Do not be in too much of a hurry to move your rooted cuttings from their first position. I like to leave them until their second spring. You must also remember that in their first summer, when they are coming up to a year old, they will not have a very large root system, and will want watering in dry spells.

6

Bat Man

When we had our stall in the market, we numbered several gardening friends among our customers. I remember with affection one elderly man who gave me some tansy, and some plants of the Welsh onion, a plant which reproduced itself vegetatively by producing a cluster of bulbils at the top of a long stem. Eventually the bulbils weigh the stem down, and as soon as it bends enough for them to touch the ground, they root into it, and the whole business starts again. Presumably to get a crop from them you have to remove the bulbils before this happens, at which time they would be about the size of small pickling onions. I am obliged to presume in this case because my own plants succumbed to being overlaid in the border rather early in their lives, and as we no longer have a market stall, I can't check the matter with the kind donor.

Another egg customer who became a great gardening mate was called Peter. He was first introduced by Ralph, a market gardener who had a stall near ours, who brought him over to see if we could help in the identity of a mystery plant that Peter was trying to track down. It was a thing he had admired some years previously in somebody else's house, so he could not produce a specimen, and from his description nobody in the market could recognise it. The best thing we could do was to put him on the track of it by introducing him to the local expert, who runs a garden centre, and who knew at once what it must be. It turned out to be something called the lampwick plant, and all that I remember about it is that its stems were triangular in section.

But if the lampwick plant turned out to be a very mere and

passing acquaintance, Peter didn't. He began to buy his eggs from us, and many a pleasant gardening chat we had over the transaction. I never saw his garden, and it must be acknowledged that in those early days I sometimes suspected him of drawing the long bow in the things he told me about it.

'I've got a strain of lettuces,' he said 'that I've been developing for years. I just let the ones that look most like I want bolt, and save the seed. And I've pretty well got it how I want it now.'

'What's special about it, then?' I asked.

'Size,' he replied, succinctly. 'They're enormous. The smallest of them'll weigh three, four pounds. I've had them up to eight or nine. And they're nearly all heart.'

'But what's the point?' I asked. 'Who wants that much lettuce?'

'Hotels,' he explained. 'When you think of how much more they don't have to throw away with mine – if you see what I mean – they're quids in. I supply quite a few of them now. And I must say, the lettuces are very nice, really sweet. I'll bring you one in if you like.'

He was as good as his word. A vast lettuce, solid as a rock, landed on my stall the following Saturday. Unable to believe my eyes, I asked one of the neighbouring greengrocers to weigh it, and it was 3 lbs. 7 oz. He was right, too, in describing his lettuce as sweet. I have never eaten a nicer lettuce; the big, solid heart, kept in a plastic bag in the refrigerator, lasted for about a fortnight, and remained crisp and snappy to the last bite.

Unfortunately, when I met him by chance in the town a few weeks ago and enquired, *inter alia,* about the lettuce strain, he told me that he had allowed it to lapse.

'I don't grow any vegetables in my garden any more,' he said. 'Haven't got room. I've got over four hundred different kinds of flowering things there now...'

After the lettuce trial, I was inclined to believe what he said, however improbable it seemed; so when, back in the market days, he told me that he had spotted orchises growing in his garden 'Dozens of 'em – all over the place – this big –' indicating a height of about three feet – I assumed an attitude of awed acceptance rather than one of scepticism.

'I'll bring you a few in one day if you'd like,' he said over his departing shoulder. I accepted the offer eagerly, and imagined that he might bring me a precious plant or two the following spring. But that was not Peter's way. The very next Saturday, he strolled into the market and casually dumped a long roll of newspaper on my table.

'There you are,' he said. 'There are those orchids I promised you. They ought to be all right. But if they aren't, you can have some more.'

It seemed impossible that they could be all right, by any stretch of the imagination. A cautious turning back of the paper revealed six plants, in advanced bud. They were on average two and a half feet tall. There was a little blackish soil in the vicinity of their tuberous roots, but the small movement of the paper revealed that this was as dry as dust, and completely non-adherent. It was then late June in the drought year of 1976; and if anyone had asked me to insure the lives of those six orchids, I should have felt obliged to refuse, however fat the premium.

They lived, though. At the end of the day I took them home, and planted them, with many misgivings, in the shadiest bit of garden that I could make a space in. The soil of their new quarters was unpropitious, to say the least of it. It was not far from the main drainage system of the house, and I think, retrospectively, it must have consisted largely of the subsoil thrown up when the drains were being laid. It was a mixture of clay and stones, yellowy-grey in colour, and of an unforgiving feel. But while we were still farming, there was little enough time for gardening, particularly with the extra problems of that droughty summer, so I just shoved them in – puddled them in, in fact – and hoped for the best.

Their response was amazing. They did not even sag. Every one of them took the transition from the fine black soil of Peter's garden to the hostile subsoil of mine absolutely in its lovely stride, and continued to open its flowers and ripen its seed as if nothing had happened. I did contrive to keep them watered; but I couldn't help wondering if I was witnessing a swan song, a last desperate effort to make seed in impossible conditions. But it was not so. The following year six little spotted shoots pierced the stony surface, and six flowers once more leaned on the summer air. And so it continued, year by year. In the unpropitious soil of my garden, their flowers got smaller, and attained on average a height of no more than fifteen inches; but by the same token, the plants themselves put on size and heft, and soon some of them were producing several flowering spikes instead of the one each that they had when I first got them.

Naturally, when I moved to Ty Arian the orchids accompanied me, and spent a year lined out in the vegetable garden. Now I have them in what I hope will be their final places, in a sunny hedgebank, as they might be in the wild, where their seed ought to get a chance to grow on. I hope that they will like it there, and colonise.

This matter of seed is a curious one. I suspect the problem is really one of time. In the four springs I had the orchids at Penllwynplan, they all flowered, and all seemed to ripen seed. To give it the best possible chance, I used to cut off the stalks when they had reached the 'burst and scatter' stage and take them to undisturbed grassy areas that seemed similar to the sort of places in which you would expect to find these orchids in the wild. I never saw any result from this, but do not entirely rule out the possibility of something having happened. It may be that orchid seedlings, thin as grass, are indeed growing in those grassy places, and will eventually show themselves as flowering plants. I hope so.

I have never been able to find a satisfactory book about the artificial rearing of our native orchids from seed. Books on exotic orchids outline such a fearsome procedure for germinating seed that one swerves away daunted from the start. After mixing composts so specialised that you feel that at any moment you may be sent on a quest for 'eye of newt and tongue of dog', you discover that you have to sterilise everything – even the lip of the flask, when you have put all the doings in, and are about to seal it! It is obviously a real enthusiast's job, and not at all the scene for a sloppy amateur like me.

But this can hardly be necessary for the cultivation of our own native orchids. Given a suitable habitat and left undisturbed, they do it for themselves; during the last two springs I have found two vast colonies of early purple orchises in the woods on the rough grazing. Here, protection from grazing animals is clearly the name of the game, for both colonies – containing two hundred or more orchids – are in little islands of open space tightly surrounded by a natural barrier of such thorny stock-excluders as blackthorn and hawthorn. Presumably there is enough shade in summer to stop rampant grasses competing too fiercely with the flowers; but of course the orchids have completed their main business of the year before the leaves are fully thick. A wide variation in colour shows that the plants have reproduced sexually, not spread vegetatively.

In my own experience, however, simply sowing the seed of the various wild orchids in ordinary seed compost is a waste of time. I have tried it half a dozen times, with such minor variations as lid on, lid off; warm atmosphere, cool atmosphere; sprinkling of compost on top, no compost on top; without even the faintest whiff of success. Presumably my stock plants will have natural increase if they decide they like their situations, but it would be nice to send the thing along faster than that, and attain, in five or six years, to the glory of really large drifts of these lovely flowers.

It is difficult to remember exactly what Peter chose from the things in my garden; I do recall that we swapped lilies. The ones I gave him were white martagon lilies, grown from seed many years ago. I had sowed the seeds in an ordinary flower pot, a big one, in ordinary soil, and had got a braird of about twenty seedlings from a bought packetful. Each one had its little seed leaf, which it flaunted bravely; in due course each one produced a second leaf too, and looked set for more.

At this stage, unfortunately, they lost my attention. I can't remember why; it was about nineteen years ago. At any rate, I forgot about my pot of seedling lilies, and when I next looked at them, they had all withered up from drought. A fortunate idleness led to their being left in their pot, and when the next spring came round, lo and behold! They all sprouted again, with one little leaf each, followed shortly by another. And *again* for some reason or other I forgot about them for a week or two ... and *again* they were stricken by drought and to all appearances perished.

I should be ashamed to say how many times this sequence of events happened to those poor lilies. Four times, possibly; surely it can't have been five? At any rate, by the time we moved to Wales, they were still slogging it out in their pot, and the five or six that had survived their gruelling initiation period accompanied us here, and were duly planted out, a year or two later, in a newly-made bed under a north wall.

Here they were safe from their previous enemy drought, but the slugs rather got at them. All but two succumbed to this; another just turned up its toes and died for no apparent reason – shock, perhaps!

This left me with only one, but one, obviously, of surpassing hardiness and will to live. Every year its polished snout used to push up through the earth in April, surrounded, as time went on, by an ever-increasing forest of other and lesser snouts. And every July it would flower, building up to a colony of about half a dozen flowering stems as well as a whole bundle of blind ones. I wondered whether or not I ought to lift and divide it, but was nervous about possibly losing, through unwarranted interference, a beauty I had waited so long for. Eventually I made a timid excavation at the side of the bulb and detached a couple of offsets without causing the parent bulb to turn a hair. These offsets grew on so well that when growth had started next spring I took my courage in both hands and inserted a garden fork under the whole mass. An astonishingly large thing came up, about the size of a dinner plate, greenish in colour, and almost infinitely divisible. You could identify the main bulbs as individuals – the ones that were going to flower that year, that is to say; and, by an act of faith, you could more or less rough out the outlines of several others. But the vast mass of the thing, seventy per cent or so, seemed to be anxious to divide itself up into individual scales, and scales, moreover, that showed promise only at one end. From the pointed top you could imagine a leaf emerging; but at the other end they were square, or at least chisel-shaped, and hardly any of them seemed to have even a vestige of root.

The garden at Penllwynplan, as I have explained, was composed almost entirely of subsoil, so planting things was not an entirely straightforward task. With a stout trowel one could excavate a little hole to pop the lily segment into, by removing about half a dozen flat, thick bits of shale. But when you had dropped the chosen one into the hole, how were you to cover it? You could hardly cram the unforgiving stones in alongside it naked; yet to go out into the field and get a bucket of mole-hill soil, or something of equivalent softness was too time-consuming in that time of maximum business when we had too much stock, and gardening, even for ten minutes at a time, seemed a bit of wicked indulgence.

I did manage to inter a fair few of the individual scales, but in the end I got impatient and began to cram them in in families. Everything grew; those planted singly came up for the first year or two like seedlings, and those shoved in wholesale seemed to find the ability to consider themselves as an individual rather than as a crowd, and to produce a proper lily-like stalk, with leaves growing all the way up it, from the word go. It was a year or two before any of them got around to actually flowering, but that didn't matter, as I had replanted the best of the original cluster in its old position and they, or it, continued to flower happily as if nothing had happened to it – or them.

So by the time I got to know Peter I was in the happy position of having white martagon lilies, as they say in Yorkshire, 'for cat and dog.' And as he was in the same situation with Pyrenean lilies, a swap seemed indicated. Pyrenean lilies have become naturalised in this country, and occur here and there in woods and hedgebanks. So for a garden like mine, whose main theme, so to speak, was to be wild flowers, they were a must. They are described rather slightingly by many flower books as being 'of a dirty yellowish colour' – a pejorative which in my opinion is completely undeserved. For my money, *Lilium pyrenaeum* is just a nice yellow turks-cap lily, and an obliging one for good measure.

Or rather, not for my money. For in due course Peter and I ceremoniously handed each other bulging paper bags in the market, and went away pleased with what we had acquired. Mature lily bulbs are very big, and I was surprised to see that the vast bag he had given me contained only two. It felt as if it would be about ten. They were splendid specimens which should flower the same year, too. I put them temporarily in the coal shed, in the cool, and wondered where to plant them. And wondered . . . and wondered . . .

The problem was not altogether simple. The lilies were handed over in our last autumn at Penllwynplan. I knew that by the time they flowered, I would be living somewhere else. But where? The sensible thing to have done would have been to have planted them out temporarily in a couple of pots; but I didn't happen to have any suitably large pots by me, and in the general business and bother of looking for another property and eventually buying it, I let it slide. I won't pretend that I totally forgot about it. When I went into the coal shed throughout the winter to fill the coal scuttle, I would sometimes see the lilies – they were in a brilliant green Marks and Spencer carrier bag by now – and think to myself 'You are a silly fool to have done nothing about those lilies. You did want them, you know you did, and you'll probably never get another chance to have any.' But this mild and occasional self-chastisement never stimulated me to action, and the winter months, as is their wont, slipped away.

It was spring when I eventually managed to buy Ty Arian. It has always seemed to me one of the nicest things about this house that I put my deposit down on it on St David's Day, and completed on May Day. And it was only after the first of these dates, when contracts had been signed, and nothing short of an Act of God could prevent the sale from going through, that I dared to begin transferring things here from the garden.

It was only now that, guiltily, and much dreading what I should see, I plucked up enough courage to look inside the emerald green bag at what I feared must be the sad corpses of two lily bulbs. But, remarkably enough, it was not too bad. The bulbs were a trifle soft, but it was the softness of dehydration rather than that of decay; and I planted them in the gentle leaf-mould of my new little wood with a good deal of hope in my heart.

Nothing happened. A dry summer followed a wet spring; everything else that had accompanied me dug its roots into the baking ground and survived somehow; *Lilium pyrenea-cum* turned its face to the wall.

But it is not for nothing that a plant gets its name on the list of naturalised species. The following spring, I was wandering round the tiny triangle of trees that I describe as my wood when I was staggered to see not two but three fat shiny snouts poking up through the winter's debris of fallen twigs and half-decayed leaves. It was the Pyrenean lily, demonstrating that you can't keep a good plant down; and heaping coals of fire on the head of its so-neglectful keeper by actually managing increase during the year that it lay, to all appearances, totally dormant under the ground.

I wish I could say that my Pyrenean lilies had totally forgiven me, and had covered themselves with blossom in the subsequent two years. But they have not. The stronger one has produced several shoots, but has not attempted to flower; the other, with just one shoot, has flowered feebly, carrying one bloom and setting no seed. I conclude that they find their situation too shady, and intend to move them to a more open place. But in the meantime I honour them highly for their fortitude and endurance, and offer them as examples of hope to any of my readers who may have some similar bulbous plant that appears to have died after being moved.

Peter had a fair-sized family, and from something he told me, it seemed that his children shared something of his own gift with living creatures, though in this case the recipient of their tender mercies was an animal, not a plant. It was, in fact, a baby bat.

They discovered this tiny creature lying on the grass in front of their house 'hardly bigger than a hazel nut,' said Peter, 'or perhaps a walnut – a very *small* walnut, though.' It had obviously dropped from its mother's fur, where baby bats cling, as she hawked after insects. Presumably, only its extreme lightness saved it from injury in its fall to the ground.

The children picked it up and took it indoors, where they arranged a soft bed for it in a cotton-wool lined box, which they kept in the airing cupboard. They tried to feed the little creature with milk from a medicine dropper, but a mother bat's teat is small indeed compared with the smallest dropper there is, and the baby could not open its mouth widely enough to get the thing in far enough to suck. 'The milk sort of splashed all round its mouth,' explained Peter. 'But some of it must have got in, because it lived. And I must say, the kids were very good. They made a rota, and one of 'em got up and fed it every two hours during the night. Of course, that was only once each, being four of 'em. But fair play to them, they stuck to it, and went on for quite a long time. Can't remember how long it was before it began to drink properly.'

Eventually, the children felt that the batlet was old enough to progress on to solid food, and set about capturing insects for its delectation. But to their disappointment, it proved exceedingly scornful of their offerings, and in fact never accepted an insect during the whole course of its stay with them. Two solid foods it did like were cheese and corned beef – particularly the latter. If a shred of corned beef was offered to it, it would hunch its way forward across the table, dragging itself along on its elbows, and eat it with every appearance of appetite. It drank milk from a saucer; I never thought to enquire whether it lapped or sucked; but I do remember that Peter mentioned that it would move straight across and indeed through its saucer of milk if it was being offered corned beef. 'But of course the kids didn't encourage too much of *that,*' said he, 'because of course then it was all wet, and they had to get it clean and dry again as best they could.'

In the end, the children managed to get it flying, and set it free. 'Hacking back' is the term falconers use for re-accustoming a bird to live wild and rely on its own resources; whether anyone has successfully hacked a bat back before Peter's children, I don't know. For several evenings they took it out and encouraged it to try its wings. At first it only clung to their clothes or their hair, upside down in the manner of bats, and when gently stimulated to take off, fluttered helplessly to the ground. But in a day or two it began to find out how to use its wings properly, and began to do 'circuits and bumps', returning after each flight to whichever child it had been clinging to. Eventually one evening it flew away and didn't come back. One can only guess and hope that its instincts were adequate to guide it in the various things a free-living bat needs to know.

This business of getting trapped as an adoptive parent strikes in an entirely arbitrary way. A woman I once met at a party told me how she and her family became foster parents to a moth. I don't remember what kind of moth it was, but she said it was quite a rare one. They were walking along the pavement in a town near their home when they saw a fair-sized caterpillar apparently determined to commit suicide by humping its way across the busy road. Pity seized them; a small box was procured, and the caterpillar was guided into it, and taken home with them. An entomologist friend of theirs identified it, and told them what its food plant was – something pretty available, like hawthorn, I think it was.

The caterpillar ate and thrived, and in due course made itself into a chrysalis. After the usual wait, it emerged as a perfect moth, and was tenderly conveyed to the frame of the open sash window, where they left it to fly away at will.

The woman who was telling me the story said, 'I went into the kitchen to get on with making the dinner, and then my youngest daughter came in and said, "Mummy! You know that moth we put on the drawing room window? Well, there are two of them now!"' And it was so. Both moths flew away, and the family thought that that was the end of that; but when they came to close the window for the night, they noticed that the moth had laid a number of eggs on the wood, near where she had been sitting.

They scraped them carefully on to some leaves of the food plant, and put it on a saucer in the pantry. 'Then nothing happened for absolutely *ages*,' said the woman. 'Weeks, it must have been. And though we sprinkled the leaves with water every now and again, of course they got all dried up. And we assumed in the end that the eggs couldn't have been fertile, or something, and I decided to throw the whole lot away. And then when I took the saucer down from the shelf to dispose of it, it looked somehow different – and when I looked more closely, lots of the eggs had just hatched out into the most minute little black caterpillars you can possibly imagine. So then of course we got some fresh leaves, which they began to eat, and the whole cycle started again. Except that this time we had lots of them.'

For several years the family cultivated the moth, even though it involved them in quite a lot of personal inconvenience. 'As it was the summer, of course, when we always had the caterpillars, we used to have to take them with us when we went on holiday. In the end we used to have two or three of those large glass terrariums full of caterpillars to carry around; people used to look at us most strangely sometimes! But in the end, I don't know why, inbreeding perhaps, they seemed to get very sickly. We began to get a lot of deaths among the caterpillars, and quite a few of the moths used to come out of the chrysalises with things wrong with them – deformed wings, and things like that. So we gave it up.'

But it does show how a family effort can be harnessed to help a threatened species.

I have not kept caterpillars since childhood, when we used to encourage large whites by feeding them nasturtium leaves in jam jars. But I did see something last spring in the butterfly line that I had often read about and never witnessed before; and that was the deterrent effect of the adult butterfly's wing markings on a predator.

It was late March, and a sunny day, with plenty of flowers out in the garden. So when I saw a Peacock butterfly, awakened from hibernation, fluttering up and down the window pane, I said to it, 'You'd probably be better off out than in' and opened the window to let it out. Unfortunately, the butterfly was not as strong on its wings as it had seemed, and when it found itself airborne, it quickly lost height, and came to rest in a patch of sunlight on the lawn. To my chagrin, its arrival was observed by a robin, which had been perching in a spirea, and which immediately hopped down to investigate this fat and meaty food hand-out. The butterfly had been sitting, as is their way, with its wings folded together like praying hands over its back. Now, however, not observing the robin, but motivated purely by chance, it opened and closed them a few times, an action that caused its white eye-spots to flash out in what must have looked a threatening way.

The robin was scandalised. It had hopped cautiously up to within about a foot of the butterfly, but now it jumped back as if it had been stung, and remained in the quaintest attitude of doubt, stretching out its neck and craning on tiptoe as if wondering what on earth this strange creature could be, playing 'now you see it – now you don't!' with such confidence. The butterfly continued to work its wings spasmodically, and the robin gave a convulsive start every time the eye-spots appeared, but was clearly not frightened enough to fly away. By ill chance the telephone rang at that moment, and by the time I had answered it and returned, both the protagonists had disappeared, but whether separately or together there was no way of knowing. Perhaps the absence of nipped-off wings blowing about in the breeze was evidence of a happy ending, from the butterfly's point of view.

It is only rarely that insects attain to any individuality in relation to human beings. But there was a bee that I got quite fond of last autumn. Some wild scabious, the field sort, was flowering under the roses in one of our sunny terrace beds, and we noticed this bee clinging to a blossom one morning, rigid with cold and dewy all over, obviously having been there all night. You could easily see that the end of its life was near. Its wings were tattered and frayed, and its fur – it was a small, yellowish bumble bee – looked unkempt and worn. Whether it was a drone, cast forth from the nest at the approach of autumn, or a used-up worker, I was not naturalist enough to know. It could have been either, for bumble bee workers do not survive the winter. Inevitably, it acquired the nickname of 'Eric, the half a bee', so one tended to think of it as a male.

When the sun got high enough in the sky to warm the scabious flower on which he was sitting, Eric revived considerably, and I was glad to see that he was crawling slowly about shoving his proboscis into the florets and presumably enjoying the resultant nectar. I did wonder if it would be a kindness to knock him to the ground and put my foot on him 'to put him out of his pain', but as he didn't actually seem to be in any sort of pain, I decided not to play God, but to let nature take its course. The next night would probably do for him anyway, I thought – and they say that it is quite pleasant to die from exposure.

But Eric had no intention of dying yet awhile. That night, instead of staying on the exposed face of the flower he had chosen as his retirement home, he crept round the back of it, and tucked himself in among the sepals in a much more sheltered position. Then when the sun became warm again, he crept round to the front, and continued to crawl to and fro, feeding, as before.

On the third day there was rain, and though I looked for Eric he was nowhere to be found. I mourned him, but briefly; for two days is not a long acquaintance, and we are all mortal anyway. But my mourning in any case turned out to be premature, for when the sun climbed the sky on day four, Eric was back again, basking and sipping on the same flower in the most agreeable way.

It was three weeks before he disappeared for ever. Whenever it rained he hid, though I never discovered where; but as soon as the sun returned – and it was, luckily for him, a remarkably pleasant autumn – he re-appeared. He even outlasted his original flower, and had to make a short move to a newly-opened one. I was glad I hadn't killed him on that first day in an access of mistaken mercy. I suppose he enjoyed his halcyon three weeks, insofar as a bee is capable of enjoyment. How impossible it is to refrain from projecting our human thoughts and emotions on to other forms of life.

Bees are important in the garden as pollinators, of course; and I have often toyed with the idea of acquiring a hive of them, being daunted more by the expense than anything else. Nobody near here has hive bees, so I assume that the ones I see on my flowers that look like hive bees must be members of the trigger-tempered colony in Mick's wood. These bees seem to get more and more aggressive as time goes by, so that one cannot go within thirty yards of their nest without being attacked, or at least 'buzzed' warningly. Luckily, they only seem to feel this access of nastiness when they are close to home. In my garden, they behave themselves quite demurely.

Bees, after all, have to have a home. But those other favourite garden insects, butterflies, are wanderers. 1981 seems to have been a singularly poor year for butterflies round here, with even the usually-common Small Tortoiseshell only putting in a rare appearance. There is no shortage of the food plants of any of the common kinds round here. Perhaps they haven't liked the weather. Or possibly there is a more sinister reason behind their scarcity. After all, there are many kinds of industrial pollution that go on quite unsuspected until they have done their dirty work and endangered something; nobody realised, for example, that our clouds of sulphuric acid gas, generated from manufacturing in the midlands and north, were drifting across the north sea and falling dissolved in rain on Norway and Sweden, until the fish in their inland rivers and lakes began to die mysteriously. It is possible that some other nasty by-product is making life difficult for our lovely butterflies. One must just hope that the Ministry of the Environment, or some other appropriate body, will be keeping its eye on the problem, and doing something about it before it gets irreversible.

It has seemed to me for many years that the day will come when it is as normal and conventional to send off a chrysalis order to your friendly corner butterfly farm as it is now to have a bulb order. Imagine the pleasure of releasing a couple of dozen Common Blues, for instance, and watching them flying around like fluttering flax flowers all over your garden. Or a noble number of Red Admirals. Or, even more *recherché*, a collection of Commas, or a lovely lot of Large Coppers. I am not aware of any technically correct collective noun for an assembly of butterflies; beside me as I write is a newly-published list, taken from a late fourteenth-century manuscript, of collective nouns, which ranges from the well-known, if rather unfamiliarly spelt 'A chirm of goldfinches' to the (surely invented) 'An abominable sight of monks', 'An incredibility of cuckolds', and 'A disworship of Scots.' But there is not one for butterflies. Perhaps one could take a leaf out of this new/old book, and invent one. How about 'A tossing of butterflies' or perhaps 'A roundabout of butterflies'?

We could certainly have used such a collective noun in the summer of 1980 for our prodigious invasion of Painted Ladies. Large numbers of these creatures are sometimes said to migrate here from the continent, but these looked too fresh, too pristine, to have come from so far away. They began to appear on 7 July, and were with us in unusual numbers until the end of the summer. In the walk across the fields between my house and Ruth and John's, which is about a mile long, one would see twenty-five or so painted ladies; and once, when walking home from there by the lane, a slightly longer way round, I saw a column of nine of them, dancing up and down almost like gnats in the warm air. You could actually hear the sibilant friction of their wings as they fluttered, a noise like a single head of ripe oats shivering its papery bracts in an almost non-existent wind. Seeing these butterflies in such large numbers, it was interesting to notice the variation in size and colour among them. Some were of a much deeper and more intense pink than the average, and some were exceptionally large. But all were beautiful, and all had that straight-from-the-maker look that seemed to imply that they could not have hatched so very far away. But for all their exceptional numbers, they obviously failed to leave a viable wintering population behind them, for not a single one fluttered across my path in the summer of 1981.

7

Garden Sundries

In their gardening careers, people become attached to certain tools. My father swears by the swoe, which looks rather like a stainless steel golf club with its head flat instead of upright. My own favourite tools are both cheaper and more unconventional. One of them is an ordinary table knife. People in books are always getting weeds out from between stones 'with a broken table knife', but mine must not be broken. That slight taper at the tip is part of its exquisite fitness for its purpose. It is an optimal instrument for pricking out small seedlings, both for making the tiny slit in the compost that the seedling is going to be dropped into, and for picking up the seedling itself. Holding the knife quite far down the blade (my grandfather, that arch-sharpener of table knives, being now dead, it is safe to do this) one can wield it as delicately as a scalpel, and persuade an individual seedling to separate from its brethren with remarkably little damage to its fine roots. Some people advocate using a plant label for this job, I know, but it seems thick and clumsy to me compared with my table knife. I don't keep a special one apart for the job, either, with the concomitant risk to it of getting lost; I just take a nicely shaped one from the drawer at need. So let anyone who comes to dinner with me take warning.

Another job your knife might have been doing if you ever find yourself at my table, is hoeing. When weeds are growing in among tightly planted things, a larger tool seems inappropriate. Take a row of peas, for example, thick with chickweed, shepherd's purse, and oxalis. Handweeding is all very well, and I am not against it. But on a dry hoeing sort of day, you can work round and among the stems of peas, themselves so juicy and snappable, without severing one, sliding your knife around just below the surface of the soil and leaving the weeds to die in the sun much more quickly than you can get them out by hand. The broader areas between the rows I usually do with a conventional Dutch hoe – though even there I sometimes find the handy knife less trouble in the long run.

My other favourite garden implement, and one which I could in no way manage without, is the bread knife. I suppose the work I do with it could be done by either the shears or the sickle, but there is a handiness and adaptability about the bread knife that endears it to me. Shears are expensive, and though a new pair by a good maker is light, efficient, and a joy to use, the cutting edge goes off the blades all too soon, and you find yourself into both expense and administrative effort getting them re-ground. The bread knife, on the other hand, seems to go on indefinitely. At least, the one I am using now has done all my garden chores as well as cutting all the family's bread for about six or seven years, and still looks to have plenty of depth left in its serrations.

The use of the bread knife as a garden implement takes one back about ten thousand years, to the early days of agriculture, when the first farmers reaped their crops with sickles made of small chips of sharp flint set in a curved haft such as a jawbone. Like them, I seize a handful of the thing I want to cut, and pull it taut, then saw across the stretched stems. It is a whole lot quicker to do it than to describe it. You can do quite large areas with it in a short time once you get the knack. Indeed, when on one occasion I had to keep the bull shut in for a few days in the summer, after a series of escapes and frantic telephone calls ('Your big black bull's outside my back door. My wife's going hysterical'), I kept his body and soul together entirely with grass harvested by this primitive method, and carried to him in the ironing blanket... A scythe or a sickle might have been quicker, but I didn't have a scythe, and I have never been much good at using any kind of slasher, like a sickle. I go through the motions, but the thing I am hacking at tends to bruise and bend rather than severing cleanly. With the bread knife, it has no option.

There is a fascinating book by Singer, Holmyard and Hall

called *The History of Technology* which shows the slow development, over the years, of the pistol hand grip in saws. Early saws have their handles in a straight line with their blades, and I was struck, when I saw the illustrations of them, by their resemblance to my faithful bread knife. The straight handle is mechanically less advantageous than the pistol grip, but it does enable you to work at any angle, and of course in a gardening situation, you are never cutting anything very resistant. I use my bread knife for trimming the grass round the edges of flower beds, on steep banks, close to the foot of a wall where a mower will not go, and round the stems of things that are flopping over on to a mown area, from beds.

A further gardening aid that I do not see in my friends' gardens, though I don't know why, is the plastic fertiliser bag. I always have a supply of them from kindly farmer neighbours, basically because round here we use them for rubbish bags, but also because they are so handy in the garden. No – not for putting things in – but for sitting on. I do nearly all my weeding, bread-knifing, planting-out, and so on, from a sitting position. I can't kneel, having a loose-jointed knee as a result of falling too hard and too often off horses, and squatting, or 'cronking' down to work is tiring for anyone over twelve and not into yoga. Sitting is the thing, and with a handy fertiliser bag you can get down anywhere, round the edge of the border, at least. I usually fold my bag into four, which gives enough thickness of material to soften any lumps and bumps in the ground; the plastic, of course, is perfectly waterproof; and though the bag may pick up the odd bit of dust or mud, it is self-cleaning enough in general to sit on in gardening trousers, unlike a hessian sack, which becomes both saturated and clogged with mud. I sit on one haunch, so to speak, and lean my weight on the left hand while the right works away. Sometimes, when I am feeling particularly sybaritic, I take along another smaller square of plastic for the left hand to rest on, for cultivated earth, particularly in a drought, can be a bit sharp and uncomfortable to lean on if one intends to go on working for any length of time. Of course, when working right inside one's flower beds there is not room to sit down, and one must adopt a stooping posture; but this much detracts from the pleasure, and I am glad that the configuration of my garden makes it possible to have access to most of the cultivated parts from round their edges.

Like many gardeners, I quite enjoy weeding. In spite of my professed dedication to untidiness, I do keep the beds close to the house reasonably clear of weeds; it is a different matter in the outer rings of my influence, nearer and nearer to my boundary fence, where what I do becomes increasingly diluted by what nature does. As I leave the house and its terrace behind, the kind of mental attitude that encourages the use of the word 'weed' seems to become less and less appropriate, and the control I exert upon what grows becomes less and less stringent.

I don't know what other wild flower gardeners do about this business of controlling the places their chosen wild species grow in – how much they leave it to look after itself, or alter it themselves. Every one must make up his or her own mind on a point like this, which is, after all, an aesthetic rather than a cultural one, and which probably depends as much on the amount of space you have to devote to wild flowers as on anything else. For my own part, when I have wild things growing in my terrace beds, I grow them just like garden flowers, encouraging them to grow thickly and to conceal the earth with their abundance, but removing any grass or other uninvited wild stuff that may put in its appearance. Then I have a sort of no-man's-land, or semi-cultivated bit, which gets weeded about once a year, and trimmed several times, but which is permitted to be pretty grassy. The outer fringes, the wood, the lower drive, the two little fields, are really kept as wild as wild, in the true tradition of untidy gardening, and once freed of the noxious things like nettles and brambles, will be expected to maintain their status quo by simply being grazed, or trashed once a year, whichever is the more appropriate. In a garden so intimately bedded into the countryside as this is, and a fairly wild countryside at that, it will always be necessary to go round once a year weeding out invading seedlings of ragwort, dock, hawthorn, burdock, and so on, but that can be done at leisure once the main armies of the unwanted have been put to flight.

I am always very conscious of my little property as part of the surrounding countryside. I want it to play its part, as best it can, in helping to conserve other forms of wild life as well as wild flowers. Perhaps fortunately for our gardening, we have no deer in this immediate area, but most of the other British mammals are to be found. I even saw a young red squirrel the other day, a particularly welcome sight, as evidence of this existence of at least one breeding pair in the vicinity.

We have amphibians in plenty round here, too. It is not often that one actually sees them, but occasional toads flattened on the road, and the bodies of slow-worms killed by the cat bear witness; and of course there is evidence of the presence of numbers of frogs in their spawn.

The frog, unfortunately, is a sharply declining species in this country. I love frogs myself, having never got over the wonder and interest of keeping 'taddies' as a child. I enjoy their whimsical method of reproduction which gives one such a splendid opportunity of looking at the whole business from fertilised ovum onwards, as through a window, and of watching the fascinating development of an embryo *ex utero*. When I first came to live in Ty Arian, I looked around for the most likely frog-spawning places, and fixed on the marsh beside the river as the most promising. Here, the springs that leak out from the foot of the hill have made a rushy, boggy area several acres in extent; occasional willows spring up among the rushes, and a strip of firmer land, intersected by one or two small drainage streams, divides it from the river proper. As you wade around among the bronzed clumps of the rushes, you find that there are pools of water round their feet, some of which expand in wet weather into quite large sheets of open water, four or five yards across. Later in the year, water forget-me-not, brooklime, river mint and meadowsweet will embroider the marshes with their fresh points of colour; earlier, clumps of water iris spear through the water, and the shiny triangular leaves of the kingcup reflect the light. Straggling grasses lie horizontal beneath the water at the pools' edges, taking their turn of prosperity during dry spells, when for a while they find themselves terrestrial rather than aquatic again.

There is an old bit of weather lore that avers that the frogs won't spawn until after the real winter weather is behind us. Naturally, the discovery of the first spawn was awaited with a good deal of eagerness that first year. We simply hadn't had any wintry weather; with February here, and the catkins already tentatively lengthening on the hazels, we didn't want to start it now. We watched our pools. 'You're looking in the wrong place,' said my neighbour, John. 'The biggest of the springs in the old farm yard, that's where we always find the first spawn. Just about the time of Cruft's.' (Being dog breeders, John and Ruth are always a bit inclined to think of dates in relation to dog shows – the dog breeders' equivalent of the churchman's 'Third Sunday after Trinity.')

Sure enough, he was right about the time, although wrong about the place. On the tenth of February, the very day after Cruft's, I found about twelve dollops of spawn in the biggest of the marsh pools down by the river; and, for some reason or other, the frogs kept on piling in and laying in that one particular place until you could really and truly see more spawn than water. The spring chamber in the old farm yard, which had been trampled by the heifers, and had got rather full of mud in consequence, was ignored. A week or so after the first batch was laid, an independent-minded amphibian couple spawned copiously in one of John's field cattle drinking troughs, a partly-sunken one which is replenished by a constant trickle of water from a piped spring. Various other promising-looking pools remained unvisited.

After a week or two had passed, and no frogs had spawned on my own land, I decided to take a hand in the matter, and, arming myself with a large white enamel jug, sallied forth in the persona of a *deus ex machina*. I scooped up a good dollop of the marsh pond spawn – choosing, from that plethora, spawn which looked good and blackish, with well-developed spots in the eggs. I carried it carefully back to my own place and dumped it into two reasonably suitable-looking pools. One was an old shallow well, just alongside my drive, which Mick had told me was there but which had been so overgrown throughout the green part of the year that I had never been able to identify it. The other was on the swampy bit below the drive where an inch or so's depth of clear water moved, over a wide expanse, across a bottom of settled muddy silt, under the shade of a whole lot of pussy willows. I preferred the well, which was much deeper and clearer. There might have been a surface area, perhaps, of two square yards in this well, and as well as flooded grass and dead leaves, it contained a good growth of bright green cloudy algae, which showed up well in the intensely clear water. Brambles and nettles draped the bit of it that caved back under the slanting, corbelled overhang, and garlic grew thickly about the rim. ('You won't have to worry at all about vampires while you're living here,' a friend once remarked, surveying the abundant growth of this plant up into my little wood.) The main inhabitant of the other pool was the poisonous water parsnip. But both were spring-fed pools, and I thought that the tadpoles must inevitably have a better chance in either of them than in that crowded marsh pool, where the spawn was still being laid with such abandon that in places it now actually stood up out of the water.

It was several weeks before any of the tadpoles hatched, in spite of the fact that the weather continued reasonably mild, with hardly any night frosts and certainly nothing that could have been described as hard weather. In the end, the tadpoles in the well were first out, closely followed by those in the willow pool.

In the marsh pool, all was definitely not well. Somewhere in the hill through which the water drains that seeps into that marsh, there must be a stratum of iron ore, because all the marsh water tends to be curiously rust-coloured, as are the algae that grow in it. An oily-looking iridescent scum sometimes collects on the surface – presumably some natural bacterial phenomenon; there simply isn't anyone in a position to have spilled oil there, or anywhere higher up, although this is just what it looks like. This mixture of environmental hazards was clearly doing the marsh pool spawn no good, and it soon became apparent that quite a lot of it was diseased, and was not going to hatch. A lot of the black dots in the spawn began to grow white coats of fungus, and, furthermore, bubbles of gas developed in some of the spawn masses, pushing them up into even weirder shapes. At about this time I discovered another pool, about a mile away, fed by a little trickling stream on its way to the river, and thickly cressed over with duckweed and water crowfoot – weeds which, according to my old riding master, showed for certain that the water beneath must be clean and pure. This pool, which I called the duckweed pool, was innocent of spawn, so, armed once more with my jug, I transferred into it a lump of the freshest spawn I could find in the marsh pool. I was careful to take spawn which showed no fungus or gas bubbles; it had all acquired by this time an orange colour, from the iron salts that were everywhere in the water; it looked rather unpromising.

My own two sets of taddies were developing quite well now. The ones in the well always seemed to do better than the ones in the willow pool, although they were litter brothers and sisters; it must have been a better environment. It was interesting to see how when the tadpoles first hatched out of the jelly they still clustered round it. They appeared to be eating it, but without examining them through a magnifying glass, which I hadn't got, I could not be sure of this. Certainly the remains of the jelly became smaller; but this may have been only the continuation of the process I had noticed in all the pools, whereby the jelly, which was stiff and upstanding soon after it was laid, slackened off in texture and spread out more sloppily on the water after a couple of weeks. By the time the tadpoles were a couple of weeks old, they began to graze the algae, and could be seen lying, mouths down, on all sorts of odd bits of refuse like decaying dead leaves in the water. I brought them dollops of duckweed and water crowfoot which spread out and looked very much at home in the water, but they ignored it.

I was interested to see how relatively inert my tadpoles were. They continued to grow quite rapidly, so presumably they must have been healthy, but they did not display the constant wriggling energy that I had been used to in bowls of tadpoles in the house. I am inclined to think that this may have been a function of low temperature. When the spawn in John's tank hatched, the tadpoles that emerged were intensely vigorous, and wriggled prodigiously – and that tank was completely open to the sun, and stood up out of the ground, so it could have been several degrees warmer than my rather shaded and overhung pools. My own tadpoles took occasional short wriggling swims spontaneously, and did indeed seem to be more active when the sun was actually shining on their pool; even at their most inert, they would swim away if I actually put a finger into the water and touched them, but they never seemed to display the almost manic activity of John's.

After waiting some days for the spawn I had put into the duckweed pond to hatch, with no result, I once more took my jug, and carried a hundred or two of John's teeming thousands up there. On this visit I noticed with disquiet that some frogs had indeed spawned into the pool, but that this spawn was just as badly infected with fungus as that in the marsh pool. But by the time I noticed this, I had already decanted the new lot of tadpoles into the water, so there was no question of being able to retrieve them. In any case, as far as my observations go, this fungus only attacks spawn, and once the tadpoles have emerged, they are safe enough from it. I took some of the duckweed back to John's tank by way of a thank-you, but once again, the tadpoles seemed to ignore it, and clustered instead round the thick clouding of algae that had developed where the tank was fed from its trickling spring.

John's tadpoles, in their sunny tank and with plenty of algae to graze on, soon outstripped all the other batches in growth, but unfortunately it was not destined to be a vintage year for froglets, however promising their beginnings. A drought which began in mid March and continued throughout April gradually dried up all the springs; pool after pool shrank away. One brilliant day, late in April, exploring with a family of friends who were staying with us, we found a sad situation where an immense number of tadpoles were eking out what had to be the last few days of their lives in a series of water-filled cows' hoof prints, at the edge of what had once been a marsh. There was nothing we could do. To put them into the river would have been death to them, creatures as they are of the stagnant pool – the brisk current would have whirled them away, and in any case, the trout would no doubt have eaten them. Besides, there were thousands of them, and we had no means of transporting them there. We just had to leave them to their fate.

Thus alerted to the dangers of the situation, we made a round of all the tadpole colonies that I had been keeping an eye on, and found them all in equally bad case. My own two springs, which I had thought would run all summer, were at their last gasp; the marsh pool and the duckweed pool had totally disappeared, leaving no trace of their former inhabitants; even John's tank was empty, the formerly flourishing weed stretched out lifeless on its muddy bottom, the large tadpoles completely gone. 'It's a megadeath,' solemnly concluded the fifteen-year-old son of my friends. Some frogs somewhere must have managed their affairs better, for we observed a few, later in the summer, in their charming, immature, thumb-nail-sized manifestation, exercising their almost transparent limbs about the roots of the meadow-rushes; but all in all, it must have been a year of regress rather than progress for the species, and it underlined for us the awful vulnerability of a creature already threatened by the destruction of large areas of its breeding habitat.

In the second spring I tried again. This time, knowing the dangers, I limited my spawn transplant to the well pool which, I thought, I could at need keep filled up by carrying bucketsful of water from the nearby river. I put only a small dollop of spawn in, thinking it better to rear a few well-done tadpoles than a lot of runty ones; I hung over them like a mother – planted up their pool once more with suitable weeds – and waited.

But once again my efforts were frustrated. A drought *did* come – not a hot drought, but a cold, miserable, east wind sort of drought, that kept all nature back; and again, the taddy-pool began to shrink. True to my promise, I carried water from the river. I carried two bucketsful a day – four – six – eight – ten. It was to no avail. It became apparent that the floor of the well-chamber was not in the least bit waterproof, and that once the spring that fed it had stopped running, all the water I could pour into it if I taxed my strength to the uttermost, would simply leak away. Before the pool dried right up, I searched for the tadpoles, meaning to put them into a bucket of water to complete their metamorphosis, but I could not find them. I had noticed and puzzled over the fact that none of the expected predators – herons, dippers, or kingfishers, for instance – had ever seemed to be seen hunting the tadpole-filled pools. Now I wondered if perhaps they were taking advantage of the tadpoles' relatively exposed situation, in water which had shrunk to a puddle, and were coming in the dawn light, and clearing them up altogether. I don't know. I never saw anything obviously trying to fish for them. But the tadpoles certainly disappeared from the well pool before the last of the water went, and not under their own steam, for they had not even got their back legs grown to any extent, let alone their front legs or their wide frog mouth parts.

I shall not transplant any frog spawn next spring. But if my plans for the little swampy triangle just inside my gate come to fruition, I shall have quite a large, deep pool. Only time will show whether or not it will be proof against the spring droughts that seem so often to be our lot here. If it does seem to be reliable, I shall be tempted to go spawn-hunting once more with my jug. But who knows? It may not be necessary. Come the season for Cruft's, two or three years from now, the frogs may discover my new pool for themselves, and spawn in it spontaneously. I shall just have to wait and see.

Efforts by other wild creatures to breed on or near my land are not always quite so welcome. I was out with Tip, my dog, one day near the beginning of July, on the rough grazing that adjoins my own fields, when I noticed a newly-excavated hole in the bank, and was surprised to see him rush straight past it, without any investigatory pause. As he is a Jack Russell terrier, his interest in holes and burrows is usually both profound and professional, so I walked over to have a closer look at it myself, to see why it had failed to interest him. It was not a very big hole, nor very deep – four inches across the mouth, and eight deep, perhaps; and for a moment I wondered what little creature had once made its home there. But then my eye was caught by a scrap of dun-coloured rubbish lying close to the excavated hole, and I realised that what I was looking at was a wasps' nest, in quite an early stage of development, that had almost certainly been dug out by a badger. These animals enjoy the grubs of the wasp brood, and, presumably, any adults that they can crunch up in the course of a nocturnal raid. Their thick coats and tough skins make them impervious to stings, though any lucky wasp that scores a bull's eye up the badger's nostril can be sure of putting its enemy to some discomfort. A few workers still crawled disconsolately over the shell of their paper nest, ruthlessly dismembered; the piece that was left was about the size of a quarter grapefruit, of four or five inches' diameter. I bent quite close to the ruin to pick up an odd piece of the rough, greyish-brown paper of which the nest is made, wanting to experience its smell and texture; but the heart had gone out of the surviving wasps with the destruction of their citadel, and though my shadow fell across them, they made no move to rise up and attack me. I supposed that they would shortly die, and though I felt sorry for them, I couldn't help being grateful to that badger which had, apparently so easily, got rid of a menace that in a month or so would have sent a constant stream of bad-tempered workers to eat my fruit, buzz about in my kitchen, and commit sticky and prolonged suicide in any pot of jam that I might have been foolish enough to leave uncovered.

The breeding of all sorts of insects seems to be fraught with peril. Shortly after discovering the scooped-out wasps' nest, I saw some ants getting themselves into trouble, through no fault of their own. I was down at my neighbours', Mick and Emerald's, watching Mick repairing an old hay-maker for another neighbour, when we all became aware that the quality of the light was changing. It had been heavy and cloudy all day, though warm, but now, although it was only half past four in the afternoon, it began to thicken up ominously, and a strange portentous pink dusk crept over us. Mick looked up at the sky.

'Better cut along home, Elizabeth, if you don't want a wetting,' he said. 'Looks as if we're in for some thunder.'

A few drops, large and warm, went splat! on to the ground, as if it emphasise his words. Pulling my coat over my head, I said goodbye rather rapidly, and hastened away home, expecting the heavens to open at any moment, and flush me down my own steep drive like a spider down a gutter. A spatter of great drops plashed on to my protective covering, but still the great weight of the storm held off. And then, as I reached my own back door, I glanced up – and what was my amazement to see, flying high, high up against that swollen, threatening, turgid bank of cloud, a great flock of hirondines, two hundred of them at least, madly wheeling, darting, diving, chasing; to and fro, to and fro they went, three or four hundred feet up in the air, among the ever-thickening drops of a storm that pretty well turned into a cloudburst before it had finished. Their flight pattern was local; it was easy to see that they were opportunely stuffing their crops at the expense of some particular flight of insects, but at that height it was impossible to tell what. Indeed, the birds were flying so high that you could not even distinguish swallow from swift or martin; there was no question of identifying their insect prey.

I am sorry to say that when the storm did eventually break, with a flash and a crash, into something rather like a monsoon, I came indoors. It would have been interesting to watch the hirondines dispersing and running for cover, but it could have been done only at the cost of a total wetting; and indeed, so high were the birds and so heavy was the rain that I imagine my vision would have been obscured by the very thickness of the rain. My eyes would have filled up like birdbaths if I had tried to look directly upwards into that lot. I am sure they would not, in the circumstances, have been any use for seeing with at all.

The puzzling thing was the great height of the insect swarm that the birds were feeding on, in such weather conditions. Anybody could have seen that it was about not merely to rain, but to pour. Insects are usually aware of approaching bad weather, and limit their flights to within a few feet of the ground, presumably so that they can easily get under a leaf or a similar shelter when the rain does come. I discussed the phenomenon with Mick when I went down for my milk next day. He was standing in his workshop ruefully surveying the havoc caused by a stream of water which the previous day's entirely unusual rainstorm had sent cascading right across his floor, but he was happy enough to re-focus his attention on the highflying swarm of insects which I described to him. We concluded that they must have been a nuptial flight of ants.

'But what would they been thinking of to go up as high as that? I wondered.

'Probably not on purpose at all,' said Mick. 'It was a funny old day yesterday – sultry. There could have been some pretty strong thermals – updraughts, pretty local. If they got into one of those, they wouldn't have been able to help themselves. They'd have been taken up willy nilly, as they say.'

I expect he was right. Poor ants, if so; whirled up into the sky in a current of air far beyond the power of their feeble wings to resist – decimated by the attacks of all the hirondines of a mile radius – and finally dashed to earth by a storm whose smallest drop would have been bigger than any ten of them. It seems a bit hard if rain stops play when you only get once chance at the game in the whole of your life. Still, anyone who expects things to be fair just hasn't been noticing what goes on, and I suppose that this applies to ants as well as to more recent forms of life.

At any rate, it must have been quite a treat for the swallows and things. The life of an insectivorous bird must tend to alternate between fast and plenty, as the vagaries of the weather influence the supply of food; and although these particular birds are summer visitors, so many of our natives are insectivorous that it is something of a puzzle to know how they do manage to survive through the winter months.

You can see how the thrushes fare well enough by noticing the heaps of smashed snail-shells lying about by their favourite anvil stones. The blackbirds, too, scratching energetically among the fallen leaves, pick up sizeable morsels of food, like slugs and earthworms. You can imagine that it is enough to live on. But little things like tits and wrens seem to spend such a prodigious amount of energy in their constant inspection of every nook and cranny of their environment in the never-ending search for food that it is hard to see how they ever manage to make ends meet calorifically. They have a high temperature to support, compared with most mammals, and a relatively large surface compared to the body weight, both adverse factors in the equation.

Luckily, though, like the bumble bees which, not knowing that the ratio of their wing area to their size and weight makes it impossible for them to fly, blandly do so, the small birds manage to support life well enough through an average winter. Minute as the morsels they find must be, presumably they pick up plenty of them. At any rate, there they still are every spring, or, at least, enough of them to breed up again, in a rural area like this one. There is evidently more food about than meets the eye, unless that eye is small, bright, and experienced in detecting insect hiding places.

Another factor struck me a little while ago when I was going to fetch my daily milk from Mick and Emerald. It was a mild, damp evening in late December, and as I walked along the wet road which reflected the gleam of the westering sun, I kept having to avoid the dancing columns of gnats which hung like smoke in the gentle air. As a summer phenomenon, this is unremarkable; the low-lying fields by the river form optimal breeding-grounds for insects of this kind. The shady side of the road is always well populated with them. But this was almost the New Year, and here were these creatures in their thousands, indulging in what I have always understood to be their mating flight. It is the same business of showing yourself off and indicating your availability that sends the young of our own species out to hang round street corners in giggling groups until pairing-off takes place, and (though we had better leave the analogy here) eggs are laid. There must be a constant population of the pupal stages of these insects waiting to attain adulthood; the surprise, when your attention is drawn to it, is the relatively low temperature – about 50°F. – that appears to trigger off the final development.

Mild spells in winter do not, of course, last very long; even if we are spared the killing east wind that brings us our snow from the cruel German ocean, we must look for cold, blustery messages from Iceland and North America; and with the temperatures in the forties or below, there are no obvious mating-assemblies of gnats to be seen. But of course, every one of those teeming thousands that so recently tangled in one's hair or attempted to invade one's trachea is somewhere, crouching under some wind-whipped grass-blade, or squeezed into a crevice on the sheltered side of a rough-barked tree. So every mild spell, however brief, that stimulates another hatch in the boggy riverside fields, re-lays the table for the small birds. And of course it is not only the gnat type of insect that is tempted to hatch by a burst of relative warmth. Driving along the lanes on one of those damp, amiable nights that seem to speak of spring even in January, you can often see pale moths dancing up and down in the beam of your headlights; and they too, if they escape the night predators, must often fall victim to the beady inquisitorial eyes of the diurnal insectivores.

8

Stealing

I wonder if there is a gardener anywhere in the country who has not at some stage in his gardening career stolen a cutting. Beverley Nichols wrote an amusing article on his own falls from grace which was published in one of the early issues of the magazine *My Garden*, in 1934; and brought down such a hornets' nest of criticism on his head from the owners of all-too-much-denuded gardens – including Kew – that he had to print an embarrassed and embarrassing disclaimer in the next issue, pointing out that he had only meant it as a joke, he didn't *really* go round stealing things, and so on and so forth.

But I frankly admit that I have two or three things growing in my garden at this moment that have no business to be there. I deplore theft in general, and I would never take anything from a garden that is thrown open to the public, on the grounds that the plants are exposed to too much risk for that to be fair. But I have on occasion snitched odd bits of things from suitable plants that have chanced to dangle within my reach; and I should not even yet like to put my hand on my heart, and swear that I shall never do it again.

I suppose that virtually everybody does a little bit of this kind of pilfering, and that the safeguard is built in. What I mean is that presumably a person who has enough gardening knowledge and skill to want to raise things from cuttings, and to take the right sort of material, will also know what they must leave strictly alone. The ultimate test, presumably, is to say to oneself, 'Would I mind if somebody pinched a few cuttings from me?' and I can definitely aver that I wouldn't mind at all being robbed, at the level I am talking about.

One of the plants I have acquired by stealth came into my possession when I had to spend a few days in a certain northern city doing publicity for my book *Yorkshire Relish*. Bored and lonely, I had gone out to pass away the long hours of a Sunday morning walking about the deserted streets, when chance directed my footsteps into a most beautiful little Georgian square. An open garden, with lawns, seats, and trees filled the centre; gracious houses, their brick faces rosy under the beneficent influence of the Clean Air Act, stood round, each with its tiny oblong of front garden, its elegant many-paned windows, and its individually designed fanlight over the door. It was a lovely place. Here, I assumed, must live the wealthy ones of the city – the barristers, the consultants, the successful business men. And how lucky they were to do so, to find this refuge of civilised urbanity in the middle of the hurly-burly, and yet to be right there, conveniently close to their places of work.

Of course, I was wrong. As I turned into the square and began to walk round it, I saw at once that it had suffered the seemingly inevitable fate of inner city Georgian properties. It had been taken over by business. Not a single house was lived in. All had experienced the melancholy desecration of being turned into offices; on looking through the uncurtained windows one could see how the rooms had been wrenched out of their true and just proportions to suit the new circumstances. Some were divided, some extended; all were a prey to that general air of seediness that seems to be inevitably associated with small businesses.

The little gardens, on closer inspection, were just as bad. Some had been entirely concreted over. Some were almost filled by overgrown privet hedges. Some were a rank growth of weeds. It was all very sad. There was just one bright spot (literally). On the corner, leading out into the road, there was a hydrangea, lovely, healthy, and abundant; and when my eyes lighted upon its deep crimson flowers and bright shining foliage, I admit that the Devil spoke to me persuasively, and at length, and that, having listened to what he had to say, I went along with it straight away. When I steal, I do limit myself to one cutting; it seems only fair – ridiculous though it may seem to use such a word in this context. So I approached the bush slowly, and paused to have a good look at it, hoping that the few passers-by would interpret my examination as admiration rather than the selection of a likely-looking shoot. As a thief, I am much hampered by self-consciousness, and I made two or three dry runs, putting out my hand but withdrawing it after simply stroking the foliage, before deciding that I was safely unobserved and actually snapping off my chosen shoot. Even when it was safely wrapped in my handkerchief and bestowed in my pocket I did not feel quite at ease, and smirked guiltily at every policeman I passed on the way back to my hotel. In my tooth-glass, the shoot remained plump and juicy until it was time for me to go home, and then, planted the same evening, flourished like a child of sin in a pot of compost, soon rivalling in growth a much earlier-struck legitimate hydrangea cutting that I had brought home from my father's garden in Jersey. The two hydrangeas, three years old now, are planted out in their permanent places, and I shall be interested to see whether the stigma of bastardy in any way inhibits the dark crimson one in the performance of its duties.

Another steal that was attended by altogether undeserved success had an ecclesiastical background. In the garden of an old Bishop's Palace – and I won't say where, because not enough time has elapsed for the Statute of Limitations to apply, and I daren't risk being humiliatingly prosecuted by 'the authorities' – I noticed a splendid row of double pinks. They were ordinary enough, of a pleasing vivid pink in colour, and warmly fragrant. The really impressive thing about them was their abounding health and abundance. In spite of the disapproval of the friends who were with me, I made a flustered grab, and came up with a stem covered with suitable side-shoots, which I shoved hastily into my pocket, wrapped in the inevitable handkerchief. When I got home, I stripped the cuttings off their central stem and put them into a glass of water on the kitchen windowsill. Then – and this is the really shameful bit, considering that I had stolen them – I did absolutely nothing about it for six weeks. At least, all I did was to keep the water in the glass topped up, and have good intentions.

Eventually, being in a domestic mood and in the act of giving the kitchen a 'good do', I decided that the time had come for the cuttings to be thrown away. There was a nasty brownish tinge in the water that they were standing in by now, and a bit of a smell with it. I did feel a pang of shame about stealing only to waste as I seized them by their still-green leaves and prepared to cast them into the dustbin.

But – what was this? Something much more solid than the slimy mess I had anticipated came out of the glass. The brownish stuff was not decay, but root formation, and instead of six reproachful corpses, I held in my hand six perfectly vigorous plants which, put straight out into the garden, grew away like Jack's beanstalk. So vigorous, indeed, did they turn out to be that they survived several other misadventures, such as being both grazed and trampled on by some young heifers which broke into the garden one night. They flowered in their first summer, lavishly, and their 'grass' is so profuse that I could, if I wished, take a couple of hundred cuttings.

The genus *Chaenomeles* is one for which I have always had a fondness. It seems to flourish anywhere, and flowers at a time of year when nothing else brings us quite that range of soft brick pinks. I have two kinds established, albeit still of course small: one is *Maulei*, and the other is a hybrid called 'Crimson and Gold'. Both were come by in the most honest manner, as suckers from my father's garden. I have also a rooted cutting of a charming semi-double that was given me by a kind friend. But there is another *chaenomeles* that I have always wanted. I rather suspect that it is 'Knap Hill Scarlet'. It is far from uncommon, but as it happens, nobody I know grows it, and the various big bushes of it that I watch with privy envy all belong to strangers, or to the local authority. It flowers a good month earlier than either of mine, and suckers freely. I must admit that I looked at all the bushes of it that I knew, and planned various Entebbe raids, but was always held back by timidity and the thoughts of shame. I remembered Macbeth and his wife:

'If we should fail – '

'We fail!

But screw your courage to the sticking-point,

And we'll not fail!'

but I felt more like him than her in the matter; and besides, he wasn't all that much of a shining example as far as actual achievement went. There were several big bushes of the thing growing outside the hospital, with super suckers on them, guaranteed to grow, and I imagined what might happen if I just went calmly up there with a trowel and took one. It might work; if you do anything with enough confidence, you can often get away with it. But just suppose it didn't? What if a hand fell heavily on my shoulder, and a stern voice asked me what I thought I was doing? I considered the possibility of saying airily 'Oh, it's all right, Mr Lewis said I could take it,' but that was too risky. After all, I had no means of knowing if the man in charge was a Mr Lewis or not. He might just as easily be a Mr Davies, or a Mr Jones. Or again, what if my captor should turn out to *be* Mr Lewis? It could have been very embarrassing. Another hideous possibility was that some hospital visitor, seeing me helping myself to public property, might make a citizen's arrest. I could envisage the small but humiliating headline in the local paper: 'Authoress in petty theft admission guilt scandal disclosure.' Thus conscience doth make cowards of us all, and I desisted.

Then one morning in early spring, I had to take my son into a nearby town to catch an early train, and, seeing the public park dewy and deserted in the morning sun, I strolled through its gates. And there was my chance. A bush of the *chaenomeles*, I knew, grew down at one end of the park, and unless some people living in the houses on the other side of the adjacent road opened their bedroom windows and shouted at me, there was nobody to see me. My mind was made up. In a moment I had crossed the soaking grass – leaving terrible evidence in the way of footprints in the dew – and was crouching by the plant, looking for a suitable sucker. Unfortunately, the park-keeper, or head gardener, or whoever looked after the place, was obviously a tidy man, and had shorn all the suckers back level with the ground. Desperately, I scrabbled. At last, right underneath the overhanging branches, I found a tiny one, about three inches long, that had doubtless been overlooked because it was growing parallel with the soil, trying, I suppose, to get to the light. A nail-file was the only offensive weapon I could produce, but with its help I scrabbled and scrooged, and in the end got my little sucker out complete, with a shoot, several new leaves, and a nice little knotty underground bit from which roots would obviously spring in due course. I smoothed back the minutely disturbed earth, and walked away, casually – my heart in my mouth, but my sucker in my pocket.

Unfortunately, the subsequent history of this steal has not been one of unmitigated triumph. It emerged a little battered from the protective custody of my handkerchief, and although I planted it out straight away in a shady spot behind a Blue Diamond rhododendron, its leaves turned blackish at the tips in a way that boded no good. But as the cool wet spring advanced, it picked up, and made new small leaves all the way up its little stem. When I saw that a fine new shoot had emerged at the top, an inch or so long and clothed in shining leaves, I thought that we were home and dry. But alas! Perhaps the Lord thought that like Job I could do with a bit of chastening. For when I inspected my little *chaenomeles* a few days later, it bore the marks of decided ill usage. The older leaves were shortened and crushed, and the brave new shoot was broken off and lay withering beside it. I did not know which to blame, the cat or the peacocks. The damage could have been caused equally easily by pecking, trampling, or rolling. In the end, the little thing died; perhaps I shall have to buy that particular *chaenomeles* after all.

Two friends of mine had a ludicrous experience of stealing which, they aver, has taught them not to do it again. Planning to visit a large garden in their area which is justly famous for its rhododendrons, they discussed earnestly the ethics of pinching a couple of suckers, if any should present themselves. 'Because,' they reasoned, one to another, 'they probably cut them off anyway, so in a way we'd be doing them a *good turn* – saving them *work* . . .' They realised that the rhododendrons might be grafted, and that they might well arrive home with nothing but *rhododendron ponticum* suckers, but being short even of that ubiquitous plant in their garden, they quieted their consciences, and decided to chance their arms.

It was early in the year when they visited the place – March or April – too early for the mass of the rhododendron family, but several early species were gracing the long alleys in towers of white and rosy blossom. There were cherries, camellias and magnolias, too, they told me, standing about the woodland walks in all the casual perfection of full maturity. A wealth of buds on the unopened rhododendrons spoke of the promise of May. But what they could not find was a sucker. From nineteenth-century giant to late twentieth-century baby, every rhododendron was clean stemmed. It seemed a pity, the more so as no other members of the public seemed to be there that day. Thwarted, they strolled down the soft grass paths. And then – speechless, the man grabbed the woman's arm, and pointed. One sucker! At last! Brave and solitary, under the spread of a vast crimson bush. Its leaves had not yet opened, but one pointed terminal bud topped a smooth grey stem perhaps ten inches long. It was ideal. Glancing furtively round, the man slipped under the overhanging branches, and, while the woman kept anxious *cave*, wrestled with the stubborn little growth with finger-nails and pocket knife. In a minute or so up it came, with a nice little bit of root on the end of it, and, having forgotten to bring anything in the nature of a polythene bag, he was obliged to button it to his bosom under his blazer and against his clear shirt, 'Where,' he told us later 'it seemed to burn a hole into my very heart every time we met a member of the garden staff on our way back to the car.'

So far so good. Its roots tenderly wrapped in wet moss, the sucker travelled to its new home, and was planted out, with a good deal of care and leafmould, in the small scrap of deciduous woodland that my friends wished to adorn. 'Even while we were putting it in I thought it didn't look *quite* right,' the woman told me. 'But I didn't like to say anything, after David had been to such pains to get it. And then we got some warm, damp weather, and the leaves came out. And what do you think? After all that, it turned out to be a seedling sycamore!'

'It made me think,' added her husband, 'of that motto you used to see hanging on the walls in some people's houses, done in pokerwork – you know – "Thou, God, seest me." Still, if that's what is was, it's a marvellous discovery to realise that he's got a sense of humour. But one shot across the bows is enough for me. I shan't go stealing again, and that's for sure.'

Saving money is one of the obvious reasons for stealing cuttings. Another is saving embarrassment. If you see a fine plant of something you've always wanted dangling over the wall of somebody's garden, you have the alternatives of either simply grabbing a bit, or of going to the door and explaining yourself, and asking. And my experience of this is that the person who comes to the door always regards you with the deepest suspicion, and thinks that you are up to no good whatever you offer in the way of swaps, or even money. Often, indeed, the custodians of especially desirable plants contrive to be stone deaf, or foreign. And because we are all mortal, and plants take a long time to grow to a size that can be seen by a passer-by, the people who own these mature plants are not as a rule the garden-conscious ones who planted them in the first place. 'Could you possibly spare me a few bits off your Mitraria?' is a request which sends them bolting back into their halls clutching their arms across their chests like Antonio in *The Merchant of Venice*; and to lower your tone and describe it as 'that red thing hanging over the wall' never seems to produce much better response either. It is difficult to convey to a non-gardening person that the small amount of material you will need will not make any noticeable difference to the parent specimen. 'But we don't want it cut down,' said the owner of a rampant rose which I believe to be climbing 'Perle d'Or', which was growing all over her garage, when I asked her if I could bring her anything from my own garden in return for half a dozen little unflowered twigs. 'And we've got plenty of plants here already. But thank you, all the same.' Poor woman; she was obviously both puzzled and a bit alarmed at my request. It might really have been kinder to have slipped over there at dusk one day, and simply to have helped myself. As it was, I walked away in the end with nothing but a red face.

These troubles, of course, only happen if the plant you covet has passed into the ownership of non-gardeners. A true gardener is notoriously the most generous soul alive, and, besides, realises that the taking of a couple of cuttings from a large plant will make absolutely no difference to it whatsoever.

One man I know has carried plant stealing to a fine art. Having satisfied himself by observation that a certain nobly-emparked estate near his home was no longer very rigorously patrolled, he went in there one day and set up aerial layers on about twenty of the choicest rhododendrons. 'You have to be careful to do 'em on what you might call the blind side of the bush,' he told me, coolly, 'and choose a position where the leaves'll mostly hide it. After all, they are evergreen. Apart from that, it's easy. You just make a little cut at an angle half way through a twig, shove in something like a grain of wheat to keep it open, blow in a little hormone rooting powder, pack it round with a fistful of damp potting compost, and wrap the whole thing up in black polythene. Tie a bit of string round both ends of the polythene, tightly, to keep it damp inside – I used that green garden string, because I wanted it to be unobtrusive – and when I went back a year or eighteen months later, they'd all rooted. So I just cut them off and took them home, and they're in my garden now, growing away. And I don't for a moment suppose that Lord Thing knows anything about it. Or, for that matter, that he's any the worse off if he does.' I was unwillingly impressed, but a little shocked at the sheer scale of the thing. The man is obviously a much better natural criminal than I am. Perhaps I should ask him to slip up to the hospital one day and grab me a bit of that *chaenomeles*...

9

Ground Cover

It is an article of faith with gardeners of our generation that ground cover is a Good Thing. The mainstream of accepted thought, from William Robinson and Gertrude Jekyll, down through V. Sackville-West and Christopher Lloyd is that you must take a leaf from Nature's book, and cover up all the earth you can. Indeed, you might as well, because Nature proverbially abhorring a vacuum, if you leave it undone she will certainly do it for you,; and as her choice for the job usually runs to things like creeping buttercup and couch grass, it will probably look better if you impose your will first.

It is not an idea with which I quarrel. But in the putting of it into practice, there are times when my experience seems different from that of most of the gardening book writers that I have come across; and I do sometimes wonder whether everything in their gardens is quite as lovely as they make out in this matter of ground cover.

'Get rid of all perennial weeds before you start, and you will soon find that your ground cover plants will thicken up sufficiently to suppress any others,' say the pundits. Well – possibly. But not all the weeds seem to have read the right books. They cheat. Take a cheerful villain like the dandelion. Arriving subtly, by parachute, in the middle of the patch you have covered with, say, a flourishing stand of bergenia, he settles down on the very crown of one of the plants; then, drawing one of its dying leaves down over his head for disguise and protection, he germinates and thrives; and before you can say 'knife' he has a good tuft of leaves, and a nice milky rootstock that is absolutely inextricably mixed up with the bergenia's, having grown over, under, round and through it. When you come to try and remove him, you find that you inevitably have to remove a good deal of the bergenia as well, and since dandelions are better than almost anything else in the world at re-growing themselves from accidental root cuttings, you may well end up with the bergenia dead, and the dandelion still triumphantly alive.

This would be rotten luck, and of course I don't mean to suggest that it happens all the time. But if you have quite a fair piece of garden to keep in order, so that you can't be tweaking out the odd space invader before it has had a chance to get fairly established, it will happen sometimes. Ground cover, just like that – covering the ground, but just the ordinary ground – is by no means the complete answer.

Towards the end of my stay in my last garden, Penllwyn-plan, by a chain of chance circumstances, I thought that I had discovered the complete answer; but before the experiment could be completed, I moved to Ty Arian, and, making my garden from scratch, I have not yet had a chance to put my tentative theories into practise again. But this is what happened.

One morning in early November, a car drew up in our yard, and, having emitted a passenger, drove away again. Our visitor, as it turned out, was the poultry expert from the feed firm with which we dealt, a young man of great charm and immense physical strength – a genial, amiable, rugger-playing young man, whose blushes I will spare by calling him Herbert, though that is not his name. He came to the door, and explained his presence.

'My car's got to go in for a service, so I can't make any calls today. And I can't stand the thought of simply sitting around all day. So I wondered if you could find me a job for the day? Anything – it doesn't matter how dirty, or heavy. I'd enjoy doing a bit of real work for a change.'

This was an offer too good to refuse, so, taking him at his word, we provided him with a fork and a wheelbarrow, and set him on to one of the hardest jobs there is – cleaning out a really deep calf cot. Most farmers raise young calves on a bed of rising dung, continually sprinkling clean straw on it as the calves dirty it, so that they lie reasonably clean and dry, but also warm, as the compacted mass of manure and bedding quietly ferments and rots beneath them. It is, in fact, a mild form of hotbed. But of course the calves, particularly as they grow bigger and heavier, trample the stuff down pretty hard, and it is quite a job to fork out by hand a large box three or four feet deep in it.

Herbert flexed his giant shoulders and rubbed his hands in pleased anticipation at the sight of the solid mass.

'Where shall I dump it?' he asked.

'Shove it here, on the garden,' I replied, thinking that he might do four or five barrowloads before shying off to easier tasks like egg collecting. But I underestimated him. Off he went with his fork and his barrow, and I occupied myself about the house for a couple of hours before going out of the back door at about eleven o'clock to see if anybody wanted a cup of coffee.

What a sight met my eyes! Herbert had gone through that Augean stable like Hercules, and instead of four or five barrowloads, about thirty-four or five had been dumped on the garden. The garden, indeed, had almost totally disappeared, and only the tips of the dying perennials waved helplessly, like flags of surrender, above the succulent brown mounds. And there was Herbert, bringing in the last load, still beaming with pleasure, bursting with vigour, and asking for some more work to do!

I must acknowledge that I was not too sanguine about the garden's chances after such an almighty great mulching as that. It was full of all sorts of plants – shrubs, bulbs, herbaceous perennials, odds and ends; could they possibly survive this avalanche of nutriment? In the event, they had to take their chance, because even though I had my doubts, I realised that I was myself quite incapable of moving away that enormous mass, and my husband was far too busy to touch it. So there it stayed. I did go round with a fork, evening it out a bit, and scraping occasional breathing-holes for plants that kept their leaves through the winter. I also tried to clear the muck away from the actual stems of the various shrubs, to protect them from collar-rot. Then I just had to wait, while the winter did its work, and see what would happen.

The garden certainly looked absolutely terrible all though that winter. The mean depth of the muck was about a foot, with lumpy bits rising to eighteen inches, and being raw calf-cot cleanings it was a pretty undigested mixture of manure, straw, and the hay that the calves had pulled down from their rack and wasted underfoot from time to time. The weather did its traditional stuff; the irregular hillocks stiffened in frost and slumped in rain; the top layer of straw, bleached by a hundred chilly dawns, fluttered a desolate grey in the untidy winds of March. Birds grabbed beakfulls of it for nesting material, and dropped it all over the lawns and the paths. And still the mountains remained.

But by the end of March, the hopeful eye began to discern at least the beginnings of a change. Lusty mat-forming plants like *Ajuga* and *Stachys lanata* stretched out their necks to see over the top, following up with spreading colonies of rampant tentacles. Daffodils and tulips, even species crocuses, defying the accepted learning about their hatred of fresh manure, drilled up through it and waxed fat; poppies, lupins and delphiniums doubled their usual size and sprawled in succulent abandon over the gradually shrinking eiderdown. And so it went on. By mid May, when I planted out my dahlias, the slabby texture of the muck had gone down to something much kindlier, so that I was able to incorporate it into the soil where I dug the holes for my tubers; and by August, when the dahlias came into flower, the garden had completely triumphed, and closed its ranks over the offending banks of manure so that they could not be seen anywhere.

There was just one difference. Whereas before, when I had pulled at a weed among my ground cover plants, it had hung on firmly in the stony soil and usually snapped off sneakily, so that it could grow again – now it was suddenly easy. Weeds did spring up, it is true, in that soft coverlet; but it was so soft that they had no purchase, and when I tweaked them, they obediently came away in my hand, root and all, leaving nothing behind them to grow on. It was a revelation. The foot of manure rotted down to three inches, and remained, a lovely, soft, wealthy, tilthy, obliging top layer, for the remaining two summers that I spent in that garden. And while it was there, my ground cover plants did as the books say they should, and did indeed suppress weeds, or at least yielded up to justice those which tried to defy their suppression.

I think that there were two factors that led to this extraordinarily deep mulching doing good and not harm to the garden in the long run. For one thing, the manure, although it was unrotted, was not exactly fresh. Most of it had been excreted by the calves for several months before it was put on the garden, so it must have had time to achieve some kind of fermentation. For another thing, the stuff was dumped out just at the beginning of winter, when the plants were inactive, so that it had been well worked on by the weather before they had to take much notice of it. The bulbs, which should have hated it, and languished to death from its proximity, presumably 'saved' as they say in Wales, because it was nowhere near their roots, and, again, had had most of the ginger weathered out of it before they even had to touch it with their emerging shoots.

In the garden I am now making at Ty Arian, I have not yet taken my courage in both hands to re-create the phenomenon. It is, by and large, a pretty wild garden. Any ground cover of the weed-excluding kind will ultimately be required to do its thing in the two main beds that I am cultivating on the terrace in front of the house. These will be mixed beds, and will need ground cover if they are not to be a constant nuisance with their weeds. So manurially mulched they must be, and it will be interesting to see whether or not I can achieve the same effect as at Penllwynplan.

It will of course be a slightly different mulch. As I do not keep calves, and for that matter no longer have access to an occasional daysworth of a Herbert, I cannot hope to slather the beds so comprehensively with the real McCoy. But in default of calf-muck I have something else which, although somewhat unusual will, I hope, fulfil the same purpose. This is a store of by now exceedingly well-rotted goat droppings and bedding, which still fills two of the boxes in my stable, and which I will try to get out and spread during the coming November. If I can get my wheelbarrow mended, that is to say—for it has been languishing with a puncture in its tyre these last eighteen months – and, such is the spirit of 'mañana' in this magical valley that it may well still be so in November, in which case it will be November twelve-months when the goat-muck gets spread; but it will be all the same in a hundred years' time.

One of the results of the Great Mulch was that the appearance of such tiny bits of soil as still showed here and there among the plants was enormously improved. Soils, after all, have their own beauty, to the eye as well as to the plant root. Handsome isn't, in fact entirely as handsome does in the matter. My soil at Penllwynplan was, in appearance, a total disaster. Actually, it was flattering it to call it soil at all. Whereas in the fields there was a kindly loam, pinkish-brown in colour, free-draining and crumbly in texture, and of a depth which we were embarrassed to acknowledge, lest people should think we were romancing, the soil in the garden was a non-event. Presumably when the site was levelled for the house, the topsoil was removed at the same time, all the way down to the road. What was left was shale. But one had to acknowledge that things grew in it. I used to help it, of course; planting holes would be filled with a juicier mixture. Still, things would grow. But although the things I planted *did* well enough, any soil that was showing always *looked* absolutely revolting, poor, stony, impoverished, and, particularly anomalous in West Wales, drought-stricken. After Herbert's mountains had rotted down, they presented an altogether comelier background. Soft, dark, and moisture-retentive, they gave the garden a trace of that lavish look that one strives for.

In the matter of moisture retention, I think that ground cover plants fulfil a curious and unexpected function. I have read many gardening books, particularly ones about vegetable gardening, which advocate conscientious hoeing. Hoeing, they explain, not only helps the plants by keeping the weeds down and reducing root competition, but in dry weather, by creating a kind of dust blanket in the top inch or two of the soil, it reduces evaporation of soil moisture and tends to conserve it for the use of the plants which are legitimately growing there. In theory, this sounds as if it should work, and I presume it must have, to some extent, for so many experts to have advocated it for so many years. But, once again, my own experience of the matter has been at variance with theirs, and though it is not great, it is genuine, and it does seem reasonable to record it.

It was in one year when I not only planted a vegetable garden, but actually followed it through with some conscientiousness. Various things were sown, ordinary enough things, peas, beans, carrots, beetroots, and so on; and, following the experts' instructions, I plied the hoe as best I could, and for a month or two succeeded in keeping the whole thing quite creditably clean and neat. It was not to last. There was a lot of work to do on the farm, and, as the haymaking season came on and the time I had available for gardening diminished, the tide of weeds began to encroach, and the perfectly clean bit of the garden shrank and shrank.

Then there came a drought. 'Ah,' I thought, looking complacently at the half-dozen or so assorted rows that I *had* managed to keep hoed out, 'those should be all right, at least. There must be the statutory inch or two of dusty dry soil on top of those to keep the moisture safe in the deeper levels. Virtue will bring rewards.' For once it seemed that I had done what I should. All the rest of the plot was swallowed up in a creeping tide of chickweed, through which the tops of carrots and things could just be discerned, and I more or less wrote that off. We were chronically short of water on that place, because our pumping equipment was old and kept breaking down; there was no question of sparing any for the garden, so the experiment had to be left to work itself out as best it could.

And, of course, in due course it did. But not at all as I had been expecting it to. On the contrary, it was exactly the opposite. The plants in the dusty, hoed bit drooped, pined and dwindled, whereas those whose tips barely showed above the weed blanket went on from strength to strength and yielded good crops. When I investigated, I found that even after three weeks of hot sun and no rain the soil under the chickweed was still dark and damp. It was clear that something – the shading, or possibly the coolness of the mass of leaves tending to make the dew precipitate at nights – was more than counterbalancing the extra loss of moisture that must have resulted from the transpiration of all those thousands of leaves. Since then I have learned that there are indeed many gardeners who do use a green mulch quite deliberately, for this very effect.

The difficulty, of course, comes in a wet year. If you could guarantee your two or three weeks of blazing drought, you could let the chickweed ramp and get nothing but benefit, but in a spongy season it provides a wonderful breeding and lurking place for slugs and snails, who hide by day and emerge at night to eat the vegetables. As in every other aspect of human life, a compromise seems to be the best solution, and, empirically speaking, a compromise is what usually happens anyway. Slug bait is sprinkled; some rows are weeded clean; others are at the stage of needing doing; and in any garden that I have ever had anything to do with, there have always been some bits that needed doing very badly indeed. So, in practical terms, one lurches along.

In the ornamental garden, too, I have found that ground cover plants do help to conserve moisture, although nothing that I have ever grown seems to do it as admirably as chickweed, which one might imagine actually leaks water, so soggy does it manage to keep the underneath of its mat. But the lamiums, the ajugas, the stachys, and the saxifrages, and so on, that one puts to wind their way in amongst the statelier border inhabitants, do undoubtedly contribute to a state of soil coolness in a difficult year.

I have no intention of writing a catalogue of plants in this book. When I am reading a garden book myself, I prefer prose, and always feel a pang of disappointment when the thing goes all alphabetical, and degenerates into a welter of appendices and lists. Anyone who needs lists can find them in good nurserymen's catalogues, or in reference books written by specialists and experts. I propose here only to mention a few favourites from the admittedly limited and chance-come selection of ground cover plants that I have grown; and of these, the one that I would be sorriest to have to do without is the indefatigable ajuga.

Ajuga repens atropurpurea is the one I am referring to, and it was given to me, along with a bit of the little pink-flowered striped-leafed lamium, by a man I didn't much like. In a way I always feel a bit of a conscience pang at so enjoying his plants when I found it impossible to warm to him.

It was at about tea-time one autumn day when I knocked on his kitchen door, to return a recipe book that his wife had lent me. She opened the door, looking vexed and discomposed, and admitted me to be the unwilling witness of an all-too-dreary scene. It was easy to see what was the matter. Their four-year-old son, choking and sobbing, sat at the table facing a nasty-looking plate of congealed dinner; the father, very red in the face, was trying to force a spoonful of it between the little boy's lips; a cooking timer, ticking away on the table, seemed to promise some even more disagreeable and violent denouement – 'if you haven't eaten all this up in ten minutes, I'll...' – as it marched inexorably on to its pinging time. The mother threw me a beseeching glance. She was almost in tears herself. There seemed only one thing to do.

'Geoffrey!' I cried, with false brightness, 'What a lucky chance to find you at home! *Do* you remember you promised me a few bits of plants – that lovely copper-leaved bugle of yours – and a bit of that pretty dead-nettle...' On a tide of chat I manoeuvred him to the door, all unwilling, and obviously thinking my importunity most inopportune. But it worked. When, five minutes later, we came back into the kitchen with the plants, the cold dinner and the cooking timer were no longer to be seen, the child was upstairs splashing in the bath, and the wife was busy with the washing up. Her eyes met mine in a silent message of gratitude; and if the dog, in his basket under the kitchen table, was licking his lips rather suspiciously, what business was that of mine?

Both the nettle and the bugle have flourished with me ever since, and have been distributed to many, many friends, though never under the same compulsion! One particularly agreeable feature of this bugle is that its leaves, being dark and shiny, reflect a lot of sky. I have often had a momentary illusion, in winter, that there was a big patch of low-growing blue flowers in the garden which has turned out on a second look to be the glossy healthy bugle responding to a bit of blue sky. I like to grow it next to another favourite of mine (and everybody's), *Stachys lanata*, for winter effect, too. The contrast of shining bronze leaf with furry silver leaf is always pleasing.

Of course there are many of these creeping ajugas. The wild form, which grows abundantly on the rough grazing, is a charmer with much lighter blue flowers than the copper-leaved form. I have imported several clumps of it, and love the contrast of the two shades of flowers. The only other kind I have is supposed to be variegated, and does, indeed, occasionally produce a tiny chip of cream on a leaf edge. But for the most part its leaves are of the same brilliant red as young beetroot leaves, and that is perfectly all right with me. It flowers in a very keen blue, and the bracts that adorn the flower spike set off those flowers to perfection, being of the sharpest Siamese pink.

I love the little lamium too, and find its orchid pink spikes of flower endlessly useful for small spring flower arrangements. This is a plant that pays for a bit of attention. If you simply let it form its mat and get on with it for a few years, it will get rather tatty-looking. It is worth the small amount of trouble that it takes, say every two years, to rip it all out, incorporate a bit of manure or compost in the place it was growing in, and replant small pieces from the edges of the clumps. This will ensure you a carpet of neat, bright, clean-looking leaves that can combine with other plants to make a very effective picture.

Just such a picture has developed, more by luck than by judgement, at the west end of one of my terrace beds. Everything seems to have grown together in a pattern of leaf and flower so harmonious, and yet so easy, that it must be worth describing its constituent parts.

The date is the twenty-fourth of September, and I am aware that this little corner of two or three square yards has been decorative for some months; but the more striking competition of the bergamots and the pink Japanese anemones further along the bed has distracted the eye. Now that they are finished and cut down, the flowery quilt of the lower-growing things that were planted as ground cover begin to assert their true value.

In the corner there is a catmint. It is, goodness knows, an ordinary enough plant, but its rounded bump of grey foliage, spreading comfortably over the path, and its succession of lavender spikes, key it in nicely with its two neighbours, *Polygonum affine* Darjeeling red, and *Geranium endressii*. The polygonum, a low-growing mat, is thickly set with six-inch spikes of flower of two different pinks – a dark intense one, and a candy-floss tint. It must be admitted that its glossy green leaves also form the background for two or three flourishing dandelion plants, but as they are happy, healthy, un-nibbled, and quite a pleasant shape, I shall delay their removal until hard frosts have put an end to the polygonum's display, which will probably not be until late in November. Even then its contribution will not be at an end, for such of its top hamper as survives the removal of the dandelions will turn a brilliant bracken red, and will remain, a spot of bright colour in the border, until spring comes again.

The geranium has been flowering most of the summer. It is the original sharp pink kind, not the more salmony 'Wargrave' variety, and when it first came out it was about a foot high. However, as it was growing rather too rampantly into an adjacent bearded iris whose rhizomes wanted the ripening touch of the sun, I yanked most of it out about a month ago, and it responded in the most obliging way by falling over in the other direction and furnishing itself with a charming little frill of new flowers at the height of about five inches off the ground. It seeds itself around the garden too, but not excessively.

The dead-nettle that I mentioned before grows on the other side of the geranium, interpenetrating it for three or four inches. It is out of flower in September, but, being a young planting, it has lovely bright striped green and white leaves, and it has arranged itself very prettily in a clump that curves round the front of the iris, hugging the ground closely.

The irises themselves – there are four of them – are the tallest things in the group. Many people cut back the leaves of bearded irises after they have flowered; I don't. I like the bold pointed glaucous leaves; they make a fine contrast to the softer and more prostrate things around them. In some years they do tend to die back at the tips, but at the moment they are still looking very much in their prime. A few leaves have died right back to the rhizomes during the course of the summer, and these I have simply pulled off; the rest are still as healthy as can be. In May, thinking that the plants were looking a bit peaky, I gave each one a sprinkle of bone meal and a thin scatter of lime, and their response has been remarkable. It surprises me that so many people think of the bearded iris as a plant to be segregated in a specific 'iris garden'; I think it pays its way in the mixed border all through the growing part of the year, and I would be sorry to lose the architectural value of those fine, solid fans of leaf.

Another low mat former in this corner is *Stachys lanata*, which makes pools of rain-washed silver in the spaces between the irises, and, like the geranium, has to submit to having great handfuls of itself ravished away when it gets too encroaching. There is a non-flowering variety of this plant called 'Silver Carpet' which is preferred for situations where tidiness is at a premium, but I am happy with the old original, as I don't care a fig for tidiness, and like to use the flowering stems for cutting. I have already referred to the lovely contrast between the pale leaves of the *stachys* and the bronze of the dark bugle in another part of the bed; in this corner it is re-created even more strikingly by planting next to the *stachys* the lovely little dahlia 'Roquencourt', whose glistening dark bronze foliage is enlivened with flowers of a truly incandescent orange.

A bland breadth of foliage belonging to various earlier cut-down flowers insulates the orange dahlia from a jolly pink *sedum* whose name I do not know, as it was a gift from a friend; and the *sedum* leans its bright heads of flower and rounded, succulent, light green leaves against the bosom of a fine *fuchsia magellanica variegata*, a nice thing, with wands of pinky-grey leaves, and a dangle of dark red, slender flowers. There is another fuchsia in the bed too, over at the other side, the much sturdier and more brilliant 'Mrs Popple'; but as yet that lady is too small to give much account of herself, and only shows up at all because she has placed herself advantageously against a noble clump of *pulmonaria*, ferally spotted in silver, and apparently revelling, all against the book, in a full south exposure. And as a final filler, clumps of the dwarf michaelmas daisy 'Little Boy Blue' (or is it Little Blue Boy? I never can remember), just coming into flower, blend their dark lavender with all the pinks and greens and silvers, and somehow hold the whole thing together.

I do not claim much credit for this nice little corner, but regard it rather as an example of the serendipitous way that good plants will combine and complement one another in contrasts of shape, colour and texture – bump, rug, spike; woolly, matt, shiny; green, silver, bronze; plain, striped, and spotted. But fortunate accidents can be built upon, and another year I must look out for additions to the scheme that will augment it, and will also help to key it into the rest of the bed. I have another polygonum, for instance – the gift of the sedum friend – that grows to three and a half feet, and carries its pinkish-crimson pokers for months. This, planted to the east of the existing group, would come into flower early enough to take part in the bergamot-Japanese anemone picture, but would carry on after their demise to add the effect of its taller flowers to the other at a new level. Then, bulbs: there are already a couple of dozen daffodils under the mat-formers; might not a few handfuls of autumn crocuses effectively join them there, sending up their amazing chalices through the leaves to augment and emphasise the lavender theme of the catmint and the michaelmas daisy?

One tends to think of the perfect ground cover plant as one that keepts its leaves all the year round, and most of my favourites do. But when I actually went out on a tour of inspection to see which of the plants was actually doing the best job of weed suppression, I found that of the two equal winners, only one had this characteristic. This was the ordinary white arabis, that simple little creature that we used to know in our youth as 'White Rock'. From a few scraps given to me a year ago, this has spread into a dense green carpet which now covers several square feet, and which is holding its own against all comers. The other, surprisingly, is the herbaceous cranesbill Johnson's blue, whose second crop of leaves, flopping outwards from the crown in all directions, have similarly protected a wide area of ground round each plant from the invasions of even such subtle infiltrators as the annual meadow grass. When I grew this plant at Penllwynplan, it flowered continuously throughout the summer, a lovely thing both in the garden and in flower arrangements, where its frail-looking buds opened one after another, sometimes for a couple of weeks. But here at Ty Arian, for some reason, although it grows heartily, it will only flower once; then it dies right back before producing a second flush of leaves that last until the frost.

'What do *you* do for an encore, then?' I asked it one day last autumn, never expecting an answer; but:

'This,' it replied, a day or two later; touched by the chilly finger of November, every leaf turned to a mixture of yellow and brilliant scarlet; and for a week it was the brightest thing in the garden until the hard weather overcame it, and it sank back into the earth.

10

Seeds

Raising things from seed used to present me with great difficulties. I went through all the motions; I put nicely soaked and squeezed-out seed compost, of one of the approved kinds, into suitably crocked pans or boxes; I levelled it off with a board; I sprinkled the seed, covered it with its own depth of soil, and put a pane of glass and a piece of brown paper on top of it, and stood it in a suitably warm place. And that was all there was to it. As a general rule, nothing germinated; if by exception there was a little flurry of green, it always turned out to be a family of weeds, from inadequately sterilised compost.

Or if I sowed seed out of doors, there would be a variation on the theme. One particular early experience is burned into my memory. The particular seeds I wanted to grow were long-spurred columbines and foxgloves of the Excelsior strain, and I had prepared what I thought was a most suitable place for their birth. It was a fair-sized piece of ground under an old apple tree, shaded, but not *too* shaded. I cultivated it into the finest tilth and enriched it with a good helping of my very best compost that I had rubbed through a sieve. I added granulated peat to help its moisture retaining qualities; I sprinkled in a judicious helping of bonemeal. Finally I sowed the seed and covered it lightly with some more peat. Then I firmed it all gently down, and watered it with a gentle but adequate spray. I even went to the lengths of spreading a piece of wire netting over it to keep any cats at bay, and of laying damp sacking over the wire netting.

The weather was mild and promising, and, having taken so

very much trouble, I was not really too surprised when tiny cotyledons began to pierce the dark rich-looking surface of the compost in a beautiful even spread. I used to rush out first thing in the evening when I got home from work (we were living in London then), and coo over them. They were the justification of all my efforts. And they certainly looked good. You could easily distinguish the two different kinds of seedlings. The cotyledons were different-looking, and then when the first tiny leaves appeared, the difference was even more marked. Some were plain – the foxgloves, obviously; and some three-lobed, which had to be the columbines.

They weren't, of course. In the end it was necessary to acknowledge the sickening truth that what I had so painstakingly reared was Upper Norwood's best braird of creeping buttercup and broad-leaved plantain... What happened to the official seeds remains a puzzle to this day.

But this is not to be a sad account of endless and inexplicable failure. The turning point for me came when I read in one of H. E. Bates's gardening books about how he, late on in his gardening life, had run into a curious patch of being unable to make anything germinate; and of how one of his friends had shown him where he was going wrong, and had made everything right again. It was the wrong use of Levington compost that was at the root of his difficulties; and though mine seemed to have been far more wide-ranging than his at their worst, I thought that at least I might as well give his friend's advice a try, and see if it could work the oracle for me. And as it did, I will pass on the method, in case there is among my readers just such another bum seed-sower as I was.

There are two secrets, according to H. E. Bates's friend, in the use of Levington compost. One is that you don't smooth it down in the container; the other is that you don't, to any extent, cover the seed. The first of these I do take quite literally. I buy the stuff dry, in a bag, from my local garden shop, and when I want to sow something, I put a few handfuls into a bucket, and add water until it is a really sloppy mix – thicker than a Yorkshire pudding batter, but sloppier than a Victoria sponge mixture. Then I just grab handfuls of it and squeeze them fairly dry and put them into my un-crocked seed containers, and poke the stuff roughly down into the corners with my fingers until the container seems about full enough.

Then I sprinkle the seeds on to the top of it. If it is really minute seed, like, for instance, that of lobelias, I do just tap it very, very lightly down on to the compost with the tip of a clean, dry finger. And if it is at the other end of the scale, really enormous, like lupin seed, I push each seed a little way into the compost so that it is half buried. And then – and this is where my own experience takes over from that of H. E. Bates's friend – I put the lid on.

For that is the third factor that I am sure has played its part in turning me, seed-wise, from a seven-stone weakling into a reasonably successful performer. I sow in plastic containers with lids to them. Not that I make any claim to have invented this method. Nor that I expect to find many people among my readers to whom it comes as a revelation. But over the years, I have tried it on many, many different kinds of seed, and I am quite sure that the atmosphere in your average margarine tub or cottage cheese container has something about it that is far more conducive to germination than that generated by a sheet of glass, or a plate, or a slate, balanced on top of an ordinary seed pan. You have to make a couple of drainage holes in the bottom of your Flora box, of course, but that is the work of a moment with a red-hot poker, and I, for one, rather like the smell. That done, you have an excellent little seed-box, and one that can be re-used many, many times; and you can even write the name of the seeds in pencil on the inside of the lid. It wipes off with a touch of Vim on the cloth when you have pricked the batch of seedlings out.

The method does not only work with Levington compost either. I find one bought compost is just about as good as another, and I generally buy whatever comes first to hand in the garden shop when I happen to remember that I have run out.

It is quite surprising to find how few people go to the trouble of chipping and soaking large seeds. Again, with large things like lupins and brooms, you can get virtually one hundred per cent germination by this simple technique. Using a sharp knife on a chopping board, you just cut a tiny corner off one of the round ends of the seed. As long as you take care to avoid what you might call the belly-button area of the seed, it doesn't really matter if you do nick the inner substance a little. It will just show up as a slight damage to its fleshy cotyledons when the seed germinates. Having chipped it, you then drop it with its mates into a mug half-filled with water – cold or lukewarm, it doesn't seem to make much difference – and by the next morning you will find that the seed has swollen to about three times its original size, and is quite obviously in the process of germinating. So you tuck it into your seed box as outlined above, and within about two days you are virtually certain to have a braird of great lusty seedlings. Any seeds that do not swell in the water have probably not been adequately chipped, and had better be done again.

One failure that I had with chipped seed was with *Cercis siliquastrum*, the Judas tree. I chipped a whole packet and soaked it; it duly took up the water, and every seed swelled prodigiously. So I sowed it, and boasted rashly to gardening friends about my splendid braird. But not one of those fat, juicy, promising seeds ever sent up a shoot. So, although the swelling of the seeds is a necessary first step towards germination, it is apparently not germination itself, and not an infallible sign that all is going to be well. As a matter of interest, the *cercis* seeds were planted in a conventional seed-pan, and not in a margarine tub. Maybe that would have been the factor that would have tipped the balance in their germination.

The most curious and unexpected braird I ever had was with some verbascums. The common wild mullein, with its spikes of yellow flowers, does not appear to be a difficult plant, yet it is not widely seen in this area. I had long wanted it on my list, so when I saw a straggling group of its spikes, half in flower and half in seed growing on a bank, I picked a couple of the ripest pods and put them in my pocket. I was wearing at the time a white knitted Acrilan jacket, with patch pockets, that I had acquired by some complex trade-off with my daughter. (One of the big advantages of parenthood is that sooner or later your children attain adult size, and then you can start wearing their cast-off clothes.) It was a useful jacket, but, being white, it had to be constantly washed, and, being of an artificial fibre, it used to undergo this process in the washing machine. It must be becoming obvious by now that on this occasion the jacket was slung into the machine with the seed-pods still in its pocket; and it was indeed only on noticing them lying lumpily there in the rinsing that I became aware of the oversight. Of course I abstracted them quickly then, and dried them on a piece of paper on the kitchen window-sill; I further wrapped them in paper, and put them in a Nescafé jar for the winter with a lot of other oddments of saved seeds. And I labelled the packet 'Verbascum; germination doubtful.' Yet when I sowed them in spring they germinated with the wholehearted joy and enthusiasm of Beethoven's Seventh symphony; and if I had wished to cover my whole property with mullein, it wouldn't have been lack of seedlings that would have stopped me doing it. In case I have accidentally stumbled upon a means of getting difficult seeds to germinate comparable to false vernalisation, or chipping and soaking, let me put on record the facts that the washing water was fairly cool, and that the soap used was Persil!

Of course, getting the seeds to germinate is only part of the battle. The after-care of the seedlings is obviously just as important. It is sickening to lose a good batch of seedlings through carelessness, but I suppose most gardeners do, in the course of a lifetime. I was certainly to blame when I lost my *Meconopsis betonicifolia*. This exquisite blue poppy is not exactly difficult to grow, but it has its fads, and it is not seen in every roadside garden. Dried seed, as provided by seedsmen, germinates erratically, and even when you have achieved a modest braird, the seedlings can be tiresome, sometimes hanging about and refusing to grow on satisfactorily, and sometimes falling victim to slugs, which are inordinately fond of them, in spite of the attractive blond hairs with which their leaves are adorned. From a puny germination of nine, I brought a mere three through the vicissitudes of youth to flowering size; and to two of them I denied the right to flower in their first year by pinching out the flowering stems. Doing this is supposed to make the thing form a many-budded crown which, in its turn, is supposed to confirm it as a perennial. If you let it flower in the first year on its single shoot, it is apt to consider itself a biennial, and die afterwards. As it happened, all three of mine died in any case, but that, although sad, is not the moral of this particular cautionary tale. That concerns the seedlings of the second generation that I raised. The one flower stalk that I permitted to develop brought three wonderful flowers, of a silken blueness that I cannot find words to describe. Cambridge blue? No, too greenish, and too pale. Sky blue? No, too harsh, and too unvarying. Flax blue? Nearer, but there was a texture, a lustre, a miracle about the *meconopsis* flowers that no flax begins to approach. Delphinium blue? No, for there was no hint of mauve or violet in the poppies. Nor was their blue as heavy as gentian, nor as bland as chicory. It was indescribable, and was set off to perfection by the great boss of golden stamens and the immaculate green pistil in the centre of the flower. These wonderful, beautiful flowers managed to self-fertilise, and produced three small seed-pods which I hung over, cherished, and harvested. I kept them as cool and dry as possible throughout the winter, and sowed their stingy allowance of seed (you can see why it's expensive) in a round flat seed-pan in the spring.

The seeds, judiciously placed in the airing cupboard, not too near nor yet too far away from the hot water tank, germinated like mustard and cress; and, the weather being fresh, cool and showery, I thought it best to put them out of doors as soon as possible. At that time we had a lorry-load of concrete blocks stacked up in a neat pile in the yard awaiting some bit of never-never building that receded like a mirage; and it had become clear, by observation, that no slug or snail ever ascended its sheer and gritty face. So the flat top of the block-pile became my favourite standing-out place for pans of seedlings, where, protected by wire cages from the assaults of the cats, they could grow on in peace. I put the unbelievably wealthy pan of *meconopsis* seedlings out there, and they grew on apace. And then I went out for the day. I went with my natural history society to Skomer, and saw puffins, and guillemots, and razor-bills, and cormorants, and shags, and fulmars – and sea, and sky, and bluebells, in long, flat strata of curiously clashing blues ... and then we came home, and I saw that as the result of one hot sunny day there was a pan of *meconopsis* seedlings all lying over higgledy-piggledy every which way, and dying ... and I cursed myself for a careless fool, and resolved never, never again to leave *meconopsis* seedlings out in the unshaded sun. More recently, Thompson and Morgan's packets of meconopsis seed have carried a printed warning against letting your *meconopsis* get sunburned. But I taught myself, the hard way.

Some seeds normally easy can take very cussed turns about germinating. Delphiniums, for instance; they like fairly cool conditions to germinate in; no airing cupboard for them. If you are unlucky enough to have sown them just before a heat-wave, then however cool the spot you choose for their seed-box in the garden, and however thick the brown paper over it, it will probably end in tears. But with delphiniums, as with so many other things, the viability is wonderfully improved by freshness. Seeds saved from your own plants (if they are good enough to be parents) gives you a much better braird than packeted seed as a rule, however scientifically it is stored.

The most wonderful braird I ever had was with some fresh seed of *Cyclamen neapolitanum*. By a coincidence, two friends, from widely different areas of the country, each gave me a couple of ripe pods of this charmer one autumn, and I sowed the whole lot together, expecting at best a small and patchy crop of seedlings. But to my amazement they started germinating in about a week, and kept on, and on, and on. I should think every single seed in the pan germinated. There were certainly more than sixty seedlings in a round pan of seven inches' diameter. They grew away lustily, and it was quite charming to watch them forming their tiny white cormlets above the surface of the soil as the minuscular leaves emerged, heads bowed and necks upwards at first, and then opening up into the characteristic pointed cyclamen leaf shape. They showed no trace of the marbling that is such a characteristic feature of *C. neapolitanum* until they were quite big.

But, lest envious readers envisage me now wandering amidst hosts of little pink cyclamen planted in every shady place, let me confess that I didn't bring many of my pretty seedlings to maturity. I sowed them in the autumn, and pricked them out of their seed pan into follow-on boxes much too late, in the following August. They did not like it, and in the course of the ensuing winter, nearly all of them died. It would probably have paid a lot better to have pricked them out a lot earlier – perhaps in May – into a nursery row, and to have put a cloche over them for the winter – or at least, to have gone round and carefully re-firmed them into the ground after every frost. For all the dead bodies seemed to have heaved themselves up out of the compost in the boxes when I discovered them.

There are some seeds which are reputed to germinate better when they are *not* fresh; the primula family is sometimes cited as having this foible. It is not a matter of vernalisation, or the alternation of freezing and thawing, which often triggers germination, because the seeds come away nicely from a spring sowing even if they have spent the winter in the kitchen drawer, a place where repeated freezings must surely be at a premium. It seems to be rather a matter of a sort of built-in clock, that instructs the seeds not to germinate, after their late summer ripening, until the worst of the bad winter weather is over. My experience of sowing the seeds of native *primulacae* is one-sided; that is to say, I have had excellent brairds by sowing them in the spring following their ripening, but I have never actually tried the experiment of sowing them as soon as harvested. So I am in no position to know whether or not what 'they' say about their germination is true.

One thing I do know is that cowslip seed, at least, retains its viability for quite a long time. I love cowslips, and allow them to grow at will in the garden, in the rough grass or in the beds as they choose. And since the one thing that every single visitor wants to take away from the garden is a bundle of cowslip plants, I try to save the seed, so that I can be sure of a good many young plants coming on to meet the demand. Harvesting it is quite agreeable; you pick the long stalks just before the seed becomes really rattling dry, and finish them off on the kitchen window-sill; then you can sit at the kitchen table dreamily bursting open the pods and scratching out the little blackish-brown seeds, and blowing on them to winnow them. It is as seductive as knitting ... only one more row ... then another ... just another cluster of pods ... this feels a good fat one, lots of seed here ... oh, yes – and that one looks good and ready ... time slips away, and you suddenly realise that you have left undone those things you ought to have done, and have done those things that you ought not to have done, and that there is no health in you; but you do end up with a really enormous heap of cowslip seed. In my penultimate year at Penllwynplan I had thrashed and winnowed to such effect that even after giving lots and lots of it away, I was left with more than four ounces of cowslip seed. And that represents an awful lot of cowslips. It was July – the wrong time to sow them by my book. So I put them in a brown paper bag, fastened it up with an elastic band, and put them into the dresser drawer, out of the way.

Came the spring and the right time for sowing, and I forgot about my cowslip seed. Came another winter. Finally came the move to Ty Arian; and, faced by a new and relatively cowslip-less garden, I suddenly remembered, and dug out the little brown package again.

But four ounces of seed is a tremendously daunting quantity, and, busy as I was with the move, I baulked at trying to find enough seed-pans, let alone enough compost, or enough cat-free standing room for such a vast lot. Besides, I knew the seed was old, and thought that it would probably not germinate very well. So, in the end, I went into my vegetable garden that my kind neighbour Mick had put into a tilth with his tractor rotovator, and sowed it broadcast. And it fell into the soft, receptive earth, and disappeared from view, and was very quickly concealed by the hearty growth of the couch grass that Mick's rotovations had stimulated. But when, the following autumn, I got around to trying to weed out some of the couch, I discovered that every single seed must have germinated, and that there were absolutely countless thousands of cowslip seedlings growing happily away down in the deep and shady area at the roots of the weed cover.

This experience confirmed something I had begun to suspect about certain seeds, which might be summed up in the advice given to Bo Beep: 'Leave them alone, and they'll come home, bringing their tails behind them.' Shortly afterwards I was glad to have the confirmation strengthened by reading an article on the subject written by a much more experienced authority than I can ever hope to be. This was Captain W. E. Johns, known to me for many years only as the indefatigable author of the seemingly never-ending stream of 'Biggles' books. I believe there were more than sixty of them in the end. But a chance discovery showed that the Captain wrote about many other matters besides Biggles, among them gardening, which he adorned with a touch as light as his knowledge was deep and wide. He used to do a regular article in a delightful little magazine edited by Theo Stephens, called *My Garden*, which started publication in 1934, and went on into the fifties, appearing monthly. When a whole set of these appeared one day for sale on a second-hand stall in Carmarthen market, my husband kindly bought them for me; and ever since, I have used them for early morning tea reading in bed, working through them steadily, and then giving myself six months to forget them before starting at the beginning again.

Captain Johns' articles are a never-failing delight, combining as they do a vein of sympathetic levity with an informed mind and an evidently humane personality. And, in a way, his experience with primula seedlings was so like mine that I feel I must adduce it. He was concerned with much more aristocratic members of the family than the humble wildlings that I was messing about with; but, sowing them ordinarily, in boxes and pans, he experienced difficulties. He experimented with varying composts; he took advice, and covered the surfaces of his containers with moss to keep them damp; he did everything that human ingenuity could contrive; and all he achieved was a thin scattering of miserable starveling specimens that miffed off almost as soon as they were pricked out. He almost despaired. And then one day his gardener (absolutely everybody had a gardener, or gardeners, in those days – it is part of the magazine's period charm) came to him and asked what he wanted doing 'With all them primula plants between the two greenhouses?' and he discovered that seeds from the discarded, cut-off pods of his bought primulae, carelessly thrown away in this unpromising situation, had sown themselves, germinated unobserved, and grown on into a generation of young plants that resembled spring cabbages in their almost indecent luxuriance. Having an analytical mind, he abstracted the circumstances that had led to this serendipitous happening, and formulated a system which ever thereafter worked for him like clockwork, and made it as easy for him to germinate the most recherché strains of primulas as it is for most people to grow groundsel.

In brief, the Captain's method was to prepare deep boxes – wine cases with the partitions knocked out were what he recommended, another nice period touch – with a deep layer of crocks over the drainage holes. Then he put in a good deep layer of garden soil, and an inch or two of sterilised seed compost on top of that. The seeds were sowed in this, lightly covered, and the whole thing watered until it was thoroughly wet. Wire netting over the boxes kept out cats and birds, and, having been watered, the boxes were put under a north wall, and just left. In that situation, he wrote, they didn't need any more watering, even in hot weather – a comment I find hard to believe, but defer to his undoubted experience and integrity. And in anything from six to eighteen months, seedlings began to appear, and could be pricked out into nursery rows, or, there being a good depth of ordinary soil in the boxes, left to grow on until they were quite sizeable plants. Peace, moisture, shade, and time were their requirements; and this was just what my cowslips got, growing away down among the grass roots in my neglected vegetable garden. I have done the same thing with primrose seed now, with equally happy results; and in another part of the vegetable garden the true oxlip, that pretty little darling, so early, so neat in its leaf and so refined in its 'drawing' has done it for itself.

It is a curious and freakish thing how a set of conditions that so cosset growth in one wildling can prove absolutely fatal to another. I lost a hundred or more lilies by allowing them to spend a summer in the very same circumstances that the cowslips so enjoyed. It was all very disappointing. There were two kinds. Most were martagon lilies, progeny of a fine fat pod that a kind reader of one of my earlier books had sent me – a pod packed tightly with flat, papery seeds that looked as if they could not possibly have life in them, but which nevertheless germinated marvellously, and in a very short time, not doing the common trick of lilies, which is to make growth only below ground in their first year, but putting up little flags of leaf from the word go. The others were tiger lilies, grown not from seed, but from a handful of the bulbils that this lily makes in its leaf-axils in late summer. Both pans had made tiny bulblets that survived the winter; when spring came and new shoots began to spear forth from them I laboriously pricked them all out into a suitably enriched patch of garden, and looked forward to having some fair-sized bulbs to plant out in twelve months' time. But alas! Their nursery ground getting rather damp and weedy during the summer, the slugs moved in unobserved, and by the time I got around to weeding and baiting in a couple of months, there was not a single trace of one lilly left. Which is why, perhaps, we see, or used to see, fields full of cowslips, but never great strands of the martagon lilly, even though it has naturalised itself in this country, and is by some authorities grudgingly accorded the status of a native.

It is partly this alluring prospect of making massive drifts of self-gardening flowers that recommends native species to me. So many of our wild-flower spectaculars are composed of thousands of individuals, growing together in perfect conditions and obviously loving it. And somehow, however brilliant their colours, you can mass them as much as you like and they never look garish. This is not true of garden flowers, even in a naturalised setting. I have often writhed in unease in too-carefully-tended woodland gardens filled with painstakingly grouped, lobster-red azaleas. They can look as harsh, as false in their tone, as any blatant bed of scarlet salvias. But who ever heard a word uttered against the heart-lifting brilliance of poppies in the corn? Except by farmers, of course.

One ought to be able to achieve this simple aim of growing great quantities of common things by simply growing them from seed. But it is not often done. Many people nowadays profess an interest in wild flowers, but few – at least, among the amateurs – seem to bring off the big effect. There is comfort in this. In writing this chapter I have been aware of admitting to a series of failures which were all the result of my carelessness and stupidity. I have been over-casual, or unobservant, and I have lost hundreds of plants in consequence. But, looking around, I conclude that everybody else probably has as well – otherwise, where are the big battalions? And that knowledge does something towards mending my wounded self-esteem and sending me forward again. Sooner or later I shall acquire another ripening pod of martagon lily seeds. Sooner or later, my own Pyrenean lilies, likewise, will marry and reproduce. And then, as a result of my humiliating earlier experiences, I shall hope to be able to avoid those earlier mistakes, and after a wait of – who knows? perhaps four years – be in the splendid position of having hundreds of bulbs to flowering size to plant out in big drifts, and enjoy.

Before I leave the subject of growing wild flowers from seed, I should like to take this opportunity of drawing attention to a fairly new and, I think, extraordinarily well-conceived scheme. This is known as the Seed Bank

Exchange, and operates from 44 Albion Road, Sutton Surrey. It is a non-profit-making store and access resource for wild seed species, particularly native seed; and members (who can join cheaply enough, one would think, at 75p) can acquire seeds they want either by purchase, or by sending in seeds which they can themselves collect, and which are on a published 'wanted' list. Naturally enough an organisation of this kind asks for a stamped addressed envelope with every communication. But what a marvellous idea! Two newsletters a year are sent to members, in spring and autumn, and lists of plants are being compiled showing their relative rarity and various other factors about them. The organisers, who must indeed be dedicated people, are also anxious to hear about members' success or failure with the seeds they acquire, and intend to publish guidelines to the cultivation of various species as the information becomes available to them. For myself, I joined as soon as I heard about the scheme, and I wish it every possible success. If it can be kept going, it must be a useful factor in the saving of our lovely and so-threatened wild life.

As well as the Seed Bank, I know of two sources of wild flower seeds, though no doubt there are many others. These are both ordinary commercial firms, where you pay for the seeds, not swap-shops; their names are Mr Fothergill's Seeds, Kentford, Suffolk; and John Chambers, 15 Westleigh Road, Barton Seagrave, Kettering Northants, NN15 5AJ.

11

Never Say Dai

Nearly every dwelling, farmhouse or cottage set deeply in the country has a reasonably cultivated garden. Many of us live five miles or more from the nearest shop and, though nearly everybody has a car, it is too expensive, with petrol going up every second Thursday, to keep popping into town. It pays us, both in money and convenience, to cultivate our cabbage patches.

There is not quite the same interest taken in flowers. A few faithful hardy perennials adorn the little front gardens; many of the women (always the women in this matter) grow bright annuals, nasturtiums, snapdragons, or geraniums, round the door. But the main interest and skill are reserved for the cultivation of vegetables, and some of our acquaintances, indeed, show an astonishing lack of information even over that. My friend and neighbour, John, was working in his vegetable garden last summer when he became aware of a looming presence and, looking up, found himself being carefully inspected by an old man who lives alone in a tumble-down cottage down the road. His local nickname is 'News-of-the-World'; and to describe him as inquisitive is to perpetrate the feeblest understatement of the century. No question is too delicate or too personal for him to ask: 'How much money does your husband have to pay you now he's run off with that woman?' – 'Is it true your an'ty tried to do away with herself?' – 'Why's your Mam left all her money to your sister and nothing to you, then?' and 'Is that new baby of your daughter from her own husband, then?' being fair samples of the enquiries with which he has shocked and affronted various

people in the last few years. John, finding this unwelcome visitor surveying his vegetable garden, wished him a cool good morning, and went on with his work. After a few more minutes' inspection, however, News-of-the-World indicated a row of flourishing French beans, and enquired, 'What's them, then? Some kind of potatoes?'
John: 'No, some kind of beans. The potatoes are those, over there.'
N.o.t.W: 'Damn, you are lucky your potatoes haven't got the blast this year.'
John: 'Well, I have sprayed them four times.'
N.o.t.W: 'There's a lot of potatoes got the blast this year.'
John: 'Well, I have sprayed them four times...'
N.o.t.W: 'Why hasn't your potatoes got the blast, then?'
John: 'Well, I have sprayed them four times...'
N.o.t.W: 'Is that good for the blast, then?'
John: 'No, it's bad for the blast.'
N.o.t.W: 'Why do you do it, then?'
John: 'It's good for the potatoes.'
N.o.t.W. 'Damn, you are lucky your potatoes haven't got the blast! There's a lot of potatoes got the blast this year!'

'At which point,' said John, 'I began to feel curiously light-headed ... It was almost like in chapel, when they get to the end of a hymn, and one of the old boys jumps up and calls out 'Repetto!' and they all start from the beginning again...'

News-of-the-World's own garden, as one might imagine from this exchange, is as run-down as his cottage. When his course is run and he goes to put his Maker to hard questioning no doubt the place will soon lapse into total ruin. His cottage is of quite a sturdy construction, with stone walls bedded in thick joints of the old-fashioned lime mortar. It will fall down once it is unoccupied, but it will not totally disappear. Many of the old cottages were built of clom, and they have vanished so utterly that it is impossible even to trace the outline of their foundations. Clom is rammed clay, the same substance that is known as 'cob' in the west of England, and 'pisé' in France, and it is often said that it will last for ever as long as it has dry feet and a dry head. But the roof of a cottage needs constant attention to keep it water-tight, and one rough winter is enough to see the beginning of the end for an empty clom cottage, particularly if it is turf-roofed or thatched. Pieces of the roofing material are whirled away in a gale; water trickles down the rafters, and, finding its easiest course to the ground, washes away so much of the packed earth of the walls that they soon collapse, bringing down roof and all in a muddle of rotting thatch and broken timbers. Dressed stone is always in demand for repair work on walls and farm buildings, so before long even the footings will have been taken away. Timbers decay; and in a surprisingly short time, all that is left of what was once somebody's home is a little mound of earth, whose extra depth encourages the growth of the encroaching brambles from the hedge. I can never pass one of these old cottage sites, indicated by the flurry of white and gold snowdrops and daffodils in the hedgebank, without thinking of the human aspect of it – the black kettle singing on the fire, the Welsh-cakes stacked, short and crumbly, on a plate on the table, the clean flannel shirt airing on the rack ... So passes, not the glory of the world, but the deep, true, essential warp and weft of human life and contentment.

So there is always something sad in wandering round the garden of an old empty cottage. Perhaps 'wandering' is an inappropriate word; the native thorns and briars take over so quickly in this lavish climate that the act of exploration partakes more of the nature of pushing, shoving, and trampling than wandering. I know half a dozen or more of these ancient cottages or cottage sites, and it has been a matter of intense interest to see what has survived in their gardens in the midst of the thorns. There is a remarkable consistency of plants, a reflection partly on the toughness of the survivors, and partly on the limited selection that was there in the first place.

The most striking plants that continue to flourish, as I have said before, are the snowdrops and the daffodils – two kinds of daffodils, *Narcissus obvallaris,* the Tenby daffodil, a small, brilliant yellow early single, and the curious tough old double, which I believe is called Rip Van Winkle. Almost as pretty at the same season are the periwinkles. Both the large and the small forms of *Vinca* – major and minor – are to be found in these little overgrown garths. Not surprisingly, they are always the original kind, the blue-purple type plants, rather than the more sophisticated white or wine-coloured; nor have I ever found a variegated specimen. Being evergreen, the vincas are able to put up with a lot of shade, and their glossy dark leaves flourish in spite of the overgrowing brambles, hawthorns, and dog-roses. Montbretia is another archetypal survivor; its sword-like leaves and gay orange spikes push up through the tangled tufts of dead grass fifty years after a cottage has been abandoned. A more curious survival, and one which I do not, myself, find pretty, is a genetic one – the survival of colour in primroses. It is quite usual to find faded, muddy pink individuals among the wild primroses round an old cottage site, and I suppose that this is the legacy of some once admired and loved red primula which flourished in the garden bed, but was unable to persist, as itself, when the jungle came back. Unluckily the bequest never seems to come through as a clear or deep pink, and I have never felt tempted to collect these strange, dim flowers.

Cottage gardeners often brought specimens of wild plants in to grace their gardens, and thus, I suppose, it is not surprising that we find them still growing there. A clump of Solomon's seal often comes up year after year: and the deep pink sedum, Orpine makes quite a flurry of colour among the roots of an old quickset hedge. Another plant whose presence seems to me to be absolutely indicative of the site of an old habitation is the butcher's broom. This curious, prickly, box-like sub-shrub seems to be so universal that I assume it must originally have been grown for use rather than for decoration. It is certainly stiff and wiry, but when I picked some to preserve in glycerine and use in winter flower arrangements, I found it so extraordinarily scratchy that I wouldn't much have liked the job of binding it to a handle and using it to sweep the hearth up with. Still, I suppose that, compared with our ancestors, we are soft.

One old stone cottage that I often used to pass on my walks was less derelict than many. There was no glass in the downstairs windows, but there were still window frames, and there was a door too, although, swollen with wet and dropped on its hinges, it always stood open. I went inside a few times to look round. A short path of slate flags led from the rotten green picket gate to the two shallow steps leading up to the doorway, and inside the slate flags continued, forming a floor that had remained dry and good throughout the two tiny downstairs rooms. Only in front of the fireplaces were the slates smashed and broken, as evidence of the curiously destructive habit of the nineteenth-century Welsh of chopping their kindling in that situation. I have never yet seen an old farmhouse or cottage without this damage; perhaps the convenience of it made it worth the trouble of occasionally replacing the ruined slates with new ones. The rusty fireplaces themselves had their own charm. One was a little kitchen range, with a raised, barred grate, an oven, a hob, and a side boiler; the other, a minuscular parlour grate, with a cast-iron mantelpiece and surround, and a prim little fender hemming in the tiles. On the mantelpiece, almost as if left there like a prop in a tear-jerking film, lay a damp and dirt-stained embroidered text that had dropped from its rusted nail in the wall above. It was crudely executed in red wool cross-stitch on a sort of flock-surfaced paper, and framed in cardboard. It read 'No Place Like Home.'

The steep and narrow staircase rose directly into a bedroom, tiny, and cramped up under the roof space. Another, even smaller, opened out of it. Both were lit by little gable windows, whose bleared glass came down to the level of the sagging board floors. I only explored upstairs once; the floors swung and bounced beneath my feet in a sinister way, and felt dangerous.

At the back of the cottage, another door opened into a little open-fronted shed which must have been the coal place, and a cobbled path, which your feet could just feel beneath the overgrown grass, led to a pointed-roofed sentry-box in the same faded green as the gate.

I had a certain affection for this cottage, because it had a homely look, and because I had acquired from its garden a plant of which I was rather fond. In the rough, ferny hedge topping the bank that divided its garden from the lane, I had noticed several bushes of a rose with which I was unfamiliar. It had small neat leaves with more leaflets on them than most roses have, and its stems were thickly set with thorns so fine that they almost looked like hairs. The flowers, when they came, were fleeting, but had their own charm, being small, pink, incurving, and very double, and borne on rather slender, nodding stems. They were like half-sized versions of an old-fashioned cabbage rose, and smelled just as sweetly. I had helped myself to a flourishing bundle of cuttings, and consequently felt a kind of cousinship with the cottage that had provided them. It seemed a pity that it should stand there empty, and obviously sliding inexorably into decay and ruin, but there was nothing I could do about it. I didn't even know who owned it.

I was glad, then, one day when I passed the cottage, and saw signs of work going about it. The long tapering triangle of the garden, previously completely overgrown, had been trashed out, and the trashings burned, in a bonfire whose last ashes still sent a fragile curl of smoke up through the still air; a neat stack of bricks and a heap of sand on the front path promised repairs, and peering through the open door, I could see two bags of cement or plaster inside, propped up against the wall. This was excellent; I enquired of my neighbours, Mick and Emerald, what was going on.

'No, it's nobody English,' said Mick. 'Not one of those holiday cottages. It's an old chap – Welsh he is, comes from these parts originally, but he's been away for years. Won a football pool or something, Glanville was telling me. Not a lot, but he's got his pension, so he's bought the place, and he's going to do it up.'

'Yes, that's right,' chimed in Emerald. 'He's been a builder, they say, so he can do it himself. He's lodging at one of the farms by there now, can't remember which one. Nice old boy, they're saying.'

'I often wondered why nobody did that cottage up,' I remarked. 'It's not too far gone, and it's so pretty.'

'Oh, well, the trouble was with that, they wouldn't sell it,' explained Emerald. 'It belonged to an old woman, a Mrs Jones, wasn't it, she was a widow. She had a big family too, eight of them there was; and then the children grew up and went away, and she was there on her own for a long while. Lovely garden she used to have there – lovely flowers. I remember it well in those days, we used to pass it on the way back from school, she was always out working in the garden, loved her flowers she did. Anyway, then she died, after the war, it was, and the cottage was left to the girls – three girls there was – and they couldn't agree among themselves, you know, to sell it. But now there's two of them died within six months of each other, old ladies they are now, of course – so the youngest one was willing to sell it. She'd wanted to sell it all along, it was the middle one was the awkward old bugger. So this Mr Williams come along just at the right time, it'll be nice for him.'

A week or two later, I met Mr Williams himself. He was in the lane, 'bending' his overgrown hedge, and replied civilly enough to my 'Good afternoon.' He was a tiny little man, less than five feet tall, with a pale, sharp-featured face, and, most unusually for a Welshman, a pair of light-grey eyes. He had lost his own teeth and his cheeks were sunken in, although the loss had been repaired with a National Health set that gave him a dazzlingly neat smile. I have never met anybody who gave a stronger impression of being 'on the ball'. His eyes positively sparkled with intelligence and irony, and he had an engaging way of bending his head to listen to what you said to him which, with his puckish cast of countenance and tidy, demure style of dress, gave him something of the air of an old-fashioned groom in good service, who defers to you for politeness' sake, but inwardly reserves his own judgement.

I might have passed on without any furtherance of our acquaintanceship, but just at that moment a mouse ran out of the hedge, and Tip instantly pounced on it. Mr Williams was delighted. 'Good boy! Good boy then!' he cried. 'Rats, is it? Rats! Good on rats, is he?'

I explained that he was more of a mouse specialist, being luckily denied much practice with the larger brethren; and then I said:

'It's Mr Williams, isn't it? Mick and Emerald were telling me your name. I live next door to them. You know Mick and Emerald?'

'Oh, aye, I know them,' he said. 'At least, I've met them. Nice couple. Oh, so that's where you're living. Not *from* this way, are you?'

This is the classic introduction to a Welsh conversation. I am happy to bear my part in the question and answer, move and counter-move by which two strangers in this part of the world get to know each other, and to place each other in the framework of the already familiar. Mr Williams and I got on well; the minutes flew by.

'Oh, but don't call me Mister!' he exclaimed, at one point, when I addressed him as Mr Williams. 'Dai's what I am – but a funny old nick-name I got with it. Know what they call me?

Dai God-willing, that's what I get. It's my initials, isn't it, see – G.O.D. – Gareth Owen David Williams – G.O.D. Will. – Dai God-willing's what I get.'

So Dai God-willing he became to me and to everybody else in the neighbourhood, though for the sake of brevity he is usually addressed simply as 'Dai.' He always calls me by my christian name, but he pronounces it rather charmingly, 'Lissabeth'.

It took him about six months to make his cottage fit to live in, and then he moved in, and has continued to improve it and fit it up ever since. With pick and shovel he dug a splendid cesspit in his garden, and installed modern plumbing; the tiny wood-and-coal shed at the back of the cottage was transformed into the neatest little bathroom. A second-hand Rayburn, bough for a song at a builders' merchant's bankruptcy sale, and transported home in a borrowed van, heats the water, and keeps the damp of the old stone walls at bay. It seems to take him no time at all to get the overgrown garden back in hand again; now, neat rows of vegetables stretch in diminishing series across the long tapering plot, and a small plantation of soft fruit bushes, carefully netted against the depredations of the birds, is just coming into bearing. There are flowers once again in the tiny triangle between the cottage front and the gate; all is cultivated and trim – there is not an inch of grass anywhere. But, busy as he is, Dai is never short of time for a chat, and many a cup of tea I have enjoyed at his hospitable fireside, from the kettle always whispering on the cool end of the Rayburn.

The subject we always seem to get on to sooner or later is Welsh social history. Dai is now seventy-six years old, and remembers the days before the Great War with considerable clarity. But even more interesting are the reminiscences of his grandfather, imparted to him in those early years, which he often tells me about; for that gentleman, a native of Pencader, not many miles from here, was born in 1851, and could speak from experience of many traditions of old Wales that are now dead, but that seemed as lively as ever in the days of his youth.

There was the tradition of the Mari Lwyd for one thing. This was a Christmas and New Year game which is supposed to have its roots far, far back in antiquity, much earlier than Christianity, in a primitive, totemic, horse-worshipping cult;

but of course Dai's grandfather never speculated about the origins, he just took part in it.

The Mari Lwyd itself (the phrase means 'grey mare') was an entirely traditional figure. It consisted of a horse's skull, with cloth ears and big staring eyes made of bottle glass which was mounted on a long pole. The pole was carried by a man, and man and pole were covered by a white sheet, all being decorated to the best of the participants' taste with ribbon knots and bows. The jaw of the skull was wired on in such a way that the man inside the Mari Lwyd could make it snap its teeth, and the horse was bridled, decoratively, with ribbon. Other members of the party by tradition were the mare's leader, Punch, Judy, the Sergeant, and Merryman. Punch and Judy would have their faces blackened, and would be dressed in rags, but the others would be in their best dress, and would wear coloured shoulder-knots of ribbon, and sometimes bright sashes. Merryman sometimes carried a fiddle.

The Mari Lwyd party would approach a house, and knock on the closed door. The householder, instead of opening it, would look out of a window, and tell them to go away. Then a singing contest would begin. 'Supposed to make it up as they went along,' explained Dai, 'but of course, that depended. Some of them was good at it, and some wasn't. If they couldn't think of anything good themselves, there was traditional things they could say, like. In Welsh it was always, of course. But if you got a couple of chaps who was a bit sharp, like, my Grandad said, they could make it up, and Damn! he said, it was funny!'

I could believe it. The Welsh have always been an exceedingly articulate nation, their whole culture oral rather than literary, and with a strong tradition of improvisation. I could easily put together a Mari Lwyd party in my mind from the men I knew – they would all be men, the Judy part being as traditionally male as the Dame in a pantomine – and picture them in the yard of any one of a dozen farms round here, doubled up laughing as the barbed insults, the unprintable indelicacies, the personal jests of the rhyming contest flew to and fro. The sort of man who would have undertaken the part of the Leader, who took the lead in the singing contest, is still to be seen in our villages. Clever, quick-witted, a natural actor, he is to be seen nowadays acting as M.C. in a local talent contest, or auctioning off the goods at a church bring-and-buy-sale. I can think of lots who would have done the job of Leader of the Mari Lwyd to perfection. Some examples of the repartee have been written down, but they are inevitably rather tame; no doubt the real thing would have been pretty topical as well as rather close to the wind.

In the end, of course, the householder would open the door, and the Mari Lwyd party would come into the house. The mare herself always paid special attention to the women, nudging, barging, snorting, neighing, and pretending to bite them. Merryman would play his fiddle; after him came Judy, who would sweep up the hearth with her broom until Punch ran into the room and knocked her to the floor. Then he ran round the room chasing and kissing all the women, while Judy pursued him and tried to hit him with her broom. It is easy to picture the scene, the laughter, the screaming, the snatched kisses, the crude jokes – literally, the horse-play.

Then of course the party would sit down to eat and drink, with special seasonal delicacies being provided, and, Dai's grandfather always averred 'Ale – oh, Dai bach! They don't make it like that now! Oh, there's lovely it was!' When everybody had been refreshed, a traditional verse of farewell would be sung before the party trooped out into the night on the way to the next house to be visited.

There are obvious tie-ups between this tradition and the wassailing that was carried on in England; Merryman and the Sergeant, too, often appear in medieval miracle plays. But the particular bit of the business that intrigues me is the Judy, with her broom, going to sweep up the hearth. Surely this must be a survival from a tradition that was very old indeed. In the days of sun-worship, the important festival of the winter solstice was celebrated by the extinguishing of all fire in the house, and the ritual cleaning of the hearthstone. When the sun rose after the longest night, the priests would kindle new fire, and this would be carried, with great rejoicings, into every house, and used to light the hearth fire again. Surely Judy's broom and abortive effort to sweep the hearth, in a festival so definitely associated with this time of year, must be a vestigial survival of this? It is curious indeed to think of Dai's grandfather, who more than once played this part, being the link between our own ordinary, everyday, living selves and a belief as ancient and primitive as this. The Mari Lwyd passed into desuetude in the last years of the last century, and Dai himself has no memory of the tradition being carried on in his lifetime.

Another old Welsh tradition upon which Dai loved to dilate was the Ty Un Nos. This was an arrangement which as far as I know has no equivalent in England, whereby a man could build a house and legally live in it as long as it was constructed during the course of one night, and by sunrise the next morning had a roof on, and smoke coming out of the chimney.

'Of course there was a lot of *organisation* with it,' says Dai, who has read about the tradition, in the public library. 'The chap'd get a gang of his friends together, and get a lot of stuff ready. Stands to reason, he'd have to. Then they'd mostly build them in winter, with the nights bein' longer. Wattle and mud I reckon they'd use, hazel or willow – they'd get the panels ready before, I reckon, get 'em hid somewhere handy. They'd get a lot of stone cut ready too, for the chimney. Then when the night come, they'd be down there, two or three of 'em – put a frame up, clap the panels on, one of 'em to build the chimney – oh, they could do it, if they was let alone. Of course the trouble was if somebody caught 'em at it. On all kinds of land they used to do it. Private or common, didn't make any difference to the law. Roof on, and smoke coming out of the chimney – that's what the law said. But not written down it was, more of a tradition, like.'

Sometimes a Ty Un Nos would be built in an exceedingly sequestered nook, for another provision of the folk-law under which the tradition operated said that if it escaped detection for twelve years, the inhabitant could claim the freehold of the property. In the days of absentee – and often foreign – landlords, this could happen, unlikely as it seems. No doubt the Agent who looked after the landlord's affairs also often lived at a distance, and would only come round at the appropriate intervals to collect the rents; as an associate and servant of the hated Saxon, he too would probably be pretty fairly disliked; it is inconceivable that the locals themselves would not know of the Ty Un Nos hidden in the wood, or tucked away in a little mountain *cwm,* but perfectly possible that they would not give it away to such a one.

Any Ty Un Nos built on private land had to pay rent to the owner of the land once he discovered it, which would have made it seem a more attractive proposition for the prospective tenant to build it on a common. But the problem with that was that the other people with commoners' rights resented such a project as an encroachment on their assets, and not infrequently would turn up, if they got wind of a building party, and tear the house down as fast as the others could put it up.

Dai always averred that the classic construction of a Ty Un Nos was wattle and daub, but some authorities claim that they were usually built of large stones, with a turf roof. Presumably they could be added to once their existence had been acknowledged, so a minimal building would do in the first instance. As well as the name Ty Un Nos (house of one night) by which they were usually known, they were also sometimes referred to as 'Morning Surprises.'

A further quaint tradition governed the amount of land that the builder was allowed to enclose for his garden. Standing at his door, he threw an axe as far as he could to the four points of the compass; a hedge was planted along the line which connected these points, and the land it enclosed was considered his.

But the bare recital, the abstract of the law, can give us very little idea of what the building of a Ty Un Nos was actually like. By thinking round my neighbours and friends, Welsh both by blood and tradition, I can easily flesh out the picture, and imagine how it must have been. The discussion – the decision – the conspiracy. Welshmen love mystery, and secret discussion; I can imagine the little group of friends or relations, meeting discreetly in one of their houses, after nightfall – heads together – the keen, dark features, lit by a wood fire or a glimmering rushlight, with here a high cheekbone, there a dark eye illumined by a flicker of flame. What plans would have to be laid, what arrangements made – 'And Ifan says we can use the mare and cart, just so's we don't get caught, can't afford to have his name brought into it, see; got to go as quiet as a mouse, man – put a bit of cloth round her hooves, grease the old wheels – ' 'Nice bit of hazel up the dingle, we can get it cut Sunday, lay it up ready ...' 'Yes, and my Da say he get the stone for me, for the chimney, like. He's putting it round that he's going to make a new calf cot, see, so it won't look so funny, cutting a lot of stone in the quarry...'

They would have had to wait for the longer nights at the end of the year to have any hope of getting the construction forward enough to be completed, as the law demanded, between sunset and sunrise. With what pretended casualness, as the time dragged by to the appointed night, would they stroll, as occasion served, past the chosen site, sizing up the risks of being seen and disturbed – noticing the proximity of the spring for water to mix the mortar – the soft bits in the ground where they would have to watch the mare and the cart when they brought in the stone – the concealment afforded by the lie of the land, or the lee of the wood, from observation by chance passers-by on the road. And always the plans, the women bearing their part as well as the men. 'And dry sticks we got to bring – only think' (with a gust of nervous giggles) 'if we got him all done, and then we couldn't get the fire to light!' 'You got to bring food, too; there's hard work it'll be, after a day's work indeed. My Mam said she'll kill you a couple of fowls, be a help, like ...' And then in the end it would all be at the mercy of the weather. I wonder how many times intending builders of a Ty Un Nos have screwed themselves up to the big adventure only to see, with sinking hearts, as the day went on, that pallid, watery greyness in the west that portends the onset of our own special, drenching, driving rain?

The eighteenth century was the great time for the building of 'Morning Surprises'; with the decline of the rural population in the early eighteen hundreds, the custom fell into decline. I know nobody who claims to have an ancestor who successfully built one; and as the law was always one rooted in tradition rather than written down – a custom, perhaps, rather than a law – nobody had better try to revive it now. For our eighteenth-century forbears may have had to contend with all sorts of difficulties, from interfering neighbours to lowering rainclouds, but at least they were spared the problem of being subject to the Town and Country Planning Act.

Most of the people who knew Dai when he was a child in this area are dead now, but he can still claim a few old acquaintances. But the district has in any case quickly taken him to its heart. He is just the sort of man that everybody likes; he is kind and friendly, handy and helpful, an amusing talker, and a great teller of tales of the old times. He is benevolent, too. I have seen him regarding the brash and over-confident young with great sympathy, and with a little amused smile. 'Oh, give them time,' he says. 'They'll come sooky soon enough. Got to have time.'

The only people for whom he is not willing to provide this invaluable commodity are the hippies, whom he despises with concentrated hatred. 'No, indeed, I got no time for them,' he told me one day. 'No time for them at all!' I had met him by chance in Carmarthen by the bus stop, where we were waiting for the bus that would carry us both home. A typical hippie family was passing by on the other side of the road – long-haired father, bearded, wearing wellingtons, jeans, donkey jacket and knitted cap; draggled mother, in long, dung-coloured skirt of sad Indian cotton; and about five elf-locked children, with runny noses and dirty faces. As we watched, the father turned aside from the procession, and, turning his back on the passing crowds, proceeded to relieve himself into a handy drain. Dai's face became a wrinkled mask of disgust and disapproval. 'There you are!' he exclaimed. 'See what I mean about those people, Liss-abeth? Typical! Just what I say – No self-control – no *birth control* – no BLADDER-CONTROL!'

12

Hot Weather

Everybody knows how difficult it is to imagine different weather from the kind one is having at any one moment, particularly when it has been the same for some time.

I know that in the winter I shall find it difficult to believe that I had to spend a lot of time watering the garden this summer; and now, while it is hot, it seems impossible to realise that last winter, last spring, and in the early part of the summer, it appeared that the weather glass had got stuck between 'rain' and 'change.' Day after day it rained. Cold winds held up plant growth; seedlings were flattened over and over again by the downpour. The spring that seeps out of the upper part of my drive twinkled busily as it ran, night and day, for weeks down over the grey stones, washing away all the odds and ends of filler with which we were trying to mend the drive's holes, and gradually deepening its channel all the time. The other spring, which fills a beautiful little corbelled pool recessed into the bank – made originally, I assume, as a drinking place for the horses – spread its limpid waters across the strip of grass that usually separates it from the drive and joined its brother, purling merrily down. Every green thing hung cold, wet, juicy, and fully charged with water.

How different it all is now. For two and a half months we have had no significant rain; nothing but 'spoiling rain' as the Welsh call it, when it gets in the way of haymaking without really refreshing the pastures. The earth is cracked and parched; even in the wood where a deep ground cover of moss, brambles and enchanter's nightshade over a soil black with leaf mould seems to promise some dampness, you can scrabble inches down among the tough stringy roots without coming to any real moistness.

So I have had to go in for watering. But it has not been a chore. If I had made a chore of it, I should have carried more water, and more things would have grown as a result, but I suppose I should not have enjoyed myself so much. Presumably, not enjoying it makes the difference between something you do being a chore, or simply being work.

One of the benefits of being middle-aged is that you no longer have to accept as gospel the gnomic wisdom of older generations. You can question their scared truths – I was going to write 'question their sacred cows', but my farming experience has shown me that enquiries made of cows, however holy, are inclined to be rhetorical.

The particular tenet that I have been calling into question is one that is often quoted by people of my own generation, as well as by our elders. 'If a thing's worth doing, it's worth doing *well*!' they say – smugly? Self-encouragingly? In exhortation? This is perhaps a saying worthy of all men to be received, but is it necessarily true? After some thought, I came to the conclusion that in my life, at any rate, there were dozens of things that were much more worth doing badly; or, at least, doing badly from the point of view of efficiency.

I tried this line on my mother, who has always been both a great advocate and a great practitioner of the 'doing-things-well' school. I should have known better. Irish-born and Irish-bred, she instantly recognised a trailed coat, and with a tactical skill worthy of a Wellington, took up an impregnable defensive position by saying that it all depended on what you meant by 'badly' and 'well', and that if what I was doing, whatever it was, was worth doing, I *must* be doing it well by some standard, even if not by the most obvious one.

Not that I really mind. I haven't got a lot of emotional capital tied up in my idea of doing things badly. And luckily for me, there is nobody in a position to criticise the way I go about my watering, and tell me that I ought to do it differently.

I fetch water, by the canful, from the river. The Arian runs at the bottom of one of my little fields, but it does not entirely lend itself to the dipping of water. There is a deep pool, it is true, and a little sandy spit running out into it, which is quite convenient, but the way to it is down an exceedingly steep slope, treacherously slippery in this dry weather, and through the branches of an overhanging willow with thickly entrenched nettlebeds all around it.

Much better is the access to the other little stream, which joins the Arian about thirty yards beyond my boundary, and whose name is variously given on old maps as the Allt Gwyn or the Gwennant. Recent Ordnance Survey maps do not dignify it with a name at all. It, too, was once a boundary of this property, but the previous owner, one Smith, sold the little field it edges to Mick, to ease a fencing problem that had bedevilled them for some years, so I have not the pleasure of owning it.

This is a pity. I should like to be able to call it mine. Not for any agricultural reason, because it is agriculturally negligible, being less than half an acre in extent, and in any case, I don't utilise even the existing agricultural potential of this place. No: the reason I would like to own it is because it is so charming. Luckily Mick, kindest and most accommodating of neighbours, has no objection to my wandering about on it, poking about in its hedgebanks and dabbling in its waters, so its charm is not totally lost to me. But I should still have liked to own it.

When I set off on a watering expedition, it is usually already hot. My house faces full south, and basks, like a great white cat, on its sunny ledge; outside, at the front, it can get blazing hot, although its thick stone walls keep the internal temperature down. I put wellingtons on for the water-dipping, and if I linger, as I usually do, to examine some flower, I can feel the sun burning my very toes through the rubber – or is it plastic nowadays?

Part of the way down the drive I plunge into shade. There is a welcome coolness; the dew lingers here, and there is a feeling of dampness, illusory though it may be. Tall, solid sycamores arch over from the south side, interspersed with lighter, more feathery ash saplings, and the birds, busy about their late summer tasks, flit almost silently among the green glooms of the branches.

After a few more yards, the drive branches, and a short spur curving off to the left leads to a field gate. Once through it you are out into the sunshine again, and into the very heart of the drought, for the rock runs very close to the surface just here. The brown, parched grass has not grown at all since Mick topped it six weeks ago, to kill the thistles. Grasshoppers chirp and leap everywhere; tiny basking lizards scuttle away into hiding; and the big dragon flies, banded in yellow and black, dart here and there with quite an audible clatter of stiff wings. The chopped-up thistles still lie, curled and brown, on the grey ridges of stone; lower down, where in winter a small spring runs, it is greener. White clover has made a second growth among the butts of the topped rushes. Its flowers attract the bees, and their hum mingles with the heavy honey scent and the faint smell of the finely-ground dust joins with the low voice of the river to epitomise the cloudless summer day.

The river is running low in its bed, and you step down about a foot into the limpid water. A shingle bank exposed in the middle divides it into two clear and shallow streams; one step through the water, and you are on the dry again, while tiny fish flash through the sunlit pools into the shelter of the bank. There are two pools on opposite banks, one upstream, and one downstream, for the river bends a little here, and the current of the winter flow has gouged itself quite a deep bed. At this time of year, the deepest bit may be two and a half feet, certainly well over wellington-top depth, and you must wade carefully into the steeply-shelving floor, for you don't want to fill your boot, however pleasant it may be to feel it abruptly cooled from the *outside*. The water is perfectly clear, and you can see every minute detail of the brilliantly illumined river bed, from the polished, reddish-brown stones that turn so puzzlingly to grey as they dry, to the clinging silt of the deeper areas that coats all the submerged stems of the bank weeds with a uniform coat of house-mouse colour.

There is an overhang of the bank as the river sweeps round its corner, and a little band of deep shade, the lying-up ground, probably, of numbers of fishes and other aquatic creatures. A foot of bank projects, unsupported, over the water, and the tangled roots of the water-rim plants hold it together. It is late August, and the best time for wild flowers is long gone by; but still a sprinkling of colour enlivens this fringe. It is surprising how many species can be found in about fifteen yards of bank. Sweet woodruff supports its fragile stems on tufts of bronzed rushes; ragwort and pink campion are enjoying a second blooming. A large plant of woody nightshade leans out over the water, showing both green berries and purple flowers. A narrow-leaved dock positively glows in the sunlight, its three spikes of flowers blood red, and a large clump of horseshoe vetch is comfortably furnished all over with its yellow flowers, in spite of the lateness of the season. Brilliant reflections of sunlight from the rippling river jump and quiver over the bankside plants with something of the effect of a mirage.

But this is no mirage. The water is fresh, and cool, and real, and plentiful. I dip in my green can (the red one I keep for noxious mixtures) and the water swirls in. It is a two-gallon can, so the weight of it full is only about twenty pounds, which is nothing. Two three-gallon buckets, which I suppose I should carry if I were pursuing maximum efficiency, would be quite a struggle up my steeply sloping drive.

The actual watering is as leisurely as the dipping up. As every gardener out of the baby class knows, it is fatally easy to pour water on to parched ground too quickly, so that it just runs away, only wetting the top half inch or so. I try to create a little saucer of soil round the plants I water, and to break up the surface too. Then I pour a little water on, and move on to the next plant and the next. Each plant ends up with its two gallons of water or so (I am speaking of shrubs here) but the water arrives in several helpings, and has time to percolate down.

You see curious things too, while dreamily waiting for the water in the saucer to disappear. I was watering a new little copper beech one day when I became aware of a strange, muffled buzzing. I looked down. When the tree had been planted, earlier in the year, I had laid some large flat stones over its root area, with the idea of giving its roots a cool, temperate and stable situation to work in. A colony of ants had taken up its abode under one of these stones, and it was from this that the buzzing was coming. I bent down to look more closely, and saw that the ants had captured quite a large bluebottle, and were forcing it slowly into the entrance of their nest. The fly was buzzing forlornly, and struggling feebly, but a dozen ants hung grimly on to it at every jawhold, and twenty or thirty others were swarming round looking for a chance to have part of the action. I felt sorry for the bluebottle, but I did not release it. It is really not possible to project one's human moral judgements into a world as different from ours as the insects' world. But, by the same token, I did not allow the presence of the ants to deflect me from my own plan. How they enjoyed the deluge of cold water which must have flooded at least part of their nest when I watered my tree, I don't know. The tree liked it well enough.

This tree was remarkably cheap. If you buy a properly grown specimen copper beech from a nurseryman, he will charge you something in the nature of ten pounds. But if instead you buy a potted-up hedging copper beech, you may have your tree for fifty pence. I suppose they are all seedlings. It might be prudent to buy the tree from your nurseryman or garden centre when its leaves are out, as there is inevitably a good deal of variation in colour and habit. My ant's-nest one was bought in winter, and was a disappointment when it first expanded its leaves, as they all came out green, and rather a muddy green at that. But after two or three weeks, it began to redden up and finished up quite a respectable copper colour. Another hedging seedling that we planted out and trained on as a specimen at Penllwynplan is now a fine young tree about twenty feet tall, and is a beautiful colour. When we planted it, about ten or twelve years ago, we were advised by the nurseryman who sold it to us to put plenty of old mortar rubble in the soil round its roots, and this we did. It was so successful that I have done the same with my first one here; and since fifty pence is so modest a sum, and the copper beech such a lovely tree, I intend to give myself the opportunity of putting mortar rubble around the roots of quite a few more of them in the next year or two.

As hedging plants the little beech trees are of course 'feathered', with twigs down their trunks. I found that it worked out quite well to remove them gradually over the course of three or four years, during the course of the summer, when I wanted some copper foliage for a flower arrangement. I started at the bottom and worked up, giving the little tree time to expand its head, and leaving a longer and longer bare trunk until I felt that it looked about right.

How quickly the summer has passed! It seems no time since I was enjoying the lyrical flourish of the unfurling bracken shoots; now that fine curl has all gone. The bracken looks rigid, awkward, ungainly. Passing traffic of tractors, trailers, and cattle has bent and broken a stem here and there, which now leans awry, untidily. The occasional plant is colouring up, in advance of the big reddening of October; it all has a used, raffish look.

The scent, on the other hand, is heavenly. Bracken always smells beautiful from the moment it pushes its fiddle-neck shoot through the turf; but in its last few weeks of greenness, when the air is mild and balmy, and you feel that any morning now you will be picking up a few mushrooms, the poignant spiciness of it tugs at your very heart strings. Is it its association with one's childhood holidays that gives it this power to evoke nostalgia? The Canadians call the wild asters 'Farewell Summers'; a name I would like to steal for this plaintive fragrance of the bracken, whose haunting fragrance meant that it was nearly time to go home again, on those farm holidays of long ago.

This year's drought has made the mushrooms very late. Wandering round certain fields in which I knew I ought to find them, I was struck by the beauty of the hedgerow trees at this time of the year. They are mostly ashes, gnarled and deformed from years of cutting and laying, irregularly performed; and I realise, looking at them, how very much I should miss them if some evil chance led me to have to spend the rest of my life abroad. The ground is very dry everywhere; the heifers have grazed the grass down short in the fields, and it has not recovered. But towards the bank where the ashes grow, there is a little length in it. Cattle always seem to find the grass under trees relatively unpalatable, succulent though it may look to human eyes; and here the broad sparse blades and surface-running stolons are left untouched even though the main meadow grass is by now barely an inch long. The trees are mossy on their north and west sides, and the moss keeps its bright green colour even though it is by now both dry and warm to the touch. The bark is astonishingly variable, deeply fissured in parts, smooth and lively to the caressing hand in others. There are little holes and entrances here and there among the roots, with evidence of occupation in the form of last year's hazel nut shells, gnawed open, littered around. Whatever it was – mouse or vole, presumably – that ate those nuts, it must have carried them for several yards, for there are no hazels in this part of the hedge. It is not a grand bit of scenery, nothing specially beautiful, but I like it very much. It is intimate, domestic, homely. And if it is home to me, how much more is it home to those other creatures, who actually pass all their time in these few square yards? To the mice, the hedgehogs denning among the tree roots – to the shining blue-black dung beetle laboriously mounting a drying cowpat at my feet? Even to the very worms in the ground, living their lives, pulling the fallen leaves of the ash into their tunnels and there eating them and excreting their elements in new combinations suitable for re-absorption as plant food? One of the chief pleasures I find in there leisurely walks round the country is the sense of integration it brings. Cut off we may be, we human beings, each globed separately in our terrible and wonderful gift of consciousness, but all the same we are locked inevitably into the system – a comforting thought. It brings a certain sense of security, like gravity, or the indestructibility of matter.

On a high branch of the ash tree sits a slender, greenish bird, pensive and silent. It is a willow warbler, or a chiff chaff. How remarkable it seems that it is sitting there thinking about Africa. This is not intended as a bit of anthropomorphising. Even if it is a young bird, one of this year's hatching, it really is thinking about Africa, whether it knows it or not. In that tiny brain, under that delicate, feather-capped skull, inherited urges are stirring. A programme, encoded in the DNA of every cell of that small, vibrant body, is working. Tiny discharges of electricity are coming from certain neurons in that brain which will soon build up to an irresistible urge to migrate. The bird's tour of duty in this country is over. If it is an adult, it has bred, and probably succeeded in rearing some young; if it is a new bird, it has lived through the riskiest few weeks of its life. Now it must go. So although, being without language in our sense of the word, it cannot give a name to its thoughts, it is 'Africa' that it is thinking as it sits there, grey-green against the grey-green tree in the late August sunshine.

The hirondines seem to have migration at least at the edge of their collective mind. Young birds migrate earlier than adults, and already I have noticed on some days swirling gatherings of birds far in excess of the normal count, which I take to be passing flocks of early passagers. It is difficult to guess what insects these birds catch that pays them, in energy terms, for all that marvellously acrobatic flying. One late afternoon as I sat on the bench against my house in the slanting sunshine, I became aware of prodigious activity among the martins that build their nests under the pine-end eaves. Thirty or forty of them were diving and soaring and wheeling in a cube of air that measured only about fifty yards each way, and in which I was sitting. To and fro they swept, passing within three feet of me time and time again, twittering excitedly and making journey after journey back to their young in the nests. And yet I was quite unaware of any insect presence in the air, look as I might, and with all the advantage of an oblique light coming from behind me.

The martins' droppings make quite a mess on the concrete path that goes round the house. This year I decided to utilise their somewhat ammoniacal guano to make some liquid manure. My father used to make this with a sack of chicken dung, which he kept suspended in a tub of water, drawing off the malodorous brown fluid at need. I scraped up what was on my path and put it in a bucket of river-water, then left it for a week to mash, so to speak, while I cast round in my mind for the most needy recipient. The shrub rose 'Felicia' was a strong candidate. Coming into her third year with me she was looking sickly, having been moved, and having suffered a bad attack of black spot which got a hold on her while my back was turned and my mind was on other things. I had controlled the black spot with spraying, but she had lost a lot of leaves, and, after flowering badly, had settled down into a kind of static sulk, with no signs of new growth, let alone the strong and vigorous young canes that I had hoped to see springing from ground level.

Having loosened the ground a bit to aid percolation, I went to fetch my bucket of magic mix. It looked loathesome. The droppings had all risen to the top of the bucket and formed a crust which bulged and heaved slightly with the fermentation. I stirred it with a stick, and cautiously smelled it. It smelled disgusting. This was good as far as it went; the peggy tub in the garden at home where my father made his liquid manure had always been a place to visit on that strange childish quest of boasting about the strength of one's stomach. But I couldn't remember the exact quality of the beastliness of the smell. This bucketful seemed ammoniacal, which, as indicating the breakdown of nitrogenous products, one felt, had to be good.

So, after giving it a final swirl with a stout stick, I swilled the whole lot in a noisesome mess on to the ground about 'Felicia's stem, and stood back to await developments. And as it sank into the ground, I realised that my martin guano special tonic had at least one side-effect of extreme brilliance. It was full of chitin. Tiny fragments of the eaten and excreted bodies of the insects the martins had fed on now spangled the ground like a covering of wonderful multi-coloured sequins. Brilliant blue, iridescent green, flashing crimson, they twinkled and sparkled in the receding tide of liquid with an altogether unlooked-for beauty. Felicia, however, stood in the middle of it all apparently suspending her judgement.

It all worked out quite well in the end, though. Three or four days after the deluge, a tiny promise of new leaves began to appear on the sickly defoliated branches; a promise that three weeks and several more cans of water later developed into a fine crop of new shoots, suitably adorned with the flower buds of the hoped-for autumn flush. The martins have continued their side of the transaction with unabated vigour. I shall feel no hesitation in offering one of my other roses the mixture as before.

13

The Primrose Path

Now that I have been at Ty Arian for two and a half years, and begin to have some idea of where I am going, I am getting fairly well confirmed in my notions of what kind of a gardener I am. That is, definitely an untidy gardener. And as my ideas about the kind of garden I am trying to create here sort themselves out and get clarified, I come to see more clearly what kinds of garden I *don't* want. People who do have and like these kinds of gardens needn't be offended with me, either; after all, I am not saying that their kind of gardening is inferior, or easy, or vulgar, or anything pejorative; but simply that it is not the one I want to pursue. I don't, for instance, want to garden with big solid blocks of brilliant colour. Perfectly grown hardy annuals, in large drifts of one kind, all of an even height, just like the picture on the packet, are not what I want. I love to see them in other people's gardens, and I do sometimes have a few small patches myself, but a classic hardy annual gardener I am not.

Even less could I have any pretensions to being a good half-hardy annual gardener. The standard municipal gardener's art, which keeps formally-shaped beds neatly bedded out with half-hardy material for as long a season as possible, is a closed book to me; and when it is taken further, to the lengths of making pictures in plants, or clocks, or representations of the city coat of arms, it goes into a book that I am sure I shall never want to open. Similarly I should hate to own a knot garden, or a maze, and have always had a secret and terrible fear that I shall one day save an old lady's life, and that she will then bequeath me a property with just such a garden, which it will be my public duty to keep and maintain. Perhaps the best safeguard is never, never to save an old lady's life, just in case; but conscience would kick against that. Luckily, the dilemma has never confronted me.

Above all, I don't want to find myself constrained by any gardening rules. Keen alpinists, for instance, who reel with horror at the idea of introducing a little liveliness into their dull rock gardens at midsummer with a few annuals; or shrub enthusiasts, who refer to such things as poppies and lupins as 'mere herbs'; or show gardeners, who see their flowers only as potential bench- and red-ticket-fodder, seem to me to have put themselves into a rather joyless set of bonds, although of course I suppose they only do it because they like it.

But enough of this negativeness; what actually do I want? Well, first and foremost, I want a garden that I can prowl in. I want it to be wild. In the more civilised areas round the house, there will, of course, be lawns, and beds, and things growing up the house walls; but as you leave the house behind, I hope it will gradually become more bosky, and lavish, and surprising, so that you can make little expeditions to the more distant parts to see if the celandines are out yet, or the magnolia has escaped last night's valley frost, or the 'Kiftsgate' rose, pouring down from the top of that craggily-gnarled old thorn, has opened its creamy, fruit-scented flowers.

I want the garden, ideally, to develop in such a way that it does not demand too much in the way of actual gardening. As I get older, I trust that the shrubs and trees that I am planting now will, in growing up to maturity, take over a good part of the decorating of the garden, and that the wild flowers, whose cultural requirements, once understood, are simple, will do the rest. With this in mind, I try to think very very hard and very carefully about how I want the wild flowers to be. One must try to get a clear mental picture of the effects one is trying to create, and guard against the various pitfalls into which it would be easy to slip by simply substituting wild for cultivated species of plants in an otherwise conventional garden situation. Because it is not much good trying to grow wild flowers formally. They are of their very nature informal, and imposing a suburban kind of tidiness upon them is working very much against the grain. It is partly because of my predominating interest in growing wild flowers that I have called this book *The Untidy Gardener*; but, really, another word is needed, a word that implies not so much the opposite of tidiness, as its irrelevance – 'a-tidy', rather than 'un-tidy.' Wild flowers want to grow very freely, but, in their heyday anyway, they are seldom messy.

Indeed, stern biological necessity forces upon them a kind of order that to my eyes is much more beautiful than the stereo-typed rows of the municipal gardener's art. I have written in another book about the lovely effect of the dog-daisies growing in a roadside bank, all leaning out, with ranks of faces turned charmingly towards one – seeking the light, of course, and the sun to ripen their pollen which will attract insects to fertilise them; similarly, I was struck earlier this year by another bit of bank cover in a very shady farm lane where the ferns had expanded to make use of every available bit of light, and had in consequence made a pattern that seemed almost magically to combine freedom and symmetry. In the last paragraph I deliberately wrote that plants were seldom messy 'in their heyday', but of course, when biology relaxes its grip and the plant's annual cycle is over, a certain messiness does creep in. Dying leaves straggle; stems, no longer held taut by rising sap, fall over, and flop every which way. But I think that the would-be wild flower gardener must cultivate the kind of eye which does not mind this, and limit himself, rather as nature does, to one good tidying-up a year, rather than keep on fiddling about and trying to impose on his wild garden standards which do not properly belong to it.

To clarify in his mind the effect he is aiming at, the gardener must look inwards and, like an artist, purge and refine his vision until its first principles are clear to him. Constance Spry pointed out that in flower arranging, you can often only achieve the effect you are seeking by emphasising and concentrating it much more than nature does. With a flower like lilac, for example, she would underline the lavish, abundant, fragrant floweriness that is its essential character by stripping off virtually all the leaves, and massing the heavy, richly-scented heads together. This was lilac used with art, and made it look much more like one's ideal vision of lilac than it would have done had it simply been arranged at the concentration in which it grows on a bush.

In the same way, the wild flower gardener, seeking the best way to dispose his chosen species into his available ground, must decide on the essential characteristics of the effects he wants. Then he must emphasise them, controlling the situation a good deal more tightly than nature does (for he cannot afford, in his limited space, her many misfires) yet not working across the grain by trying to impose such alien qualities as perfect tidiness on to the picture.

Perhaps I might give a few examples of what I mean by the essential characteristics of an effect. Take cowslips, for instance. Now the cowslip is an exquisite flower anywhere, and does not disgrace itself even in quite formal border situations. But I think it looks at its most *cowslippy*, if you will permit the word, when it is scattered, irregularly and fairly sparsely, in very fresh young grass. Solid drifts are alien to its nature, and look inappropriate; it is a child of the 'flowery mead', and requires its scattering to give its optimal embroidered effect.

Wild daffodils, on the other hand, do suggest drifts. In nature, they seed themselves around to some extent, but each successful bulb increases massively by offsets, and forms a clump, the eventual result being a series of clumps of various sizes growing fairly close together, and all bedecked with flowers ranging through the full age cycle, from the sharp, upright-pointed green bud to the fluttering, pale yellow, fully-expanded bloom. The effect comes from the contrast between the bright, downward-looking flowers and the closely-ranked, tightly-packed upright leaves and buds, and it is lost if the clumps are too widely scattered, or, for that matter, too formally disciplined.

Bluebells make one think of carpets. The magic of a bluebell wood lies not only in the colour but in the astonishing evenness of the sheet of flowers, so fragrant and so lavish, winding away among the trunks of the trees in the lightly dappled shade of May. Try to envisage a bluebell wood in which the flowers appeared on plants that ranged in height from six inches to four feet, and at once the picture is spoiled. And for my money, at least, the bluebell demands a little shade and the complementary colour of fresh yellowy-green to look really like itself. One May I went on a trip to Skomer, the island bird reserve just off the Pembrokeshire coast, acres of which are covered by bluebells, in contrast to the remainder, which is gnawed down to the merest stubble by the rabbits. I thought that these sheets of bluebells in their open, windswept situation, backed only by pale fawn earth, looked quite peculiar. And when one saw them in a long stratum between the other blue strata of the sea and the sky, the three shades of blue, each beautiful in itself, absolutely killed each other for me.

There are other plants whose beauty is that of an individual, which would not be improved by repetition, but which depends rather on background and placing. One fine plant of tutsan, for example, displaying itself against a rough hedge, is probably more handsome than half a dozen, possibly crowding each other and preventing the full display of the noble flowering stems which will later, with luck, be adorned with splendid shining berries.

Of course upon reflection it becomes clear that the concept of a plant's best and most characteristic way of displaying itself is based on the plant's own biology, its method of seed distribution, and its adaptation to the particular environment it grows in. There is no particular surprise in this. But it is important, I think, that in planting up our wild-flower gardens we should be aware of it and work with it. Thus, even from the first, we shall perhaps get the effect we are looking for and, if we are lucky, and do succeed in truly naturalising our wild flowers, nature will continue to distribute them in the way we like.

I should like at this point to enlarge upon a matter I referred to earlier, and to discuss the extent to which we need actually to *garden* our wild flower plantings. Do we need to cultivate them to some extent, once they have got going, or can we leave it all to nature? The difficulty about that is that, aiming as she is at a biological rather than an aesthetic target, she is inclined to hit the latter only at random; and for every entirely wild display that seems to us to be perfectly beautiful, there are probably a hundred that would bring the words 'if only...' to the lips, rather than the spontaneous 'Wow!' of ungrudging admiration. If only those harebells had chosen to grow five yards to the left, so that they could have contrasted with that crimson ling ... if only that yellow-catkinned willow had arranged itself in a threesome in the hedge with the foaming white blackthorn and the dark, polished holly ... if only that spatter of scarlet poppies had been concentrated into a blaze, rather than an almost unnoticeable trail of sparks ... how much better it would all have been. And of course in our own gardens, these 'if only's' are quite easily within our grasp. We can trim, weed, thin, and transplant, until we achieve a picture that comes as close as possible to our original conception. We may even be so lucky as to surpass it.

But what we hope to achieve in the end is a picture that is like the very best that nature shows us, and yet that does *not* require this regular input of ordinary gardening labour. Indeed, if we are to be successful not only in making our pictures in the first place, but in keeping them as we wish to see them, we must think very carefully about the whole business of 'gardening' them, and get clear in our minds what is the particular sequence of acts of ours that will ensure their continuity.

At first glance, once you have properly suited species to environment, any idea of 'gardening' seems ridiculous. Whoever heard of 'gardening' a bluebell wood, for instance? Or a honeysuckle hedge? Or a buttercup meadow? Yet a brief reflection will show that it is not so silly as all that. Not all woods are full of bluebells, hedges draped with honeysuckle, or meadows sheeted with buttercups. Why? It is because only certain woods, hedges and meadows have suitable conditions for these species; and the suitable conditions include not only the basic requirement of a suitable soil, but also an ongoing situation, throughout the year, that enables the species to complete their cycles and perpetuate themselves. Very, very little of this island is in a truly natural state. Almost all of it is subject to the influence of man. The environment, then, in which these wild flowers make their best effect, is a man-made one, and would not exist any longer if, having got them into our gardens, we then just left them alone. They used to do well enough in the man-made situation as it existed in the days from the dawn of agriculture up till the agricultural revolution of our own times. So what we must do is to try and reconstruct in our minds the sort of treatment under which they did flourish in those earlier farming systems, and analyse what it was about it that suited them. Then we can devise means, within our capabilities as gardeners, of re-producing that treatment; and, if we have got it right, we should reap the rich reward of an ever-increasing abundance of our chosen wild flowers in return for a pretty simple series of cultural acts.

Thus, the honeysuckle in the hedge benefits prodigiously from the hedge's annual trimming. Its own thin, whippy, quick-growing shoots recover easily from the cutting, and contrive to grow both upwards and outwards above the mutilated host species into the best possible situation to get access to the light. This makes it flower with delirious abandon, until the hedge looks as if it had had a wonderfully rich and subtle embroidered Eastern shawl cast over it. I can never stop marvelling at the wonderful variation in colour of the common wild honeysuckle, which ranges, in different plants, through pink, soft purple, amber, ivory, gold, tawny, tea-rose colour, and straw yellow. But it is only in the hedgerow situation that I can enjoy this riot of colour. In a wood, though there may be ten times as many honeysuckle plants, there is hardly a flower to be seen. Presumably some of them do manage to work their heads out into the light sufficiently to flower but, at least in our woods here, their numbers are negligible compared with those of their hedgerow sisters. The implication is obvious. If we wish to enjoy the honeysuckle in our wild gardens doing its ebullient best, we too must give it a chance to overtop its host, and reproduce, for a different reason, the situation the farmer creates when he goes round in autumn and winter with his hedge cutter. His primary intention of course is to keep his hedge dense and stock-proof, furnished with twiggy growth down to the bottom; it is for this that he cuts it so ruthlessly back. But as we can see from the roadside examples that the honeysuckle takes and likes this harsh treatment better than anything else, we too must be bloody, bold, and resolute, and hack it back just as hard.

The bluebell, too, has its cultural requirements. Here, the requirement is also light, but light at a rather particular time of the year. Growing in their favourite deciduous woods, the bluebells have attained their full growth before the canopy of leaves has closed over their heads; the dense shade of the later part of the year protects them from too much competition from such things as grasses; the rich leaf-mould provides adequate food for their fleshy quick-growing leaves and succulent bulbs. So if you want to create a bluebell wood in your wild garden, you must provide them with the same sort of conditions, and not try to naturalise them under heavy-leaved evergreens, or even allow such light-blockers as brambles to overshadow them.

Of the various things that happen to wild plants in their natural habitats, perhaps the most difficult thing for the gardener to simulate is grazing. The trouble is that it is so selective. Anyone who has watched grazing animals closely must have observed the semi-automatic choice of the next bite, avoiding this, reaching out for that. In just the same way we, faced with our plate of dinner loaded with about six different constituents, build ourselves appetising forkfuls – a piece of turkey, a sliver of stuffing, and a nice brussels sprout, perhaps – with a sort of George, an automatic pilot, that can do the choosing and arrange the order in which we eat our food while we, perhaps, are keeping the table in stitches between gulps, with a vivid version of what the Irishman said in the hot bread shop. This same George, working for cow, sheep or horse, leads its busy lips, tongue and teeth around and about, here and there, among the plant species in a system which, in the right circumstances, is capable of creating a balance based on that happy situation known as symbiosis. In the symbiotic situation, our wild-flower population, though probably subject to local fluctuations as a result of special conditions, were basically fairly stable. The wild flowers, in great number and variety, were there; people took them for granted.

In modern farming, it is easy to see, this symbiosis between plant and animal is gone. And it appears to have been going, faster and faster, since about the time of the Great War. People who can just remember back into the last century speak of a country-side laced all over with abundant flowers; what was the system of grazing management that produced that effect? And how, allowing that grazing itself is rarely practicable, can we reproduce it in our gardens?

One thing that is quite obvious is that there was a lot less stock carried on farms in those days. My neighbour, when I was a farmer, milked about sixty cows, and raised all his own followers, as well as carrying a few bullocks. His father, who farmed the place through the 1930's, thought he had a big herd if he had twenty-five milking cows at any one time. And yet the farm was the same, the land was the same, the weather was the same; only the techniques were different. But, obviously, increasing the headage of stock in this way is bound to increase the pressure on the grazing, even allowing for the increase in production that comes from artificial manuring and the sowing of modern strains of grass. A cow grazing in a tightly-stocked pasture is not going to turn aside from the next bite because it contains a herb that is slightly unpalatable; willy-nilly, off it will be bitten; and so a plant that has protected itself quite adequately throughout all the centuries by having mildly acrid juice will be eaten before it has a chance to ripen its seed and, before long, will die out. What we are looking to simulate, then, is half-grazing rather than what we moderns think of as efficient grazing. We must attempt to find a system that differentiates, even as the grazing animal on an extensive pasture does, between lush grass, which we want to keep in check, so that it does not overwhelm our flowers, and the flowers themselves, which are not expendable until they have set their seed and distributed it.

I used to think that the only way to manage this awkward requirement was to grow together all the species that flowered at the same time, and to mow them, when the time was ripe, equally, all together, right across the board. Not that I wish to imply that this is a bad system. It works; it can be seen to work. Round here, at any rate, it is very obvious how, for instance, such a species as the dandelion is favoured by just such a system, which is what it gets when it elects to grow in a hayfield. Flowering and seeding early, the dandelion has done its reproductive work for the year before the hay is cut and carried; it has enjoyed the protection from grazing animals afforded by the closed-up hayfield; and when the crop is finally taken off the field, its seedlings have already germinated down among the damp roots of the grass, and are ready to appreciate the extra bonus of light that they receive when it is cut. In consequence, the hayfields of traditional farms are golden with dandelion in May, whereas it is a much more struggling competitor in a pasture. So the system of putting all the things of the same flowering time together, and then mowing them, does work; but it has some disadvantages.

Part of the trouble lies with things that are particularly slow in ripening their seeds. In my own garden, I find that cowslips and primroses often seem to maintain their swelling seed-pods in a most irritating stage of greenness when many of the other things that flowered at the same time as them have finished the whole job, and are beginning to get to a stage of untidiness that even I want to clear up. Wild orchids are another lot of heel-tappers. And even though you may think to yourself that you will avoid the difficulty by keeping these slow ripeners in a patch by themselves, it is not always the perfect solution. Man proposes, but God, after all, distributes, and after a few years, with any luck, he will be scattering the offspring of your cherished wildlings rather arbitrarily over the whole area of your pretend pasture. And it does seem a pity to behead a pretty, lusty fertile flower that wants to give you a whole generation of grandchildren when you don't have to.

And really, nowadays, you don't have to any more. For a new tool, developed some years ago, but only lately seen on every side, has come to the aid of the wild-flower gardener, and, using it, he can graze round his field like the most selective nibbler, skirting his cowslips and orchids while beheading his ladysmocks and bugles; I refer, of course, to the strimmer. To anyone who is gardening with wild flowers in an area that is too big to be comfortably trimmed with shears or a knife, a strimmer is an absolutely invaluable aid, and I am sure will in a few years come to be as widely distributed as the ubiquitous and equally indispensable rotary mower.

My own experience with wild flowers growing fully naturalised, as I would wish to see them, is as yet rather limited. When I first realised in 1975 how threatened our commonest wild flowers were, and began to try to do something about it, and to write about what I was doing, people tended to credit me with both more knowledge and more success that I then had. 'We want to see the wild flower reserve,' they would say, arriving out of the blue on to our farm, even in muddy February; and I used to feel rather a charlatan as I showed them my few pathetic little specimens and tried to explain to them that it was really a very long-term project. Many of my early experiments had negative results, too, and were actually none the less useful for that. What I wanted to find out was whether it was possible to keep up a high wild-flower population on a reasonably profitably-run grass farm, and it was only after I had satisfied myself that it wasn't, that I began to attack the problem from another angle. But, useful or not, negative experiments don't make very good showbiz, and I am sure that many of the visitors went away puzzled and disappointed in spite of my explanations, having credited me with much more both of knowledge and achievement that I had ever claimed for myself.

But those apparently fruitless years at Penllwynplan were not entirely wasted, because even though the cattle instantly ate everything that I tried to grow in the fields or hedgebanks, I never ventured my whole stock in that way and, in the protected environment of the garden, I potched around, and gradually began to put together a little foundation of useful knowledge based on experience.

It still strikes me as ludicrous and absurd that one should have to struggle to grow what are, after all, weeds, but I will not deny that I have so struggled, and still do with certain species – and at that, I have never attempted anything really awkward, like some of the rare orchids. So when I see a really measly bit of wild-flower gardening in somebody else's patch, believe me, my feeling is of fellowship, not of scorn. With a few exceptions, my wild flowers at Penllwynplan were as pathetic as anybody's could be, and even here at Ty Arian, where the conditions are so much more suitable, only a few plantings are yet doing what I hoped they would. But at least now I do see the light at the end of the tunnel, and I know that if I am spared in health for, say, another ten years, I should have something to show by the end of it.

I have written in another chapter about the importance of choosing appropriate species for your area if you want to grow wild flowers. This demands a constant self-discipline; you see something that particularly takes your fancy, and an unregenerate little imp of covetousness in your soul whispers 'I'd love a piece of that plant', even though you know in the top part of your mind that your circumstances are quite different, and that it would never grow with you. It is not a new problem. Between the wars, the country was swept by a craze for rock gardening, and addicts drove themselves demented trying to grow high alpines in Barnstaple or Bedfordshire; referring to the ensuing problems as 'a challenge' rather than recognising them as a just punishment for perversity. If you will try to grow *Eritrichium nana* in Nuneaton or *Corydalis cashmeriana* in Crewe, you are going to find it difficult. I would find it similarly difficult to grow the chalk-loving orchids here, so I control my longings for them, a discipline rendered easier by the fact that our native orchids, although available from a few nurseries, are fiendishly expensive. Similarly, when I visit certain areas of the Pembrokeshire coast, I have to stop myself collecting seed of such lovely but strictly littoral species as *Aretmesia maritima*, which, adapted as it is to the constant flushing to and fro of the salt tide, would surely perish in my sheltered inland situation. Luckily, a lot of our loveliest flowers seem to be far from choosy about their situation, and will grow for pretty nearly anyone. This was brought home to me when I remarked once that the finest cowslips I had ever seen were on the chalk hills behind Caterham, and the friend I was talking to blinked with amazement, and said that he had always associated them with the deep, strong clays of Essex. I also remember them up on the high limestones of the Yorkshire Dales, and they certainly flourish here, in the acid loam of Carmarthenshire. Probably, when it comes down to it, this obliging behaviour is the norm, and extreme specialisation the exception; so none of us need feel too deprived, even though a few haughty beauties may be forever beyond our reach.

One useful file of information that I began to compile in the course of my earliest efforts was on the influence that the quality of the soil has on wild flowers. And I do mean quality, fatness or poverty, not, in this instance, merely kind, because this has a very real bearing on the way wild flowers behave in the garden. At Penllwynplan I grew quite a lot of different things in the garden, and noted the effect that civilisation had on them. Some of them behaved themselves, and continued to do the thing that had made me love them in the first place; other ran rank, lacking the hard living and tight competition of the natural environment, and soon became ugly and overdominating. The gardener in a small garden, where all the soil is likely to have been cultivated and improved, must be careful to confine his wild-flower gardening to the goodies; a larger garden, with peripheral areas that are no better than they should be, can chance its arm with the thugs.

I have already mentioned that the cowslip is absolutely

unexceptionable as a garden flower. In my experience, all the common wild primulas of this country – the primrose, cowslip, true oxlip and false oxlip, will adorn any garden, wild or tame. Their response to good living is to get bigger, but the flowers keep in proportion to the leaves, and the appearance of the plants is hearty rather than coarse. I have no experience of the bird's-eye or Scottish primulas, but all the others listed above (except the false oxlip, which is a natural hybrid, and sterile) seed themselves about very freely, as long as they have a chance to cross-fertilise. My first clumps of cowslips were all one clone, made from dividing the original clump I was given, and as there were no others in the area, I never got any seeds until somebody else gave me some other seedlings, when cross-fertilisation took place.

Another of the first-rate wild flowers in the garden is the wild poppy. This is of course an annual, and dies right off in winter; but once you have got it in your flower beds, it sheds its seeds everywhere, and the resultant seedlings come up like mustard and cress as the ground warms up in spring. It is of course fairly obvious that this flower will not react badly to rich land, for its most splendid effects in the wild-flower heyday were seen in wheat fields, which were always of necessity heavily manured. I have never managed to get the poppy to establish itself thickly and permanently in the wilder parts of the garden, which is a pity, for it is one of the most brilliant of our natives. I keep on trying, though, for I know a number of road verges and railway embankments where you can be sure of finding what Gerard Manley Hopkins described as the 'Blood-gush blade-gash of crush-silk poppies aflash'; and what it does for itself there, it may one day do for me. In the meantime, I let it riot in my cultivated garden beds, and am never without my fine scatter of scarlet from June until the end of October.

Perhaps it is a little unfair to cite as good garden plants ones which originated in gardens, and only naturalised themselves when they escaped. They ought to be good garden plants, after all. But their relevance to the wild or semi-wild garden is such that I feel I must at least mention their names – the sweet rocket, the old-fashioned columbine, the early blue pulmonaria, the red valerian, the montbretia, the pale mauve single michaelmas daisy, the monkshood – these, and many others that fall into the same category, are jewels for our purpose. They seem designed to be the link men, so to speak, in a garden, between the truly wild parts and the more formally cultivated parts which, in most people's book, are round the house. They will grow happily in the cultivated beds without becoming too rampant or coarse, yet they can rough it in a much wilder situation if that is what your design requires. Just a mile up the road from Penllwynplan there was a patch of blue-purple monkshood in the roadside hedge that never failed, in its due season, to make a pool of colour about five yards long; and the only treatment that it ever received in the way of cultivation was a harsh going-over from the Council's trashing machine once or twice a year. Another wonderful roadside display was provided by a great long stretch, more than a hundred yards, I am sure, of dark blue columbines that edged the steep road up out of the pretty little village of Gellywen, not far from here. And of course, sweet rocket, or dame's violet, to give it its older and more charming name, will adapt itself to bed or bank as occasion demands. In the village of Meidrim where I used to live, it has entirely covered one end of the steep, rocky bluff that the church stands on; another fine show of it has self-sown in the bank of a new bit of road, less than ten years old, where it joins with the brisk yellow horseshoe vetch to make a lovely picture. Honesty is another garden escaper that will seed itself cheerfully along the road edge and in amongst the roots of the hedge. Its flowers are magenta, but coming out quite early in the season, before our eyes are sated with that colour, are none the less welcome for that.

There are some flowers whose classification will depend upon where you put them. Give them room, and you will be inclined to count them among the goodies. Plant them in a bed with other things, and you will see them as thugs of the purest breed. I made this mistake when I was given a few fragments of the double soapwort, *saponaria officinalis flora plena*. It makes me laugh now when I remember how carefully I planted the scraps of woody root in deep, fertile soil, and how I congratulated myself when shoots began to appear, followed by leaves, stems, and in due course, pretty pink flowers, rather like doubled phloxes – as if I had had anything to do with it! Experience proved that it was the saponaria, not me, that was in charge, and that, had I simply thrown it down on a heap of concrete building blocks, it would probably have managed to establish itself just as effectively. In a short time it was bidding fair to take over the whole of the bed in which I had so incautiously given it a foothold; and, trying, but always failing through the years to eradicate it from there, I remembered that the friend in whose garden I had admired it had it growing as a sort of tall edging along the edge of a gravel drive, insulated by many yards of desert territory from any possibility of getting into her cultivated borders. Wise woman. Since I became familiar enough with the look of it to identify it easily from one flashing glimpse, I have often noticed it making big colonies on the sort of unpromising land that you see beside railway lines – not on sheltered embankments, but between the points, and among the sidings, where, in company with such other jolly toughs as the Oxford ragwort, it adorns the later months of the summer with cheerful insouciance.

I left the double soapwort behind when I left Penllwynplan, not relishing a continuation of the struggle I had been having with it, though I might eventually go back for stock of it and start a colony in one of the outlandish bits of Ty Arian. Another plant that I ducked out from under at the same time was the Himalayan balsam. A friend I had made through my writing sent me the seeds, and, again, I was delighted with the ease with which they germinated, and the willing, healthy way in which the seedlings grew on. It really is a very pretty flower, with its dark pink sizeable blossoms dangling on their thread-like stems, and coming so conveniently to adorn the waning months of July and August. It seemed too good to be true. Why, I wondered, did we not see it more often in the wilder sort of garden? I know the answer now – in a word, it is self-preservation. For the Himalayan balsam turns out to be a sort of Triffid – not poisonous, it is true, nor even 'carniferous' (a splendid word used to describe the shrubs planted around a house that was advertised for sale recently in our local paper), but at least determined to take over our island to the absolute exclusion of any other form of vegetable life. Like the other wild balsam found in these parts, the jewel-weed or noli-me-tangere, it has an exploding seed capsule that shoots the seeds off in all directions, a most effective form of distribution; and, being a quick-growing and sappy sort of plant, it overtops and smothers all normal competition, and asserts itself as the all-too-dominant species. If you get hold of the seed-pods lightly while they are still quite green, the heat of your hand will often make them explode with a curious wriggling feeling that is quite uncharacteristic of anything vegetable. I felt quite shocked the first time it burst a capsule in my hand, and flung the seeds away with as much horror as if I had felt an insect walking about on my palm; but it was such an unusual sensation that I experimented cautiously again, and eventually developed such a taste for it that I would go over the plants every time I passed them, hopefully massaging any likely-looking pods, and enjoying the frisson that resulted from any success. The result of all this was, of course, an enormous distribution of seeds around my garden, and an immense tide of Himalayan balsam plants the next spring. I weeded up what I could of them – they are very lightly-rooted, and come up at the merest tweak – but even so, many survived, and I fear that it has become the dominant weed of that garden. Another place in which it has made itself very much at home is in a stretch of water meadow that can be seen from the train near Cardiff, where you can look out upon acres and acres of it, marching steadily towards the city in what always looks to me a rather threatening way. I don't think I shall risk another invasion of the Himalayan balsam. Like the willow herb, and the exquisite white convolvulus, I shall be content to admire it on other people's land.

There are some plants, however, that I have grown whose fault was only that they were ill-adapted to garden life, and became too presumptuous. These I shall certainly have again. The obvious thing to do is to give them a niche exactly like the one they adorn in the wild, so that they will be mortified into good behaviour, and not get too overweening. One that will be with me as soon as I can get around to re-collecting it is the common toadflax. I had this in a garden bed at Penllwynplan, and this was definitely a mistake. It grew tall and coarse, flopped about in an ugly way, and never seemed to produce enough flowers to justify itself, though the clump from which it was taken was always admirably free with its charming sulphur, orange-lipped blooms. A meagre diet is what the toadflax wants; given that, it will be most reliable in adorning the July hedgerows. I committed a similar error when I introduced a strand or two of the lovely native *potentilla*, silverweed, into a bed as a carpeting plant. My plant came from the very edge of the road, where it made an exquisite feature, creeping out on to the very tarmac with its small silvery fern-shaped leaves, pink stems and generous light yellow buttercup-shaped flowers. But within a month, the good living in the garden had turned it into a monster. The leaves, four times their original size, became the dullest of dark greens; the pink creeping stems were totally obscured; and as for flowers, it never bothered with them at all, obviously feeling that it could do all the colonising it needed to by simple spreading. All you could have said for it was that it was at least successful as a carpeter, indeed, too successful. So deep was the pile of this most lavish of carpets that everything else in the bed began to sink out of sight into it; and, unlike the toadflax, it proved quite difficult to eradicate, being only too willing to regenerate from even the smallest bit of root left behind when weeding. I do not have to collect silverweed again – it grows of itself all over the place on this weedy and neglected property; but I know enough now to realise that the colonies I must enjoy and encourage are the ones that eke out a hard living on the edge of the stony drive, and not the would-be upper classes that are struggling to take over my well-manured vegetable garden.

In the bit of land I have here at Ty Arian I am lucky enough to have examples of most of the good wild-flower environments – wood, hedgerow, pasture and marsh. The one thing I have not really got is a bit of arable, in the agricultural sense of the word. I have already referred to the difficulties of growing the poppy in a pasture situation. It is not the only species that presents something of a problem. There is a whole range of arable weeds that I would like to grow – fumitory, corn marigold, heart's-ease, cornflower, lesser bindweed, and so on. But my vegetable garden is the only cultivated area of any significance around the place, and I don't really want them there. Possibly the answer is to try to cultivate the whole of it – it is much too big for my needs as it stands – and to use the spare bit to grow a patch of corn every year for the peacocks. At Penllwynplan I once grew a tiny square of wheat, intending not so much to harvest a useful crop of grain as to get material for making corn dollies, a craft I should still like to pursue. It was not much of a success. The wheat grew up quite satisfactorily and produced a crop, but it was disfigured by a blackish stain here and there which I was not arable farmer enough to identify. The troubles of wheat are legion, and are only rendered tolerable by the wild and unintentional poetry of their names, which run to such improbable extremes as 'loose smut' and 'glume blotch'. If I do grow corn here at Ty Arian, it will be on a slightly larger scale than my two-square-yard crop, the piece of ground that suggests itself being about fifteen yards by twenty. It will be rotated on a three-course system with a) potatoes and b) all the rest of the things one grows in a vegetable garden; the arable weeds will have to survive such anti-fungal sprays as I am obliged to administer to control the stinking bunt, glume blotch, et caetera, but will probably manage. It is not these sprays, I think, but the hormone weed killers that have banished them from the large-scale cornfields of proper, commercial farms, and with these, of course, they will not have to contend here.

If I do manage to get my mini-cornfield going, what a joy it will be. Not since my childhood have I seen the poppies growing as I used to love them, beautiful at every stage of the corn's development – scarlet, in vivid compliment to the blue-green of the young wheat shooting into the ear; or even more glowing, blazing vermilion in the red-gold of the ripe field. The poppy conflagration must be one of the high-lights of the wild flower year.

But there are others. Bluebells in the woods – buttercups, sorrel and ox-eye daisies in the hayfields – honeysuckle in the hedges – kingcups in the marshes – bugles and tormentil in the pastures – the seductive list is endless. And even though, here at Ty Arian, many of the pictures are still only the merest embryos or, even less than that, seeds in the imagination, yet the potential is there, and the will. And in a world with as much violence and fear in it as ours seems to have in it nowadays, that is a lot. Anyone can account themselves blessed who can look forward to a future of the sort that I envisage for this little place, as a refuge for these lovely wild flowers of our countryside; for it is a future of beauty, and of hope.